The Rising

Other works by Buffy M. Brinkley:

There Are No Monsters Here
The Blazing: A Vampire Story
The Awakening: The Blazing Book Two

The Rising

The Blazing Book Three

Buffy M. Brinkley

Library of Congress Control Number: 2021901662
ISBN: Hardcover   978-1-6641-5468-1
                 Softcover   978-1-6641-5467-4
                 eBook   978-1-6641-5466-7

Print information available on the last page.

Rev. date: 02/04/2021

To order additional copies of this book, contact:
Xlibris
844-714-8691
www.Xlibris.com
Orders@Xlibris.com
804467

CONTENTS

VIVECA

RICHARD

THE RISING

I dedicate this book to myself. It is a love letter from me, to me, in celebration of all I am and all I hope to become.

ACKNOWLEDGMENTS

My sincere appreciation to my best friends: Michele, Candida, Maxine, Laura, Pamela, Carla, Judy, and Lexi. Your belief in me lifted me up when I was down. You have been my Northern Star, my compass, and my light in the darkness. I found my way because of you. Thank you.

Candida, I'm not sure where to start, except to say thank you, Big Sister. The wealth of knowledge you have shared with me is priceless. I can never repay your patience, your kindness, or your indelible spirit in all the moments you spent answering my questions, listening to my ideas, and encouraging my imagination.

Richard, thank you for being the man worth dreaming about.

THE BLAZING

Viveca Moreau was eight years old when she met Richard Ambrose. He saved her life, and she believed him to be her guardian angel. But Richard is no guardian angel. He's a vampire with a yearning to become human again. There's only one way, and Viveca holds the key. She is a dream walker warrior, and she is just learning to use her special gifts. The blazing is the cure, and as Viveca grows up, all the necessary factors align. She's in love with him, and she will do anything to save him, but Richard knows the dangers all too well. Can he allow her to risk her life for him once he realizes how much he loves her?

THE AWAKENING

When Viveca Moreau pulled Richard Ambrose through the blazing, he became human again for the first time in two centuries. He wants nothing more than to have a life with her. An ordinary life as an ordinary man. When he takes Viveca as his bride, their future seems bright. And when Viveca becomes pregnant, the couple couldn't be happier. But some enemies refuse to stay buried, and when an unspeakable enemy awakens to take its revenge, it will stop at nothing to reclaim Richard to the darkness.

PROLOGUE

December 20, 2016, New Orleans, Louisiana, 1:27 a.m.

The phoenix surrounded Richard's body, but Viveca could barely hear his heartbeat. She removed her overshirt and wrapped her son in it, careful not to stretch the umbilical cord too much. Then she pulled her knit pants back on, careful of the same umbilical cord. Wet with blood and afterbirth as they were, she had no choice. She projected the tigress again, and it lifted Richard in its massive jaws.

There was no way she could climb the ladder. She looked down at her son, who was whimpering in her arms. "I need your help, Liam. I need your eagle to help us out of here."

Liam had been born and no longer a physical part of her except for the umbilical. She hoped that would be enough of a bond for her to still use his power and for him to realize they were in trouble. She made her way back out of the adjoining church and back toward the mortuary. Quiet and careful as Malcolm could be waiting in ambush.

She came out into the cavernous area and approached the kiln. With all her might, she used her left arm to shift the latch on the kiln door and swung it open. She stood back while the tigress leapt inside with Richard. She commanded it to lay him on the slab. She climbed in after it and called the tigress back to herself. "Liam, please. I need your eagle to help us out of here. Do you remember when you saved me? Can you help your dad? Can you lift him out of here?"

Liam stirred in her arms and then became still. Around him, a golden light radiated from him and filled the room. Then, it condensed and formed an orb around Richard. The orb began to rise from the slab and out through the chimney. Then, it returned and carried Viveca and Liam out and next to Richard.

She projected the tigress again. It came to crouch down beside her. "I need your help, my friend." She gingerly climbed atop the tigress's back, cradling Liam close to her. It stood, lifting her and Liam, then took Richard once more in its jaws and began to run toward Viveca's car.

Viveca opened the rear door, and the tigress climbed in to place Richard on the back seat. Viveca shut the door and climbed behind the wheel. She'd barely called the tigress back when she started the car, threw it into gear, and sped toward the hospital.

The emergency room entrance was blessedly clear of vehicles when she arrived. She blew the horn, then stepped out and opened the back door. Richard's blood had begun to soak into the seat. "Richard," Viveca yelled, "don't you dare leave me!" She tucked Liam close to her chest and slammed her free hand onto Richard's chest. A tremendous jolt passed between her and her husband, one that weakened her and sent her flying back as if she'd come into contact with an electrical charge. She hit the pavement behind her with Liam still safe in her arms.

Hospital attendants rushed through the automatic doors with stretchers. Liam and Viveca were loaded onto one while Richard was loaded onto the other. The darting brilliance of overhead fluorescent lights moved like road striping around a fast-moving vehicle. "Can you hear me," a man asked. "What is your name?"

"Viveca Ambrose," she answered. "Please help my husband. Please."

"We're doing all we can for him. But right now, let us focus on you. I'm Dr. Goodman. When did you give birth, Viveca?"

"An hour ago, I think."

"We need to cut the umbilical cord, Viveca."

She nodded, and Dr. Goodman proceeded to separate her son from her. He handed Liam to a nurse, and she moved to another table.

"What are you doing with him?" Viveca asked, looking around wildly, trying to see past the crowd of hospital workers surrounding her.

"He's going to be just fine, Viveca. We're just cleaning him up and examining him for injury."

"Where's my husband?"

"Your husband is in surgery," Dr. Goodman said. "We'll have word soon. We're going to get you out of the rest of those clothes, and we can get you cleaned up as well. You've been through quite an ordeal. Can you tell me what happened to you and your husband?"

"We were attacked. Just managed to escape."

"You're a very lucky woman, Viveca. Can you tell me how your husband sustained his injuries?"

"I don't know," she began and then tried to sit up.

"Whoa, take it easy," the doctor said kindly, placing a hand on her shoulder to press her back onto the bed. "You have to lie down. We've called for the police so they can help you."

"I am the police," she said.

"Then, your colleagues are on their way. Is there anyone else we can call for you?"

She thought of Nana safely tucked away ahead of all the chaos. She shook her head. "No one. It's just me and my husband."

"And now, your son. I am going to step out so the nurses can assist you, and I'll be back soon to check on you and Liam."

"Please check on my husband, Richard. Please find out how he is."

"I will," he said, but she could see a sadness in his eyes that alarmed her. He left the room before she could ask any more questions.

"Okay, dear, we're going to cut away the rest of your clothes so we can clean you up and get you into a hospital gown," the nurse nearest her said, and she could feel hands on her body and the coolness of the room as her clothes were removed.

Tears began leaking out the sides of her eyes. *Richard.* She lay there and focused on the strength of the tigress. Within her, the tigress's strength quietly spread throughout her body. She lay still as the nurses began to wipe her down with cleansing cloths and antiseptic. Rolled one way, then the other, she was carefully moved around the bed so that the sheets were removed and changed. A hospital gown was provided, and then her son was brought to her.

Liam was calm and staring up at her as if she had all the answers. "It's best if you feed him right away, dear. If you want, I can show you how."

Viveca nodded. The nurse lowered her hospital gown to just below her left breast. Liam's lips were guided to her nipple, and the nurse showed her how to massage her breast to entice the flow of milk. Liam closed his eyes and fed, and Viveca marveled at her body and at her son. "You are a beautiful boy, Liam. You look just like your father." She smiled down at him and allowed a few tears to fall. "He would have been so proud of you. He would have loved you so much."

Sometime later, the nurse brought a hospital crib into the room. She lifted Liam from Viveca's arms and showed her how to burp him. Then, she laid Liam inside the crib where Viveca could see him. Viveca's tears continued to fall. *Too soon*, she kept reminding herself. It was too soon to contemplate a life without Richard, and yet she had just referred to him in the past tense. *Don't*, she chided within herself. *Make them say it. Don't grieve until they give you a reason.*

"I'll take him back to the nursery now," the nurse said.

"He can't stay here with me?"

"We keep a close watch on the newborns and bring them in for feeding. In another day or so, he can stay with you. Okay?"

"Okay," Viveca said and watched as the nurse wheeled her son away. She laid back on the bed and adjusted her gown. She looked toward the window at the far end of the room. In a few hours, daylight would illuminate the panes. She thought of Malcolm and hoped that wherever he'd gone, it soon would be someplace sunny.

The hospital room door opened and pulled her from her musings. Frank came in. Upon sight of him, Viveca burst into tears. "Frank," she sobbed. "Oh, god! Help me!"

Frank perched on the side of the bed and pulled Viveca into his arms. "Viv. What happened? Who did this?"

She brought her mouth close to his ear. "Vampire," she whispered. "He might've killed Richard." The words caused her to cry harder.

PART ONE

VIVECA

CHAPTER 1

December 20, 2016, New Orleans, Louisiana, 5:28 a.m.

"Jazz!" Malcolm's booming voice echoed down into the pit. His skin, which had been singed in places when the eagle had come forth, was starting to heal. The body he found himself in was stronger than his own body had been. It was more athletic, healthier. He did miss his own face, but he was glad to be back. He began to descend the steps of the great house. She was somewhere in this place, and he would find her. "Jazz!" He yelled her name again as he came to the bottom of the steps. She had lit candles. Upon the slab where he slept, a woman lay unconscious. Then, he saw Jazz cowering in a corner, her knees drawn to her chin and her arms wrapped around her legs. He leveled his stare upon her. "Come here," he said calmly.

She rose with all the uncertainty of a child in trouble and walked toward him as if she were heading toward the guillotine. All her usual confidence was gone, and she came to stand before him afraid and ashamed. "I am sorry, Master," she said quietly.

He reached out and forced her chin up with his fingers so she would look at him. "You betrayed me, Jazz," he said calmly.

"I did not mean to, Master. I was afraid."

"You are young, and you are clumsy, but I will teach you to be loyal."

"Please don't hurt me, Master. I was afraid."

"When I first saw you dancing on that stage, I knew I would have you for my own. I'm not going to destroy you, Jazz, but I am going to punish you. I made you for myself. You must learn to remain by my side, even if it means your death. Do you understand?"

"Yes," she whispered.

"Now, tell me: why did you not return when I called for you?"

She tried to lower her head again, but he kept his fingers firmly under her chin. She met his eyes, and her expression screwed up in fear. "I was afraid."

"Of what, love?"

"Of the dream walker. She was going to kill me."

"Do you think I would have allowed her to do it?"

"Yes."

He smiled without humor. "If it meant bringing my brother back here with me, you are correct."

"Where is your brother?"

"The dream walker wrested him from me and let him die."

"I'm sorry, Master."

"Are you?"

"Yes."

"Show me how sorry you are."

He lowered his hand and gave her full range of motion again. She stepped out of his reach, then approached the slab. "I brought her for you. A gift. You must be hungry."

Malcolm approached the unconscious woman. "And you believe this blood bag will make us even?"

"No, Master. I only meant her as a start. A new beginning between us."

"A new beginning. Yes, we must have one. Gather Bain and the others. Make sure they are upstairs by nightfall."

"But the sun, Master."

"You'll figure it out, Jazz. I know you will. If you don't have them here by nightfall, don't return."

"Yes, Master." She cursed herself as she climbed the stairs. She'd left her phone in the car, and she'd have to retrieve it.

Outside, the darkness was beginning to sap away, and she knew the sun would soon cast its rays over the horizon. Jazz moved quickly, but the impending dawn had already begun to drain her vampire strength.

∞

Bain couldn't say he hadn't been expecting the call, but he was surprised at who was on the other line. Jazz's voice came waxen across the phone line. "Gather your fledglings and meet us at the house."

"Is that a request or an order? Because I only answer—"

"It's an order from the Master," she said with more force than she felt. "If you doubt it, stay away and reap your punishment." Jazz had made herself as small against the side of the car as possible. The sun had begun to rise, and her skin had started to burn.

"Oh, I'll be there. What of Turner?"

"He's dead. The dream walker destroyed him."

"I knew he was not ready. So eager to prove himself. Tell me, vampire, what time does the Master wish to meet?"

"Sundown."

"And the dream walker?"

"She lives, but the Master said his brother is dead." The urgency of her voice did not seem to register with Bain.

"That's too bad for the dream walker's sake. Master will seek his revenge now—"

"She is very powerful, Bain. She will not be killed easily."

Bain laughed, a deep-throated laugh that might have sprung up from the pit itself. "Her husband is dead. Everything she lived for is gone. She may even hold the door open for us."

"The Master was hurt, wounded as if scorched by the sun."

"How did that happen?"

"I don't know." Jazz took in a sharp intake of air as more rays found their way to her skin.

"Weren't you there?"

Jazz hesitated. "I ran away."

Bain laughed without humor. "There will be a price for that, vampire."

"I'm paying for it now. See you tonight." Jazz hung up the phone and stepped away from the car. She hurried across the yard to the porch. The morning sun had already caused damage to her skin. Her dark skin was seared black in places and bubbled up on her arms, chest, and face. In the relative shadows of the porch, she tried the door to find it locked. Desperation drove her to try the handle again, harder. Still, it did not budge. Her vampire strength was all but gone and Malcolm's words echoed in her mind: *You'll figure it out, Jazz. I know you will …*

"Bastard!" Jazz cursed. She needed blood, and she needed rest in the darkness. No blood was to be had in the daytime; only death waited for her outside. Then she remembered, and quickly, she made her way around to the side of the house where a bit of the lattice was loose. She pull back on it to create a gap, then slipped within the gap to crawl under the house. The ground was muddy, and she hated feeling dirty, but the cool mud acted as a salve against her burning skin. This would have to do.

When the sun set, she would have blood. She closed her eyes and allowed the vampire sleep to come over her. Hate rose in her heart—not for her master, but for herself. Never again would she leave his side, even if it meant her death. Lesson learned.

∞

Frank held Viveca as she wept. She shook against him, and he reached up and stroked her hair away from her face. "Oh, Viv. He's not gone. Try to hang on to hope," he said. The door opened again, and the captain, along with Grant and Ferguson, entered the room.

Frank stood up from the bed to allow the others to get closer to Viveca. She sat up as best she could and tried to introduce some order to her appearance. "Take it easy, Viv," the captain said as he came to stand by her bedside. Not once in all the time she'd known him had he called her by her first name.

"Captain. Thank you all for coming."

"Of course, we're here, Viv. We're family," he said and placed his hand on her shoulder. "Can you tell us who did this to you and your husband?"

"I don't know," she replied calmly.

"Did you get a good look at him?"

"It was dark. It happened so fast. I just don't know."

"Okay, you just rest easy. Frank will keep in touch with you. If you think of anything, please let us know. We want to catch this guy."

She nodded and tried to hold back her tears. The captain had turned to move away from her and allow Grant and Ferguson to get close, but then he hesitated. "You know you can count on us, don't you, Viv?"

"I know. Thank you. Means a lot." Suddenly, paranoia rose within her. Quietly within, she let the tigress rise, and she switched on her vision. The captain was human, and so were the others. She tried to calm herself, but anxiety rose within her like a wildfire.

"Are you okay, Viv?" the captain asked.

She nodded.

"Are you sure? Are you remembering something?"

"No. I think I'm just tired," Viveca said, taking a deep breath and letting the tigress settle.

"Okay, well, if you think of *anything*, you let us know," the captain said and then stood aside.

Grant came close and took her hand. He said nothing, just stood in quiet communion with her for a moment, then stepped back and let Ferguson come forward. He, too, took her hand and held it gently, then he met her eyes. "I'm so sorry, Viv. Is there anything I can do?"

She shook her head, and he gave her a weak smile. All of them were counting her husband as lost, and it was as though she were standing at Richard's funeral. People coming up to her, taking her hand, and not knowing what to say. All of them muttering how sorry they were, but with no idea how to make her circumstances better. She would start now with what she had already planned to do. She returned his weak smile, squeezed his hand, and said, "No. There's nothing you can do right now. Thank you."

Ferguson released her hand gently and stepped back from the bed to rejoin the captain and Grant. "Anything you need, you just say the word, Viv," the captain repeated then led the others out of the room.

Frank returned to her bedside and sat down. "They don't know what to say, but they mean well."

"I know."

The door opened again, and Mike and Stan entered. "I texted Mike while you were talking to the captain." Frank rose from the bed again, and Mike and Stan flanked both sides of the bed to gather Viveca up in their arms.

"I can't believe it, honey," Stan lamented. "Do we know how Richard is?"

Viveca's emotions broke open again, and she wept. Mike said nothing, but she could feel his body shaking next to her. When at last the hug was spent, Mike and Stan sat on the bed on either side of her. "Who did this, Viv?" Mike asked, his voice a quiet simmering rage.

"I don't know, but—"

From across the room, Frank interrupted. "Aren't these your closest friends?"

She nodded. "Yes, they are."

"And you've never told them?"

She shook her head.

"Don't you think it's time?"

"What is he talking about, Viv?" Stan asked.

She looked between Mike and Stan and took a deep breath. "You're not going to believe me."

"I've never known you to lie, kid. What's going on?"

"Richard's brother, Malcolm, attacked us. Only he'll now look like Rainier's son, Philip."

"What?" Mike's eyes were wide with a thousand questions.

"Malcolm is a vampire. He hates me because I pulled his brother through the blazing."

"Um, the *what*?"

"Until the solstice last year, Richard was a vampire. I saved him. I am a dream walker warrior."

"I'm confused," Stan said. "A vampire? Like Dracula?"

"Not like Dracula. The vampire is a spiritual cage that traps the human soul and then wears the human's body. The blood they drink restores their immortality. If the human remains at war for the control of the body, then a dream walker, provided she meets the criteria, has the power to pull the human free."

"Like an exorcism?" Mike asked.

"Kind of, I guess. Basically, when the solstice moonlight falls upon the vampire, the blazing, which is like a portal, sparks wide, and the dream walker can pull the human free of the cage. This drives the vampire out of the human. That's why a dream walker is needed. So she and her warrior spirits can kill it. But apparently, there are ways for it to return. I destroyed Malcolm when I saved Richard. Rainier's son died, so Rainier injected his dead son with vampire blood. Malcolm's blood. Because Philip was already dead, there was no soul to cage, and Malcolm took reign over the body."

They sat in silence for several minutes. "It's true, guys," Frank said. "She can prove it. I've seen her in action."

"Frank, watch the door, will you?" Viveca asked, then she took Mike's and Stan's hands. "Do you both trust me?"

"Yes, we do, kid," Mike said, and Stan nodded.

"Close your eyes," Viveca commanded, and both obeyed. In another instance, the smells and environment of the hospital room seemed to vanish, and both Stan and Mike could feel the breeze of the open air around them. "You can open your eyes now."

When Stan and Mike opened their eyes, they were standing in a beautiful field. "This is my dream walk," Viveca said, then projected the tigress. "And this is my spirit warrior, the white tigress." The tigress came to sit in front of Viveca and lower its head to her. "Don't be afraid, guys."

"This is incredible, Viv, but why did you never tell us?"

"I didn't know what I was when I met you. I've only learned to how to use my power within the last year or so. Please forgive me for not telling you both sooner. But now that you do know, you must keep my secret, and you must keep your wits about you. Malcolm thinks Richard is dead and he'll be coming for me and my son. He may try to get to me by hurting the people I love."

"You'll have to teach us, Viv. And please be patient with us. The whole world just changed," Stan said.

"I understand. I owe you my story and everything that's happened over the past year and a half. But now we have to get back." She took their hands again and led them from the dream walk.

In the relative coolness of the hospital room, Frank came back to her side. "Okay, that was pretty cool."

"What was?" Viveca asked.

"When you took them to your dream walk, you all disappeared. A dome of light formed around you, and then you were gone. When you came back, the dome formed again then disappeared."

"Wow, I didn't know that's what happened." She turned her attention to Mike and Stan. "Are you guys ready to learn about vampires and ghouls?"

"Ghouls?" Stan's eyes widened with fear.

"They are the servants to the vampires. Humans who have been fed vampire blood."

"This is getting crazier by the minute, Viv," Stan said.

"I know. I'll be released from the hospital soon, and then I'll come by to—"

The hospital room door opened again, and the nurse wheeled Liam to her bedside. "It's almost feeding time, Mrs. Ambrose."

Viveca gave her a small smile. Everyone turned their attention to Liam. Mike spoke first. "Well, will you look at that? He's awesome, Viv."

She took a deep breath. "Liam John Ambrose."

Stan smiled down at her son. "Do you think you might want to change his middle name to Richard?"

"No. Richard and I decided on his name together. I don't want to change the decision we made."

"Understood. Well, he's a gorgeous kid."

"He is," Viveca smiled at her son.

The hospital room door opened again, and a different doctor stepped in. "Hi, Mrs. Ambrose. I'm Dr. Morgan. How are you feeling now?"

Her lip trembled. Something about being asked if she was okay made her feel like she wasn't okay. She decided to go for broke. "My husband is dead, isn't he?" Mike gathered her hands in his.

"Mrs. Ambrose, your husband's doctor will be in soon to talk to you."

"Just say it. Don't leave me in this agony. Please."

"I will page the doctor for you in a moment, but first, we need to check your vitals. You delivered your baby under stressful circumstances, and it is my job to make sure that you and your son are okay."

"Look, Doctor, you seemed to be in the know here," Mike said. "Can't you just give her an answer? Don't you think she's waited long enough for the confirmation?

"I understand. I will get the doctor in here after I've taken her vitals. I promise." Mike and Stan rose from the bed to give the doctor access to Viveca. "Would you gentlemen kindly wait by the door? I'll need to pull the curtain so Mrs. Ambrose can have her privacy."

"Of course," Mike said. The three of them moved to the door and waited patiently as the doctor checked Viveca's vitals.

When the curtain opened again, Dr. Morgan addressed them quietly. "She's going to be okay. Her vitals are good, and there don't seem to be any after-effects of childbirth. We will keep her here for observation for another day or two. Her son is also doing well. Now, I'll get her husband's doctor for you."

"Thank you, Dr. Morgan," Frank said, and he and the others moved aside to allow the doctor to leave the room.

"Are you sure you're okay?" Mike asked as he sat next to Viveca again.

"Yes, I'm okay," Viveca said. "I just wish they'd tell me about Richard and get it over with."

"The doctor is coming, kid. And we're going to sit right here with you."

The door opened, and Dr. Goodman came in. "It's good to see you again, Viveca. I am very sorry to have kept you waiting." He took a deep breath, then continued. "Your husband suffered massive blood loss. He was moved to emergency surgery to close the wounds and replace the hemoglobin. Viveca—"

"Please just tell me. Don't drag this out with all your explanations. If he's dead, just say it."

"Viveca, we can't explain it, but your husband is alive. He's very weak. He's unconscious, but he's alive."

Viveca felt Mike's hands squeeze around hers. She took a series of quick breaths of relief and then pulled a hand free and pressed it to her mouth. Then the worst idea in the world fluttered in her mind's eye. "I have to see him! Now."

"You need to rest right now. You can see him in a little while."

"No. It's important. I have to see him now." Mike released her hand and rose from the bed to return to Stan's side.

"Viveca," Dr. Goodman said calmly, "your husband is barely hanging on in there. Give him some time to recover."

"Did he ever flatline?"

"I'm sorry?"

"Did he die at any time before, during, or after the surgery?"

"He did flatline about halfway through the surgery, but we were able to pick up his heartbeat quickly after."

"I have to see him! Now! I can't wait!" Viveca sat up, and Dr. Goodman put a hand on her shoulder as he'd done earlier to press her back down to the bed. "Let go of me! I need to see my husband!"

"Viveca, please be calm."

"You don't understand. My husband was dead, and now he's not," she said pointedly and looked at Frank. Frank's eyes widened, and he whispered to Mike and Stan.

"He is alive, Viveca. I would say it's a miracle," Dr. Goodman spoke evenly and calmly.

"I have to see him. It's so important. Please!"

"I can let you see him in a couple of hours."

She changed tactics. "Is he in a room with windows?"

"I believe so."

Viveca's panic became palpable. "Keep the curtains shut. Don't let any sunlight in the room for any reason. Do you understand?"

"What is this all about?"

"You must trust me, Doctor. Please keep the curtains shut. He has to stay in darkness. Do you understand?"

"No, actually, I don't understand. Do you mind telling me why?"

"He has a skin condition. A very sensitive condition to light. He could blister."

"Okay, stay calm. I'll make sure the curtains are kept closed."

"Thank you." She settled back down to the bed and took a few ragged breaths. Her anxiety rose within her. She feigned calm, but she felt anything but calm as she forced herself to lay still on the hospital bed.

Dr. Goodman left the room, and the nurse turned her attention to Frank, Mike, and Stan. "It's feeding time, gentlemen. I'm afraid it's time for you all to go. You can visit her later."

Each of them came to Viveca's side and said goodbye. "Thanks, guys. I can't tell you how much I appreciate you all being here."

When they were gone, the nurse handed Liam to her. Following the instructions given to her earlier in the morning, she began feeding her son. Her thoughts wandered to Richard. If he died, then there was a very good chance he was once again a vampire. The doctor said she could see Richard in a couple of hours. Oh, how time moved so slowly in hospitals.

CHAPTER 2

December 20, 2016, New Orleans, Louisiana, 11:28 a.m.

When Viveca finished feeding Liam, the nurse laid him in the crib. "I'll leave him here for a while."

"Thank you," Viveca said. She watched the nurse leave the room, then looked over at Liam. "Oh, baby, your daddy is alive. Isn't that great news?" Despite her fears about Richard's future, she comforted herself in the fact that she hadn't lost him. At least not yet.

Liam didn't open his eyes, but his lips moved up in a smile. "You already knew, didn't you," she said, then laid back on the bed and closed her eyes. She was exhausted. She tried to project the phoenix to help relieve her stress, but it wouldn't answer. It didn't matter anyway at the moment. She could feel her eyelids getting heavy. She looked once again at her son. Liam was sleeping peacefully. She contented herself to do the same. Her eyelids drooped, and she was nearly asleep when movement played out at the corner of her eye. An animal. She could see it sitting in the doorway. A dog?

She tried to focus on it, but her vision wobbled in her exhaustion. Maybe it was a service animal taken in to soothe the patients. She'd certainly heard of that. She tried to stay awake, tried to make it out, but her body had had enough, and she slipped, struggling, into sleep.

∞

"Hey, little man," Frank said as he stepped back into the room. The captain and the others had gone back to the precinct. He had called his new partner to discuss their current case and informed him that he would catch up later.

Liam looked up at Frank and smiled. A tiny hand reached out toward Frank, and Frank lifted the boy from the crib. Liam's tiny hand wrapped around Frank's free index finger. Frank carried the boy to the chair next to Viveca's bed and sat down. "You are a sweet boy, Liam. Your Uncle Frank is going to spoil you rotten."

Viveca opened her eyes and watched quietly as Frank held her son. For as short a period of time as she'd known Frank, they had become very close. In Frank, she'd found a friendship she'd known in just four other people: Brenda, Mike, Stan, and Richard. Her circle of friends and family was very small and very well-guarded. She didn't make friends easily; she never had. But when she did, those friendships generally lasted forever. She and Frank were more than partners. They were friends. They were family. His loyalty to her as her partner and as her friend wasn't something she would ever take for granted. She knew well how quickly life could change.

Frank smiled down at Liam, and Liam looked up into Frank's face with a kind of serenity she'd only seen when Liam looked at her. Liam, she was convinced, was born with all the secrets of the universe. He would be a great spiritual leader and a powerful dream walker warrior. His sight was something she could sense was already at work in him. Liam squeezed Frank's finger a bit tighter and let out a laugh that brought a dazzling smile to Frank's face.

Viveca switched on her sight and watched as a golden light surrounded Liam and moved to envelop Frank. At first, Viveca thought it might be some sort of protection, but she realized quickly that it was no such thing. Her son was blessing Frank with a part of himself. Nature erupted all around them in that moment, and Viveca marveled at how magnificent her son really was. It was something Frank would probably never know, but something by which Liam would always be able to recognize in him. The golden light enhanced Frank's aura for a moment, amplifying the good in him, almost as if Liam had sought out the goodness in Frank and placed it under a magnifying glass. Then, Frank's aura returned to normal.

Frank looked up and saw Viveca watching him. "Did you hear that?" Frank asked.

"What?"

"I don't know, exactly."

"What did it sound like?"

"I don't know. For a moment, I felt this incredible warmth and then I could hear birds and the wind. Then, an incredible peace washed over me. Did he do that?"

"You did feel it, then. I don't know if he can do it yet, but those are the sounds from a dream walk. He's amazing."

"He is," Frank said. "I can't tell you what I just felt. It was like he was telling me that there was nothing I needed to be afraid of."

"I think he loves you, Frank, and he's telling you so."

Frank smiled broadly. "Well, his Uncle Frank loves him too. And by the way, you owe me a dollar. The captain squealed like a schoolgirl when he came by yesterday."

Viveca laughed. "Put it on my tab. I figured I owed you the dollar when I opened the carrier car seat combo."

Frank chuckled. "Buy me a coffee one morning. We'll call it even."

"You got it. So, Frank, I see you're bonding with my son."

"Of course I am. He and his Uncle Frank are going to be best buds, Viv."

"The doctor should be by soon to take me to see Richard. Will you stay here with Liam?"

"Sure I will," Frank said, then seemed to cut himself short.

"What?"

"Oh, nothing."

"Spit it out, Frank."

"It's an errant thought, Viv. One I shouldn't have had anyway."

"Tell me."

"I hope Richard is going to be okay. I'm praying for that, I really am."

"But?"

"Not really a *but*, more an *and*."

"Okay. And?"

"I'm your partner, Viv. I'm here for you no matter what. I hope Richard is going to be okay, *and* I'm going to be here for you and Liam too."

"I know," Viveca gave him a weak smile. She'd meant it to reach her eyes, but it hadn't. "You are a good and trusted friend, Frank. I appreciate all you've done for me."

It was Frank's turn. "But?"

Viveca chuckled. "There's no *but* to that statement. I am sincerely grateful. I don't know what I would have done without you this past year, my friend."

Frank rose and placed Liam back into the crib. "I have to meet with Watson in an hour or so. I better get going. I'll be back later to check on you. Can I bring you anything when I come back?"

"French fries."

Frank laughed. He pursed his lips in humor and nodded his head. "French fries," he echoed. "You got it."

∞

Frank made his way from Viveca's room to the Intensive Care Unit. He had the choice of three hallways. He bypassed the nurse's station and began making his way down the first hall to the right. He kept his expression light, giving the impression he knew where he was going. At each door, he read the room number and patient's last name. At the end of the hall, he turned around and made his way back and down the hallway to the left.

As he made his way back toward the third hallway, he spotted Richard's room. Room 234. The name Ambrose printed on a tab that had been slid neatly into the patient identification slot. He stepped cautiously to the door and slipped inside, letting the door shut quietly behind him.

Richard was lying on the bed. Bandages covered his neck and several other injuries had been attended to. An intravenous line that was hooked to his left arm was delivering fluids in rapid fashion. Another line that was hooked into his right arm was delivering a half-empty bag of blood. An oxygen line was inserted into his nose, and he looked beat to hell.

Frank came to the bedside and sat down. "Hey, Richard. It's Frank." Frank moved his eyes across Richard's body in concern. The EKG monitor etched his heartbeat across a screen, and its rhythm played aloud in little beeps from the monitor. "Viveca did everything she could to save you, didn't she? She loves you more than anything. I hope you know that. You should know that she's okay, Richard. Viveca and Liam are okay. Now, you hang in there and you come back to her and your son. They need you."

Frank laid his palm on Richard's arm and gave him a light squeeze. Richard's expression changed in quiet micro muscle spasms, little tics that played themselves across his face. His eyelids fluttered but did not open. "Hey, man," Frank said. "It's okay. Just rest. Viveca and Liam are fine. Just rest now."

From behind him the door opened, and a nurse stepped inside. "Who are you? What are you doing in here?"

"Just visiting my friend," Frank replied.

"Only family is allowed to visit," the nurse said patiently.

"His wife is my partner," he said and then showed her his badge.

"Even so, you aren't supposed to be in here, sir."

"I'm sorry."

"You should go now."

"Okay, I was just leaving," he said, then paused. "Can you tell me how he's doing?"

"I'm not sure I—"

"Please. His wife is frantic, and I know she won't rest and recover the way she needs to if she doesn't receive some kind of word soon. She doesn't know I'm down here. I just wanted to be able to tell her he's ..." Frank trailed off.

"He's showing small signs of improvement, which is a good thing considering he was practically dead when they brought him in."

"*Practically* dead or actually dead?"

"I'm not sure what you mean."

"Never mind. Do you think he'll pull through?"

"I think that depends on him and how much fight he has left."

"Thank you for speaking to me. I know you weren't supposed to," Frank said, offering the nurse a kind smile.

The door opened again, and Dr. Goodman stepped inside. His eyebrows knitted together harshly upon seeing Frank. "Nurse Jenkins, what is this man doing here?"

Before she could answer, Frank spoke, "I snuck inside the room, and she was just about to escort me out when you came in."

"Sir, I met you upstairs. You knew very well no visitors other than family were supposed to be in here."

"And yet you won't let his family come visit him."

"Detective, I don't think you understand the severity of this man's injuries or the state of his wife's injuries."

What do you mean, 'the state of his wife's injuries'? What's wrong with Viveca?"

"They both suffered severe trauma. Mrs. Ambrose gave birth under extremely stressful conditions. How she managed to drive in her condition is beyond me. Her husband lost a tremendous amount of blood. Whoever attacked them meant to kill them, there's no question. And that's as much as I can say. The best thing for you to do is try to find out who did this. The best thing for me to do is try to make sure they recover."

"I'm not trying to give you a hard time, Doctor."

"Do you see this man's condition?" Dr. Goodman waved a hand toward the hospital bed.

"His *name* is Richard." Frank's tone had transitioned from sheepish to impatient.

"Do you see Richard's condition? His wife is in a very fragile state. Seeing him like this may upset her and she may take steps backward in her recovery. I need her to wait a couple of hours until the counselor arrives."

"So you don't think he's going to make it, do you?"

"Mr. Ambrose lost a lot of blood. We've done all we can for him. While he's shown small signs of improvement, his overall condition is very critical."

Frank nodded. "He's a fighter, Doctor."

"I pray so, Detective. If you want to be present with Mrs. Ambrose in a couple of hours, you may do so with her permission, but for now, I need you to leave. And I ask for your discretion."

Frank nodded and turned to Richard. "I'll see you in a couple of hours, my friend."

∞

Viveca held Liam and sat at Richard's beside. The fluids intravenous line was still attached, but the blood bag had been removed before she entered the room. Frank sat in a chair next to Viveca to provide support for what he knew the doctor would say. While Richard's vital signs had improved slightly, he was still critical overall—unconscious, and that, above all else, concerned his doctors.

"When will he wake up, Dr. Goodman?" Viveca asked.

"We're not sure, Viveca." He stepped to the bedside and pointed at several distinctive wave patterns playing themselves out on the monitor. "This one here is his heartbeat. His heart is beating steadily, but it's not as strong or as fast as I'd like to see. These here are his brainwaves. Again, steady, but not as active as I'd like to see."

"Would you consider this a coma?"

"It's not a coma in the traditional sense. He's suffered severe trauma, and he's lost a tremendous amount of blood. We're not sure when he'll wake up, or even if he will."

Viveca shot him a quizzical look and then glanced back and forth between the doctor and her husband. Then, she shook her head. "He has to wake up. If this isn't a coma, then he has to wake up, right? Richard wouldn't remain away from me and our son. He has too much to look forward to. Are there any other tests that can be run?"

"Not right now. We may want to do another MRI in another day or two if—"

"If?" Viveca steeled herself.

"Viveca, we've done all we can for him. I'm afraid it's up to him at this point. We will monitor his vitals, and keep him as comfortable as possible, but—"

"But what?"

"You should prepare for him not to recover."

"You think he's going to die?" Viveca held Liam closer to herself.

Dr. Goodman looked down at his shoes. He hated delivering bad news. When he looked up again, the crisis counselor, a woman named Dr. Delphi Williams, spoke up. "This is one of the reasons I'm here, dear."

Viveca gave the counselor a hardened glance then refocused her attention on Dr. Goodman. "So you kept me from my husband until she," Viveca pointed harshly at Dr. Williams, "could arrive?"

"It's standard procedure to have a counselor in the room when—"

"I don't care about your freaking standard procedure!" In her arms, Liam began to cry. Viveca turned to Frank and handed him the baby, then she stood. Richard's hospital bed separated her from the two doctors. "For this whole day, I've been going out of my mind, worrying about Richard, and you maintained that I was too fragile to see him or that he was in recovery and I could see him soon. Now, I know this was not the case! You just wanted to make sure this woman was here to help you do your job! You know what, *Doctor*, my husband is *alive!* He's alive, and until his heart stops beating, no one in this hospital is going to give up on him! You understand? You be his doctor, or I swear to god, I'll find a new doctor!"

"Viveca, I know you're upset, and I am sorry I delayed you seeing Richard. I honestly thought it was best for you. You were in a very fragile state yourself, and I did not want to risk your recovery. You gave birth under extremely stressful circumstances."

"Why does everyone assume I don't know that? I was there. I know what happened. I also know I am recovering quickly. So the next time I ask to see my husband, someone is going to take me to him. No questions, no delays, no excuses. Am I understood?"

"Viveca," Dr. Williams said gently. "Why don't you and I go to my office where we can talk?"

"No. I'm staying here with my husband. You both can go have a talk in your office. Start with how to treat your patients with dignity and the truth."

"We do need to talk, Viveca. You're very angry right now, and—"

"You bet your ass, I'm angry! Now, I may want to talk to you later, like tomorrow—maybe—but right now, I want to sit with my husband. I want to let him know I'm here, and I want to be left alone with him."

"Viveca, it's not a good idea to let yourself get stressed out, and—"

"Okay, for the cheap seats: get the hell out of this room! Both of you! Now!"

Goodman and Williams made their way to the door. Goodman opened the door for Williams, and she stepped out, but Dr. Goodman lingered a moment. "No one in this hospital is trying to hurt you or Richard, Viveca. We're just doing what we think is best. If you want to visit your husband, I don't see a reason why you cannot. You obviously can handle it. But the ICU has rules. You have thirty minutes."

"Fine. Come back in thirty."

∞

"Holy shit, Viv!"

"I know I was harsh, and I'll apologize later, but I had to get them out of here. Time is of the essence."

"What are you going to do?"

"I'm going to pull him into the dream walk. I'm going to try to find out if he's still my Richard."

"What can I do?"

"Guard the door. Do not let anyone in here, no matter what. If it's over thirty minutes, make something up. Do whatever you have to."

Frank nodded, moved his chair to the door, and sat like a barricade. Liam had fallen asleep in his arms, and the baby seemed to be the only peaceful thing about the room. "No one is getting in here, Viv."

"Be back soon." Viveca reached over and took Richard's hand. In another moment, she and Richard were in the luscious green field once more. She smoothed the hair away from his face as he opened his eyes to look at her. "Richard," she said, the hope of a thousand worlds in her voice.

"Where am I?" He asked as he sat up next to her.

"The dream walk."

"Malcolm!"

"He got away."

Richard reached over and touched Viveca's belly. Still swollen from giving birth but nowhere near her pregnant girth. "Liam."

"He's beautiful, Richard! Frank is taking care of him while we're here."

"Malcolm left the vampire with me."

"I know. I can see it. Fight it, Richard! Can you fight it?"

He shook his head, and his eyes held a stark sadness. "When I wake, I'll be a vampire again."

"You controlled it before. Maybe you can prevent it from taking hold altogether."

He shook his head again. "All I feel is cold and weak. I haven't any strength to fight it, my love. Can you wield the phoenix to burn the vampire from me? Like you said you separated the ghoul from that Price fellow?"

It was her turn to shake her head. "I lost the phoenix when we arrived at the hospital. I've been trying to call her back, but she won't come."

"So there's no hope," Richard said, resigned to fate.

"Your heart still beats, Richard. As long as it does, there's hope. Keep your heart beating."

"I love you, Viveca."

Tears stained her cheeks. "You're making it sound like goodbye. Please. Fight. Don't give up!"

"How? I can feel the change trying to happen even as I sit here."

"We've come so far!"

"We're running out of time, sweetheart. Tell me you love me."

"I love you! I'll love you forever, Richard. It's you. It was always you. And it's always going to be you."

Richard leaned over and kissed her gently, then they emerged from the dream walk. Richard was, once again, lying in repose. His vitals were growing ever more slowly. Viveca sat beside him with her head in her hands. She felt her heart breaking. The dream walk had taken so much more out than it had put in.

Frank moved his chair from the door and came to sit next to Viveca again. "What's the verdict?"

"The vampire is with him, but—and I don't really understand it—it hasn't yet taken hold of him. He's tired and weak, and he doesn't think there's hope. He believes that when he awakes, he'll be a vampire again. He's waiting for his body to die."

"So what does that mean?"

"It means that when my husband wakes, he might very well be a vampire, and then we'll be separated forever."

"But could Richard fight it?"

"I know on some level, he'll try, but he's so tired, Frank."

"But what if he could find the strength to fight it?"

"He could hold onto the cage the way he did before, but he'd still be a vampire. We'd be starting over, except this time, I won't be able to save him."

"Is there any chance he could go back to being Richard?"

"I don't know. It hasn't taken hold yet, so maybe there is a chance. But Dr. Goodman is right. Richard lost a lot of blood. Let's say by some miracle he can recover and defeat the vampire. He may never be my Richard again."

"What would he be?"

"I don't know. It would all depend on how much damage the blood loss did to his body. He could have brain damage, organ damage, heart failure. It's possible he could emerge in a vegetative state. It's the toss of the dice."

The door opened, and Dr. Goodman stepped into the room. His tone was gentle. "I'm afraid time is up, Viveca. You can see him again in the morning."

"Thank you. I'd like to apologize for earlier, Dr. Goodman. I shouldn't have spoken to you or Dr. Williams like that. I know in my heart you are doing all you can to help me and Richard."

Dr. Goodman gave her a kind smile. "I understand, Viveca. And I accept your apology. If you'd like to speak to Dr. Williams, I can bring you to her office."

"Please. I do think it's good to talk to her."

Dr. Goodman stepped out of the room a moment, and when he returned, a pretty nurse entered the room after him. "I'll just take the baby back to the nursery, if that's okay."

Viveca nodded, and Frank handed her the baby. The two shared a quiet smile, and then she was gone with Liam toward the neonatal wing. "I've got to meet Watson about the case, but I'll be back tomorrow, Viv," Frank said.

"Thanks for being here for me, Frank."

"Anytime, partner."

∞

"Are you comfortable, Viveca?" Dr. Williams asked once Dr. Goodman had stepped out of the office. Not far from the desk, on a large plush pillow, a medium black dog was curled up in slumber.

"Is that your dog?" It sounded like a stupid question, but hadn't she seen an animal sitting in her doorway?

"That is Shadow. She's a Labrador. She's a service dog."

"She's beautiful."

"Thank you. Now, let's get back to you. How are you feeling? Are you comfortable?"

"I'm fine. Thank you. Dr. Williams, I'd like to apologize for the way I spoke to you earlier. I know you're here to help me."

Just as Goodman had done, Dr. Williams gave her a kind smile and accepted her apology. "We all have our moments, Viveca."

"I'm afraid," Viveca admitted, keeping her eyes on her hands.

"I know you are. And that's what we're going to talk about. Your fear, how you feel physically, mentally, emotionally, and spiritually."

"Spiritually?"

"Of course. Our belief systems go a long way in regulating how we feel about the world. Oh, it's not going to be a revival meeting in here, but rather a general discussion about how you see things and what you believe helps you manage how you see things."

"Okay, I think I understand."

"We don't have to get started today, but I do want to ask you a few questions to start your file, and then we can schedule regular sessions while you're recovering, and then once you're discharged, we'll maintain a schedule that works for you."

"How long does this last?"

"The sessions usually last about an hour. How long your therapy will last will depend on you and how long you feel you need me to help you."

"So I'm not committing myself to anything?"

"Not at all."

Viveca sighed and closed her eyes. "Okay. Let's get started."

"Were you born in New Orleans?"

"Yes."

"What was your childhood like?"

"My parents died in an accident when I was six. I grew up at St. Mary's Orphanage."

"I see. And how well did you get along with the other orphans?"

"Can I ask what that has to do with me, my husband, or our son?"

"Nothing at all, but it helps me to get to know you. The better I know and understand you, the more helpful I'll be to you."

The pleasant demeanor of Dr. Williams helped Viveca relax. Viveca called the tigress and began assessing the woman. Something about her instantly relaxed Viveca. There was a distinct aura about her that reminded her of Nana. She looked over at Dr. Williams's dog. Even the dog seemed to be a source for relaxation and calm. Was this woman a visionary, she wondered. She pulled the tigress back and remained silent.

Dr. Williams sat forward a bit in her chair. "Viveca?"

Viveca's mind raced. If this woman was a visionary, why was she really here? She thought quickly, desperate to find a response that would satisfy Dr. Williams and keep her thoughts to herself. Again, Dr. Williams called for her attention. "Viveca?"

"I'm sorry," Viveca began. "I've just got so much on my mind." She looked around the room and began taking note of her surroundings. The office was more dimly lit. The blinds were inordinately thick for office blinds, and the sun was barely peeking through them. A small desk lamp burned with soft ambient light. All of it would serve to keep Viveca's vision at a minimum.

"Of course you do. A lot has happened to you in the past few days, and you may be facing a choice soon."

"A choice? What do you mean?"

"Dr. Goodman has tried his best to prepare you for—"

Viveca held up her hand. "Not right now. He's alive."

"He is, Viveca, but he suffered significant blood loss. Oxygen deprivation, especially to the brain in these cases, can prove devastating. You must know that he may not be the Richard you knew if he wakes up at all."

Viveca closed her eyes a moment. When she opened them again, she looked up at Dr. Williams. She allowed her anger to bubble to the surface of her emotions. "I have to believe he will be fine. For our son's sake, and for my own. Dr. Goodman also said that Richard's brainwaves are steady," Viveca challenged. She took a breath and continued, "At least for now, he's doing well. I have to hold on to that. It's all I have."

"Viveca, I'm here to help you keep a healthy perspective on the situation, be a listening ear, and help you manage your emotions. Sometimes just talking about it will help."

Viveca stood and locked eyes with Dr. Williams. "Look, I'm telling you I'd rather remain positive and hopeful, and you are resigned to believe that I should prepare myself for my husband to die. I don't choose to accept that, and I'd appreciate it if you would keep your crystal ball to yourself."

"I'm sorry, Viveca. It isn't my intention to upset you. I only thought you should at least prepare for the possibility that—"

Viveca shook her head. "No. I'm not going to prepare for anything but for him to come home. I'm not going to grieve him while he's still alive! How dare you even suggest that I do that!" She didn't wait for an answer. She turned on her heel and left the room. So much time had passed. Only moments ago, the afternoon sunlight had been peeking around Dr. Williams' blinds. Now, dusk lay behind them with night not far behind. How did she lose time?

She didn't know where she was going. She should have been headed back toward her room, but her feet took her elsewhere. Down one corridor, then another. Her anger brought tears to her eyes again. She would *not* cry. *He's alive,* she thought. *Don't grieve him!* When she turned the next corner, she found herself at the cafeteria. Next to it, a door leading to a stairwell. The smell of food and coffee rumbled her stomach. She was hungry, but she resisted. Instead, she entered the stairwell and made her way up. She let the tigress loose within her spirit and raced up each flight. At the uppermost landing, there were two doors: one which led back into the hospital and another which led to the roof. The roof access door held a sign at her eye level: *Roof Access: Authorized Personnel ONLY.*

A quick try at the handle. Unlocked. She wasn't authorized to access the door, she knew, but she nevertheless entered through it and made her way to the rooftop. Outside. Fresh air. The assailing scents of latex and bleach sealed off behind her. She took a deep breath. She could feel the tigress yearning to run. "Okay, my friend. Let's race!"

The tigress burst from her. The rooftop was a flat panel of concrete with several air units arranged around it, each sending recycled air into the building. Each standing like a large hurdle. It wasn't a rooftop; it was an obstacle course! A place she could burn off her nervous energy and clear her mind. She ran, the tigress at her side. Coming toward the first of the air units, she leapt and cleared the obstacle with ease. Around and around she ran, leaping, allowing the power of the tigress fill her until she became the dream walker warrior. She could feel her hair growing, could see it turn to its beautiful stark white of the tigress's mane. Her muscles felt stronger. Her vision acute and taking in everything the night disclosed.

At long last, she returned to her room. A moment later, an orderly entered with her supper. She thanked him kindly and settled in to eat. Hospital food wasn't the greatest, but she was starving. The baked chicken breast and vegetables needed salt, but otherwise were delicious. A soft bread roll was her favorite part of the meal.

When she put her fork down, her thoughts turned immediately to Richard. She knew his battle would soon be over. Would he wake a vampire, or would he still be her Richard? Her mind filled with conflicting thoughts. In the dream walk, he was still her Richard, determined to fight the vampire as he had done for over two centuries. Still, she couldn't help but wonder if he would be able to fight it this time. When he was first turned, the repulsion of seeing Malcolm murder an innocent girl had inspired him to wage war against the monster within. But now, he was so tired. Stress and worry had compromised his strength, and she had been the cause of a lot of it.

She sensed he was on the verge of a new becoming, and there wasn't a damned thing she could do about it. Time was running out, and the phoenix was not responding to her call. If she could regain the phoenix, she could destroy the vampire before it could claim him. She had projected it in healing protection of him, but she feared she had wielded it to its limits. Mr. Eaglefeather had warned her about that. Like any energy, it would need rest to regenerate its power. She brought her hands to her face and tried to focus on the positives. He was still alive. The vampire had not yet taken hold. Richard was a strong man with a strong will. Hadn't he proven that over two centuries of living in that cage? He waged war against it before. He could do it again.

She pressed her hands more firmly over her face and tried to hold back the sob that was rising within her. *Don't grieve him!* she reminded herself. *Don't grieve him until his heart stops beating!* After a moment, she let her hands drop to her lap. An errant tear, large and purposeful, traced a path down her cheek. She hated to admit it, but Dr. Williams was right. She had to face the possibility that Richard would not come home. She had to face it. It was the only way she was going to make it through should the worst happen.

Then, suddenly, Frank's voice was in her head. He had told her that he would be there for her and Liam. She realized then that Frank had believed Richard would not survive. It occurred to her that if not for the vampire within him, Richard would most likely be dead already. Then, hope rose anew. That determined, hard-headed, stubborn part of her that refused to give up or give in allowed her a final glimmer of optimism. He had been a vampire when they'd met. He had loved her with all his heart. Maybe, just maybe, he still would.

CHAPTER 3

December 21, 2016, New Orleans, Louisiana, 6:47 a.m.

"Did you have any trouble getting in?" Viveca asked when Frank entered her room.

"No. Everything was right where you said it'd be," Frank replied and held up the items he'd retrieved from her house. "Where you want it, boss?"

Viveca smiled. "On the chair is fine. Thanks, Frank."

"Any time. I brought your key with me. Hope that was okay."

"Yes, fine. Will you please place it in my jacket pocket?"

"Sure," he said and slipped the key into the jacket he'd retrieved and zipped the pocket.

"So how's work?"

"It's busy. There's a new string of disappearances, Viv. Men and women from all different backgrounds. Literally, there's nothing to connect them."

"What are your theories?"

"I don't kn—"

"Frank, you're a good detective. What are your theories?"

He shrugged then said, "Maybe the vampires are up to something."

She nodded. "Yep."

"So what is it?"

"Malcolm thinks Richard is dead. He'll come for his revenge."

Frank shook his head. "There has to be a way to protect you, Viv. You and Liam."

"Frank, I need you to promise me something. If anything happens to me and Richard, please take care of Liam. I need to know that he's going to be okay. Can you promise me that?"

"Viv, nothing is going to—"

"Promise me."

He nodded. "I promise. I won't let anything happen to him." Frank came toward her and sat on the bed next to her. "They're going to discharge you today. Are you okay to go home?"

"I'm not going home. I'm going to see Nana. I need to introduce her to her grandson, and I need to let her know what's happened with Richard and Malcolm."

"Do you want me to drive you? Your car was towed to evidence. I got your other keys off the ring, though."

"What vehicle did you drive here?"

"Richard's truck, as you asked."

"Good. I'll need it. Can you be here when I'm discharged?"

"Of course I can. Do you want me to drive you?"

She shook her head. "No. I need to go alone. I'm going to ask Mike if he can pick you up and bring you home or to the station."

"I can call ahead and have one of the guys come here."

"No," she said urgently. "You and Mike and Stan are the only people I trust right now, Frank. I don't want anyone else near me right now."

"You're even more scared than you're letting on, aren't you?"

She looked up at him, and the expression she wore told him everything. "I'm afraid for my son and my husband."

"And what about yourself?"

She shook her head again. "I'm not worried about me. I'm a warrior. I was born to handle these things."

"Viv," Frank said, touching her arm with his hand. "You don't have to be strong all the time, you know."

"Yes, I do. I've known this for a long time. It was only reconfirmed the moment Richard lay dying at my side."

Frank moved his hand from her arm and placed his fingers under her chin. "You are the bravest person I've ever met," he said and leaned down to brush his lips against her cheek. Then, he gathered her into his embrace and held her close. "I'm worried about you, Viv."

She didn't say anything at first. She sat in his embrace a moment and listened to his heartbeat. "I'm worried about you too. Malcolm is going to come for me and Liam, and he is sure to destroy anything and anyone in his way."

She felt him stiffen in his posture for a fraction of a moment, then he released her and stood from the bed. Looking down at her, he nodded. "Then, we'll figure out a way to destroy him for good."

She smiled despite herself. "We?"

"Yes, 'we.' You aren't going to fight this alone. I'm your partner, and I've got your back."

"It's going to be dangerous."

"I'll wear my bulletproof vest and garlic garland."

Viveca laughed. "Garlic doesn't bother vampires, Frank. Or ghouls."

"Then, I'll speak softly and carry a big stake."

Viveca laughed harder. "Stakes don't kill them either. Stakes might just serve to piss them off."

"Well then, I'll Paul Bunyan the damned thing and carry my big ax."

"Now you're getting with the program! Remove the heart or the head."

He gave her a half-hearted smirk and feigned an ego. "Yep. Totally know what I'm doing." Then he and Viveca laughed for what seemed like the first time in a really long time.

∞

Frank was right on time. Mike and Stan were just behind him, waiting for vehicles to change hands. The car seat the captain had given Viveca was secured in the back of the double cab. Viveca placed Liam in the car seat and came around to take the keys from Frank. He pulled her into his embrace again and lowered his lips to her ear. "You be careful," he whispered.

"I will," she whispered back. She moved from his embrace to wave at Mike and Stan, then she hauled herself into the cab and began her journey to see Nana.

The old house was nestled deep within the bayou south of New Orleans. Nana had promised to go there and not return until Viveca had come to get her, and as Viveca approached the old place, she could see Nana's car parked close to the front porch.

The sound of an approaching vehicle had called Nana to the porch. The sight of Richard's truck pulled a sigh of relief from her, but the sight of Viveca emerging from the driver's side gave her pause. "Where's Richard, dear?" she asked as Viveca moved around the truck to open the rear door of the double cab. "Viveca?" Nana called.

Viveca came back from around the vehicle with Liam in his car seat. The car seat converted to a carrier, and Viveca toted it by the handle. She had slung the bag Frank had packed over her other shoulder.

The sight of the baby moved Nana from the porch to Viveca's side. "Oh my goodness! He's beautiful, sweetheart!" Viveca gave her a half-smile and handed Liam to her. "Oh, Viveca, he's perfect!" She looked over at her granddaughter. Viveca, usually full of spark, looked to have the weight of the world on her shoulders. Nana took a breath. "Dear, where's Richard?"

Viveca crumbled under her emotions. The stress of the past few days caught up to her at once. She fell to her knees and sobbed. Nana immediately knelt down beside her. "Viveca, I'm so sorry, sweetheart. I'm so sor—"

"He's in the hospital, Nana," Viveca said through her sobs. "But he's not well. And if he dies, he'll rise a vampire."

Nana placed a hand on Viveca's shoulder. "He's been a vampire before, darling. He was able to fight it then, I'm sure he'll be able to fight it n—"

"Yes, but this time, I cannot perform the blazing. And he's weak. He may not be able to fight it, resist it, or keep it at bay. I just can't think of a way around it. I really do hope Malcolm comes for his revenge. I'll take great pleasure in flaying the skin off that asshole!"

"Dear, it may not come to that. You know there's always a chance."

Viveca let out a rueful chuckle. "Now you sound like me last year."

"Come on, honey. Let's get inside. We'll figure it all out over tea."

Viveca rose and followed Nana inside. "Nana, I just don't know what I'll do without him. I'm so scared."

"I know you are," Nana said and laid Liam on a blanket. "Come here, sweetheart," Nana said and opened her arms. Viveca entered her grandmother's embrace and wept. Nana stroked her hair and tried to soothe her. "It's going to be okay. Richard has always looked out for you. He'll find a way to keep looking out for you."

"I love him so much! I can't imagine being without him, Nana. He was made for me. I know he was!"

"Of course he was, dear." Nana said.

Within minutes, Nana had poured tea, prepared it as she knew Viveca liked it and joined her granddaughter and great-grandson in the living room. Viveca held Liam close to her, a small blanket over her shoulder, shielding his head and her right breast. Nana smiled. When Viveca looked up to see her grandmother, she blushed slightly. "I'm sorry, Nana. I can move to different room."

"Oh, no, dear. Don't leave. There's nothing more natural or beautiful than a mother breastfeeding her child. It's just us. Nothing to be embarrassed about."

Viveca smiled. In another few minutes, Liam was ready for burping. Viveca laid another cloth over her left shoulder and placed Liam against it and patted his back. He made a small hiccupping sound and a small amount of spit-up was absorbed by the towel. "That's my good boy," Viveca said, rubbed Liam's back, then moved him back into her arms to clean him up with some baby wipes she had placed on the coffee table.

Nana beamed at them. "You're a natural at this, Viveca."

"You really think so?"

"Yes, I do. Just look at you, sweetheart. You're a wonderful mother. I can see that honey."

Viveca smiled and looked down at her son. "He's so gorgeous! He looks just like his father."

"There's some of you in him too. He's got your cheeks and your hands."

"He's got Richard's eyes and smile. I think he might have my nose and chin, but that will remain to be seen," Viveca said and then reflected on meeting her son in the dream walk. If he really would look like the child in her dream walk, he would look more and more like Richard as he grew up.

"How are you feeling, Viveca?"

"I'm tired. I'm a bit stressed out. I'm a bit scared. I'm a bit angry. I'm a bit of everything, I think."

"Why don't I take him while you take a nap?"

"Oh, we'll be okay, Nana. You need your rest too."

"Not as much as you need yours, sweetheart. Come on. He'll be fine, I promise. I may be old, but I remember how to take care of a baby. You'll be right in the next room if we need you."

Viveca looked thoughtfully at her son and then at her grandmother. It would do them both some good to bond. "Okay. Thanks, Nana." She stood and laid her son in her grandmother's waiting arms. Seeing Nana hold Liam brought her emotions full circle.

Nana looked up at her. "Go on, now. We'll be fine. Get some rest."

Viveca nodded and made her way to the first bedroom. She entered the adjoining bathroom and took a shower. She hadn't thought to bring the bag in with her, but there were towels she could cover up in long enough to retrieve her bag. The car seat carrier combo the captain had given her would the best thing to put Liam in for the night. She should have thought of all this before she took her shower, but Nana was right: it was just them.

∞

In the living room, Nana held Liam and rocked him gently. She hummed a little tune under her breath and stroked his hair. He was a beautiful child, and she smiled down at him lovingly. "You are the sweetest boy in the world, Liam Ambrose. Your Nana has something for you. You're going to need this, my child. You will remember this moment when the time comes, Liam, and when you do, you will know what to do with it."

Nana placed her free hand over the baby's face, her fingers splayed wide, the tips of each gently touching the top of his head. The palm of her hand barely rose above Liam's mouth and nose. She closed her eyes and focused her energy. In another moment, a brilliant light emanated from her palm and suffused into the baby's skin. When she moved her hand, Liam had his eyes open and was looking up at her. She smiled down at him. He reached up and grabbed hold of her index finger. Then, he offered a soft, but knowing smile. In response to her energy, a delicate golden light radiated around him. A warmth—beautiful and serene—rose with the light, and Nana marveled at her grandson.

In another moment, the golden light subsided, but the warmth remained around him. He smiled up at her again and let out a small gurgle of happiness. Nana smiled. "You are incredible. That's what you are."

∞

Viveca stood in the doorway and watched Nana rock Liam in her arms. She allowed herself a moment's happiness over the scene. In that moment, nothing was wrong. Liam was a perfect child, and they were just waiting for Richard to come home from work.

Nana looked up to see Viveca. "Oh, hello, dear. Did you have a nap already?"

"No. Just took a shower. I forgot to get my bag. Can't get dressed without it."

"Why don't I turn down the bed for you and set up Liam's carrier, sweetheart?"

"Oh, you don't have to do that, Nana. I can certainly turn down my own bed. Besides, you look very comfortable holding my son."

"I do, but I also insist." Nana rose from the chair, and Viveca took Liam back into her arms. Nana smiled up at her. "I'll be right back, dear."

Viveca took Nana's spot in the rocking chair and contented herself to hold her son. In another moment, she began to sing a lullaby. It was a song she knew but could not remember hearing. When she came to the end of it, she began it again. Then, she repeated the song a third time. Where had she heard it?

"I used to sing that song to your mother," Nana said from the doorway.

Viveca looked up with a smile. "She must have sang it to me, then."

"I don't doubt it, dear. When she was a little girl and I would sing to her, she'd always say she couldn't wait to have a baby so she could sing it to them."

Viveca smiled. "How is it I can remember all the lyrics? I looked at my son and started to sing. I wasn't even thinking about it. The song just came to me."

Nana moved to sit on the sofa next to the rocking chair. "Viveca, there are moments in our lives that transcend our conscious, and even our unconscious minds and find their way to our very souls. What your soul remembers, you can never forget. Things which are imparted to us through love—especially unconditional love—stay with us forever. We pass these down the generations. I believe even if your mother had never sung that song to you, you would still know it."

"I believe you."

"Why don't you try to get some sleep now, sweetheart?"

"Thank you for turning down my bed and setting up Liam's carrier."

"I placed your bag on the floor by the nightstand."

"Thank you, Nana."

"You're welcome, dear. Now give me my grandson. I want to rock him a while longer. I'll place him in his carrier before I turn in."

Viveca rose from the chair, and Nana took the seat. Viveca laid Liam into Nana's arms, then kissed Liam's cheek and then Nana's. "I'll be right in the next room."

CHAPTER 4

December 22, 2016, New Orleans, Louisiana, 4:57 a.m.

Her phone was ringing. She struggled to consciousness and clumsily reached for her phone. She pressed the green answer button and held the phone to her ear. "Hello?" she asked groggily.

"Mrs. Ambrose?" A clinical voice asked.

Viveca sat up quickly, her eyes opening fully to her surroundings. "Yes," she said breathlessly.

"This is Amber Wakefield from New Orleans General."

"Richard! Is he okay?"

"He's awake, Mrs. Ambro—"

"I'm on my way!" Viveca hung up the phone and moved from the bed quickly. She pulled on the first pair of jeans from her bag and slipped on her shoes. Liam was sleeping in his car seat. Nana had apparently placed him in it as promised when she decided to go to bed. Waking him up meant feeding him, but she'd have to. Liam came first, no matter what.

She forced herself to slow down. Her heart had been racing. She unstrapped Liam from the car seat and picked him up. He stirred and then he started to cry. "It's okay, baby. Momma's here." She felt his diaper and realized he needed changing.

Frank was a world-class bag packer. He'd thought of everything—her clothes, Liam's clothes, diapers, wipes, baby blankets, bibs, burping cloths, and changing pad. She definitely owed him one. She spread the changing pad over the bed and laid Liam on it, then went about the business of changing his diaper. "That's Momma's good boy," she cooed. That done, she disposed of the dirty diaper, refolded the changing cloth, and prepared to feed her son.

A soft knock came to the door. "Come in," Viveca called, and Nana entered the room.

"I heard a commotion. Is everything okay?"

"Richard is awake, Nana. I've got to get to the hospital."

"Of course. Do you want me to keep Liam?"

"No, I want to take him with me. I know Richard will want to see him."

"Of course, sweetheart."

"Is everything okay, Nana?"

"Everything is fine, dear. Do you want to some coffee or breakfast?"

"I don't have time, but I appreciate it."

"Please tell Richard I love him and can't wait to see him."

Viveca nodded. "I will." Then, she took in a sharp intake of air. "Nana?"

"Yes, dear?"

"What if he's not my Richard anymore?"

"You will know what to do if he's not."

Viveca took in another deep breath. She nodded sadly then looked down at her son. "You just about done there, young man?"

"He's got a healthy appetite. That's a good sign that he'll grow into a strong man."

"Yeah, well, I believe it. This kid has more suction than a hoover vacuum!" Viveca suddenly burst into laughter, and Nana joined her.

"Viveca, I love you, dear. You and Liam."

"We love you too, Nana."

∞

The plan was to see Richard then return to Nana and escort her home. Viveca had no illusions that Richard would be released from the hospital. She spoke aloud to activate the dial assistant on her phone.

Her cellphone assistant asked how it could help. "Call Frank Taylor," Viveca commanded.

"Calling Frank Taylor," the dial assistant announced.

On the second ring, Frank answered. "Taylor," he said sleepily.

"Hey, Frank, it's Viv. I'm sorry to wake you."

"No problem. What's up?"

"Richard's awake."

"Are you headed to the hospital now?"

"Yes. Do you think you could meet me there? I'm sorry to ask, but if this thing goes south, I'll need you to take Liam away quickly."

"I can be there in fifteen minutes."

"I'm about that far away myself. Thank you, Frank."

"See you soon, Viv."

∞

She parked in the closest visitor space she could find and lifted the carrier from the back seat. "We're going to see Daddy," she said, her voice shaking. She took a deep breath. In the east, the sun began to peak over the horizon. Viveca picked up her pace.

At the nurse's station in ICU, Viveca saw Frank waiting for her. "Give me the baby," he said, and she handed the carrier to him.

"Are his blinds closed as I instructed?" she asked the nurse.

"His blinds?"

"Yes, the blinds on the window in my husband's room. Are they closed as I instructed?"

The nurse's eyes went wide a moment. "I don't think so, Mrs. Ambr—"

Viveca rushed past the nurse's station and toward Richard's room. If he had awakened a vampire, he was in a lot of trouble. Down the hall, she ran, dodging orderlies and nurses making their rounds. She reached her husband's door and threw it open to see daylight streaming through the window. Her heart lurched, and she forced herself to make the few steps it would take to move beyond the tiny hallway that housed the bathroom.

He was sitting up in bed, watching television, several rays of sun falling over his skin like a spotlight. She could not believe her eyes. She took in a deep breath and allowed her vision to assess him. As perfect as the day she pulled him from the blazing, Richard sat before her as a human man. He retained no traces of the vampire spirit Malcolm had tried to force upon him. But was he *her* Richard?

"Richard?" she asked gently.

He moved his attention from the television to her and smiled. "Viveca," he said quietly. "I can't explain it, love, but I'm not a vampire."

Tears sprung to her eyes, and all the tension she'd done her best to suppress over the past seventy-two hours came rushing forward to cripple her and send her to her knees. In another moment, Frank appeared in the doorway holding Liam's carrier. "Viv?" he asked gently. "Are you okay?"

She said nothing, but she pointed toward the hospital bed. He looked up to see Richard sitting in the sunlight. "My god," Frank uttered, then helped Viveca to her feet and to a nearby chair.

"Are you all right, love?" Richard asked.

Viveca stared at him. Marveled. "I'm fine. Oh god, Richard, I was so afraid I'd lose you!"

"I'm not going anywhere, love."

Frank unstrapped Liam from the carrier and picked him up so Richard could see him. "Hey, my friend, want to meet your son?"

Richard gazed awestruck at his son, then held his arms out toward Frank. "Can I hold him?"

"Of course you can." Frank moved to the other side of Richard's bed and laid Liam into his arms.

"My son," Richard said. "Look at him! He's perfect, Viveca. I love him so much."

The hospital room door opened, and a nurse stepped inside. "Is everything okay in here? How are you feeling, Mr. Ambrose?"

Richard beamed at the nurse. "My son," was all he said.

The nurse moved past where Frank was standing to check the intravenous line. The bag was half-full. "Your doctor should be in soon,

Mr. Ambrose, and your breakfast will be delivered shortly. Is there anything I can get for you? Water? Are you in any pain?"

A tear escaped Richard's right eye and tracked down his cheek. "I have everything I need. Thank you," he replied, never taking his eyes from his son.

The nurse smiled, then focused her attention on Viveca and Frank. "He's still going to need his rest. I'm sorry, but ICU restricts visits to thirty minutes."

Viveca looked up at the nurse and smiled. "I understand, but I'm his wife, and he's holding our son for the first time. I'll need to stay with him at least until his doctor arrives."

"Oh, I'm so sorry, Mrs. Ambrose. I didn't realize you were his wife. You can stay, of course, but your friend will have to leave in thirty minutes."

"We understand. Thank you so much for everything you all have done for my husband."

"We've all been praying for him. We're so happy to see him doing well."

"Thank you."

The nurse smiled and left the room. Frank came to her side of the bed and sat on a rather uncomfortable sofa. "Geez! Who designed this sofa? Josef Mengele?"

"Yeah, well, imagine sleeping on it." Viveca laughed, then returned her attention to Richard. "You okay over there, Daddy?"

Viveca's use of the noun drew his attention to her. He offered her a smile that bespoke his happiness. "I'm a daddy," he said, the smile becoming boyish with wonder and pride. Then, the smile beamed again.

"I better get going," Frank announced.

"Already?" Richard asked.

"Yeah, have to meet with Watson in an hour."

"Any leads on those disappearances?" Viveca asked.

"Not yet. No real blood evidence. No bodies have turned up. It's like they were kidnapped by aliens or something."

"What's happening?" Richard asked. Liam had fallen asleep across his chest, and he had his right hand over Liam's back. His left arm was still hooked into an intravenous line.

"People have been disappearing all around and outside New Orleans. There's no trace of any of them," Frank offered.

"Malcolm," Richard said. "He's creating ghouls, isn't he?"

"That was my first instinct too," Viveca said. "What I don't understand is how there haven't been any homicides in connection with the disappearances. Ghouls have to eat, don't they? Wouldn't there be some sort of trace?"

"We'd be happy for half a clue," Frank said. "I'll check on you guys later. I called Mike and Stan on the way here. I'll give them a call to let them know Richard is okay. Welcome back, Richard! It's good to see you. This one just about lost her mind worrying about you, my friend."

"Thank you, Frank. Take care and please keep us informed on the kidnappings," Richard said.

"Will do," Frank said and exited the room.

Richard turned to his wife. "You nearly lost your mind?"

"It wasn't quite that bad. I was really scared, though."

"I'm sorry, love."

"This isn't your fault, Richard. I've got to tell you something, though. Malcolm thinks you're dead. He's sworn his revenge."

∞

Nana's phone rang, and she picked it up quickly. "Hello?"

"Hi, Nana," Viveca said.

"Oh, Viveca, dear, I've been so worried!"

"Richard is okay, Nana. If his vitals check out, he'll get to come home tomorrow."

"Oh, sweetheart, that's wonderful!"

"Thank you for letting me and Liam stay with you last night."

"Of course, darling. Will I get to see you tonight?"

"Yes. Then, when Richard comes home, I'd like for you to stay with us for a little while."

"You and Richard aren't going to want me around when you get home, sweetheart."

"It's for the best, Nana. I think you're safe where you are, but you can't stay there forever. You're missing out on your friends and your social events. You deserve to get back to your life, but I don't want you to stay alone. Malcolm is still out there and he's going to make good his promise," Viveca said and looked up as the doctor entered the room. "Nana, the doctor just arrived. I'll call you back in a few minutes."

"Okay, dear. Talk to you soon."

∞

"Hello, Mr. and Mrs. Ambrose. I'm Dr. Kent Battiste. I'm assisting Dr. Goodman with his patients today while he's in surgery."

"It's nice to meet you, Doctor," Viveca said.

The doctor looked at Richard and noticed Liam sleeping on his chest. "Now, either you have the cutest tumor in the world, or that is your son all the nurses have been gushing about."

Richard smiled. "My son, Liam."

"Do I need to take him, Dr. Battiste?" Viveca asked.

"Oh, no. I'm just going to check Mr. Ambrose's vitals. No need to wake a sleeping baby." Dr. Battiste looked to be about thirty with light caramel skin, dark eyes, and a bright smile. His manner was easy-going and relaxed. He was kind. Even when things were at their worst, she imagined him to be a force for positivity. As was her habit of late, Viveca switched on her vision. He was human, and he was also something more. A visionary spirit shone out from him. Like Nana, like Delphi Williams, a special sort of aura surrounded him. She wondered if he recognized her for what she was.

Dr. Battiste examined Richard for blood pressure, heart rate, and lung function. He laughed delightedly when his stethoscope picked up both Richard's and Liam's heartbeats. Then, he moved on to check Richard's vision, then used an instrument to peer into each of Richard's ears. "You're doing well, Mr. Ambrose," he said, then began checking the bandage around Richard's throat. "It's interesting, these marks. Can you remember how you got them?"

"No," Richard lied.

"Two neat little holes just above your jugular vein. One might think you were attacked by a vampire."

Richard forced a laugh. "That's funny."

"No, it's not. Not really. And, yes, Mrs. Ambrose, I do recognize you for the dream walker you are."

Viveca sprung up from her seat, ready to defend her family. Dr. Battiste held up his hands and stepped away from Richard's beside. "What do you want?" Viveca asked.

"Nothing more than to make sure your husband is ready to be discharged. I mean you and your family no harm. In fact, we're on your side, Viveca."

"How do you know me?"

"I'm a visionary, like your grandma, like your mom. I've known Enola Hampshire for fifty years."

"You don't look old enough to have known her for so long."

"Visionaries age more slowly than normal human beings. It's nothing to be afraid of, it's just a fact of life. You can trust me. Call your grandma if you don't believe me."

"I believe you. It's just been a very rough few days."

Dr. Battiste gave her a reassuring smile. "I understand. Do you know where the vampire is who attacked your husband?"

"No. He ran away when my son was born."

Dr. Battiste looked admiringly down at Liam, who was exuding a beautiful golden aura. "I don't blame him. Your son has the light of the golden eagle around him. Liam must have scorched him good."

"The vampire has sworn revenge on me and my family."

"A darkness is coming. We all can feel it," Dr. Battiste said then turned his attention to Richard. "I'm going to discharge you today. If you start to feel dizzy or disoriented, you'll need to return."

"I understand, Doctor," Richard said then turned his head to smile at Viveca.

∞

"Hello?" a shaking voice asked.

"Nana?" Viveca asked.

"How's Richard?"

"He's doing well. He's being discharged today. What's wrong? You don't sound like yourself."

"Oh, I'm all right, dear," Nana replied.

"Are you sure?"

"Yes, I'm fine."

"Well, once he's been discharged, we're coming to get you."

"No! Don't come here!"

"Okay, something *is* wrong! What's happening, Nana?" Viveca listened as her grandmother cried out. Raspy breathing came onto the line. "Who is this?" Viveca demanded.

"Three years, dream walker!"

"What? Who *is* this?"

"You have three years to love your family, dream walker. That is the deal your grandmother made. Three years," the raspy voice announced.

"What is in three years?"

"The master comes for his brother."

"Let me speak to my grandmother!" She listened as Nana cried out again. Her voice came nearer the phone. "Nana!"

"Viveca," Nana said, her voice was weak. "I love you."

"I love you too, Nana!"

"Viveca, prepare for the rising. Prepare for—" Her voice was cut short, and Viveca distinctly heard a gasp and the sound of bones breaking.

"Nana! Nana, please! Nana!"

The raspy voice returned to the line. "Three years, dream walker," it said, and then the call was disconnected.

∞

"Taylor," Frank answered.

"Frank!"

"Hey, Viv, how's—"

"Frank, do you know where Old Tarver Road is?"

"Yes, what's wro—"

"Please get there now, it's the third house on the left. They're spaced out about a half mile apart."

"What's happ—"

"Oh god, please get there! I'm on my way. It's Nana!"

"I'm going!"

∞

"Viveca, please slow down, love. I know you're worried, but we won't do Nana any good if you get us killed."

"I'm fine, Richard," she said calmly and took the next curve at fifty miles per hour. The tires squealed, but she maintained control. The drive from New Orleans General to Old Tarver Road normally took forty-five minutes. Viveca made it in thirty. Only when she was near Nana's driveway did she slow down. She turned in and drove the truck all the way to the porch and parked next to Frank's sedan. "Stay with Liam," she said and exited the truck.

Richard watched as she approached the porch. Frank stepped from the doorway and began speaking to her. Suddenly, she tried to move past him, but he held on to her, effectively preventing her from entering the house. She attempted to throw him off her, but he kept his hold on her and brought her down to the porch steps. She continued her useless struggle a moment longer, then leaned against Frank. He heard her cries of anguish from where he was and knew the worst had happened. Behind him, Liam started to wail.

PART TWO

RICHARD

YEAR ONE

December 31, 2016, New Orleans, Louisiana, 6:12 p.m.

Nana's funeral had been devastating, and Stephanie Vaughn had insisted everyone return to her home for refreshments. Pastor Hawkins had delivered a very moving eulogy, and several members of the congregation had taken the time to say a few words. Viveca had stepped to the podium and told them all how much Nana had meant to her and how much she appreciated each of them for attending the services. When emotion began to overwhelm her, she pressed her hand to her mouth and stood there shaking. Pastor Hawkins had placed a hand on her shoulder and helped her down to the pews where she retook her seat next to Richard. Richard shifted Liam from his right arm to his left and took Viveca's hand in his.

When they arrived home, Richard unlocked the door and held it open to allow Viveca to pass ahead of him. Liam was asleep in her arms. She'd check his diaper, change him, feed him, then put him to bed. She was exhausted.

She began to ascend the stairs. "Viveca," Richard called up to her. She stopped at the first landing and looked sadly down at him. He gave her a small smile of sympathy. "Viveca, it wasn't your fault. You know that don't you?"

From where he stood, Richard could see the tears forming in her eyes again. Then, she shook her head. "I should never have gone there. I should have known they'd follow me."

"Viv, it's not your fault, honey."

"Do you honestly believe they'd have found her otherwise?"

He stood there in silence, then he looked up at her and spoke with conviction. "I think they were following everyone. I think they already knew where she was."

Viveca shook her head. "They would have killed her long before then, don't you think?"

"Not if Malcolm gave orders otherwise. Don't you see the game he's playing? He wants you to doubt yourself, Viv! He wants you to blame yourself!"

"I'm tired, Richard. I can't have this conversation right now. I'm going to feed Liam and then I'm going to bed. Are you coming?"

"I'll be there in a minute, love."

"Okay," she said and made her way to the second floor.

∞

When Richard entered the bedroom, Viveca was lying on her side with Liam cradled close to her. Liam was suckling at her left breast, his little hands pressed against her chest. She stroked his back with her left hand and massaged her breast with her right. Richard looked admiringly at his wife. Her quiet strength carried her through each moment they'd experienced together. She was his match in every way.

He made his way to his side of the bed and stripped to his boxers, then crawled in beside Viveca, put his arms around her, and placed his right hand over hers on Liam's back. He kissed her shoulder, nuzzled her neck, and kissed her neck just below her ear. "I love you so much, Viveca."

She turned her head to look back at him. "I love you too," she said and brought her lips briefly to his.

When Liam had had his dinner, Richard positioned the burping cloth over his right shoulder and held his son, patting his back gently. A soft hiccup was followed by a small amount of spit-up. Richard smiled down at his son. "Good job," he said lovingly, then proceeded to carry his son into the nursery for cleaning up and diaper change.

When Liam had been placed into his crib for the night, Richard returned to his wife and joined her once again on the bed. He held his arms open to her, and she immediately entered his embrace. "I just want to be in here with you for as long as you can be in here with me," he said. He stroked her skin with his hands and kissed her hair. "Rest now, love."

Viveca kissed him tenderly, then laid her head against his chest and closed her eyes. With his arms around her, she felt protected. She drifted into a peaceful sleep and left the hardships of the waking world behind.

∞

December 31, 2016, New Orleans, Louisiana, 11:33 p.m.

"Why did you give them three years?" Jazz asked sulkily. "We could have killed them easily in the hospital."

"Do you not understand? My brother is alive! He's alive, and he's *not* a vampire."

"So?"

"*So?* I bit him. I drained him. He should have turned, but he didn't. I gave them three years because that's what the visionary asked for in exchange for her life. I gave her my word. I keep my word, Jazz. You most of all should know that much about me."

"Oh, I know you do, Master," Jazz said and ran a hand across the right side of her face where her skin was still healing.

Malcolm closed the distance between them and touched her face. "This ought to have healed by now, my sweet. Have you been feeding enough?"

"You said to keep a low profile, Master. I haven't been killing them."

"Take one tonight, my precious. Keep to the homeless. You'll be safe to take someone who will not be missed."

"Thank you, Master."

∞

January 1, 2017, New Orleans, Louisiana, 5:37 a.m.

Liam was crying. Viveca woke to his cries coming from the baby monitor and rose and slipped on her robe. Richard stirred and sat up. "Do you want me to go, love?"

"No. You've been up with him all night. It's my turn. Go back to sleep."

"You sure?"

Viveca smiled. "Get some sleep, honey. I'll be back soon."

He smiled and snuggled back into his pillow. "Hurry back, love," he said, his voice sleep-muddled.

Viveca stood there a moment longer and watched her husband sleep. He'd been up every time Liam cried during the night. The nursery was the next room down from their bedroom, and she'd heard him singing to their son, his beautiful voice filling the room and echoing down to her. She hadn't had any idea he could sing, and she'd drifted back to sleep to his soothing voice.

She stepped over to him and kissed him on the temple. He stirred quietly but did not wake. "I love you, Richard," she whispered and made her way to the nursery.

Liam was on his back, wailing up at the Noah's Ark mobile Pastor Hawkins had given them as a baby gift. Lions, tigers, giraffes, and elephants chased each other, two by two, under the plush ark. "What are you crying about, little man?" she soothed her son. She picked him up and brought him to the changing table. She began to sing the soft lullaby she'd sung to him at Nana's not long ago. "*Little dreamer drift off to sleep. Dream of blue skies and fields of green. When you wake tomorrow, all will be fine. Little dreamer, little dreamer of mine.*"

"That's beautiful," Richard said from the doorway.

"I'm so sorry to wake you," she said as she changed Liam's diaper.

"You didn't wake me, love."

"I heard you singing to him last night. Your voice is amazing. What was it you were singing?"

"A lullaby my Mum used to sing to me and my brothers."

"It was lovely. She must have been such an incredible woman."

"She was. She would have loved you and Liam. She would have been so happy," Richard said affectionately.

"My parents too. Nana was overjoyed to see him," Viveca said, her expression turning a bit sad. She lifted Liam from the changing table and moved to sit with him in the nearby rocking chair. Holding him, she unbuttoned her nightgown, exposed her left breast, and lifted Liam to her nipple.

"I don't think I'll ever not be amazed by you, Viveca," Richard said.

She smiled up at him. "I'm not the first mother to breastfeed her child. I'm not doing anything amazing, Richard."

"Yes, you are," he said, stepping from the doorway and coming to kneel down beside the rocking chair. "You are the most amazing woman I've ever known. I love you." He leaned forward and kissed her, then he stroked his son's head gently.

"What are we going to do about Malcolm?" Viveca asked quietly.

"He's given us three years to love each other."

"And then?"

"And then he'll come for me."

"I won't let him take you away from me and Liam."

"I won't allow him to hurt you and Liam. If becoming a vampire again is what will keep you both safe, then that's what I'll do."

"I know you, Richard. If you become a vampire, we'll never see you again. You won't risk it."

"Maybe."

"What are you thinking?"

"I'm thinking that I'm not sure what happened in the hospital or why I didn't turn. Whatever it was, maybe it'll happen again."

"Malcolm will continue to create ghouls. Three years is a long time to amass an army. And forgive me, but your brother is a coward. He's not going to fight me himself."

"First, there's nothing to forgive. Malcolm isn't my brother. He may have once been, but he's not been for a very long time. Next, I'm sure he'll use the ghouls to try to weaken you. Then, once you cannot defend yourself or—well, let's just say that's when he'll come."

"So what do we do?"

"We prepare as best we can, but we focus on loving each other and raising our son. If I only have three years, I want to spend them loving you with all my heart."

Viveca placed her free hand on the side of Richard's face. She nodded. "I'm going to spend them loving you with all my heart too."

Richard took her hand in his and kissed her palm. Then, he stood and tossed a small towel across his right shoulder. "Looks like our little man needs burping. Here, I'll do it."

Viveca handed Liam to his father and stood to right her nightgown. She heard Liam hiccup and watched as Richard laid him back onto the changing table and cleaned him up. "Richard," she began. He lifted Liam into his arms and turned to face her. "I just want you to know that I will do everything in my power to protect you and Liam. I'll die trying if I have to."

"Don't die for me, Viveca. Not for me, love."

"I won't lose you, Richard."

He gave her a weak smile and stepped to pull her into his embrace, Liam nestled between them. "Viv, I may have to make that sacrifice, and if I must, I won't hesitate. Please know that I will do all I can to fight it just as I did before. I will fight it, love, with everything I am. I promise I will."

"But you won't come back to us. Even if you fight it, you won't chance hurting him or me. How many times did I try to draw you near only to have you distance yourself from me?"

"Because I loved you so much, I sometimes lost my grip on that cage. I was unprepared for how much the vampire would fight me falling in love with you. Now, I know the lengths it will go to. I will find a way back to you and our son if that's what it comes to."

"But it will take time, won't it?"

"Yes, I'm afraid it will."

∞

January 15, 2017, New Orleans, Louisiana, 7:47 p.m.

The body was found beside the trash dumpster behind Drake's Restaurant. Frank began his assessment, calling out important details as Watson took notes. "Who the hell dismembers a body like this?" Watson asked.

"I don't know," Frank answered, but his instincts bubbled up and sent a shiver down his spine. The body had been dismembered at the major joints from what he could tell and placed haphazardly into a garbage bag. Why the bag had not been tossed into the dumpster itself, he couldn't say.

"Have you seen anything like this before?" Watson asked.

"No," Frank answered. He wanted to shed the gloves he was wearing and take out his phone to call Viveca, but he kept his cool and tried to think through the situation.

"Do you have any idea what was used to, you know, cut it apart?"

Frank turned his head toward Watson and gave him an impatient expression. "I haven't the faintest idea. What I need you to do is be quiet and take notes. Okay?"

"Yeah, okay. Sorry. This is freaking me out!"

"I get it, Watson. Trust me, I do, but we've got to keep our heads. So calm down, take notes as I give them, and pray the coroner turns up soon."

"Yeah, I got you. Um, the new coroner is some guy named Max Ryan. I'm sure he'll be here soon." Watson joined Frank and peered down into the bag. "Jesus, what the hell?" Watson suddenly turned and moved away quickly.

Frank could hear him retching. "Please tell me you at least made it to the bushes."

Watson stood upright and did his best to wipe his mouth clean. As he was doing so, the forensics van pulled up. A moment later, another van joined them. Watson looked back and announced their arrival. Frank joined Watson as forensics approached. Behind forensics, a woman approached. Frank stepped forward and effectively blocked her path. "I'm sorry, ma'am. No press allowed."

"I'm not the press. I'm the coroner," the woman stated patiently.

"I think we're expecting a guy named Max Ryan."

"Yes, I'm the *guy* you're expecting. I'm Maxine Ryan. People call me Max."

"I apologize, Dr. Ryan. Forensics should be done soon, then I'll escort you in. Is your team with you?"

"I did send out a text to the former coroner's team. Rainier, I think it was. They should be joining me soon."

"This is my partner, Detective Harrison Watson. I am Detective Frank Taylor." Frank held his hand out, and Dr. Ryan shook it.

She turned to shake Watson's hand, watched him wipe his mouth again, and thought better of it. "Well, while we're waiting, can either of you cast any light on my predecessor? I understand his death was very sudden and unexpected, but that he had been involved in several kidnap murders?"

Frank gave her a short-lived smile, then turned to Watson. "We need to start questioning the restaurant employees. Do you want to start that while I wait to turn the body over to the coroner?"

"Sure, I'll go on ahead," Watson said and made his way around the building to the front entrance.

When Watson was out of earshot, Frank turned back to Dr. Ryan. "Rainier was a good man. Please don't start off on the wrong foot, Dr. Ryan. Don't spread rumors."

"But I understand he was arrested for the crimes. How is that spreading rumors?"

"He was being held on circumstantial evidence, Doctor. He had not been formally charged with any crime by the district attorney's office."

"That's not what I heard, but you are right. I do not wish to start my dealings with the police on the wrong foot. So what do you say we start over?"

Maxine Ryan was a short wisp of a woman. She stood around five feet tall. Her inquisitive brown eyes noticed everything and missed nothing. Small lines flanked her eyes and mouth. She probably laughed and smiled a lot when she wasn't examining dead bodies. He gave her a more genuine smile than before and stuck his hand out again. "Detective Frank Taylor. It's nice to meet you, Dr. Ryan."

She took his hand again. "It's nice to meet you too, Detective."

Forensics completed their examination of the scene, collected the evidence, and returned the scene to Frank. Frank led Dr. Ryan to the body. "The body appears to have been dismembered at the major joints. It's definitely a man, but that's all we can really tell on first impressions."

Maxine Ryan crouched near the body and drew on a pair of gloves. She lifted open the bag more fully and began assessing the body, making preliminary judgments that would have to be proved in the lab. "Rigor mortis has begun to set in. The body looks mauled in places."

"Mauled? By what?"

"Well, the autopsy will tell us more. He was found in a garbage bag, Detective. Anything might have taken a nibble, and—"

Frank came to stand next to where she was crouching. "What is it?"

"This man's heart has been removed. And not just removed. Torn out." She looked up at him with a puzzled expression. "What the hell is going on here?"

From behind them, they heard a voice. "Hey, Frank," Paul said as he approached with the rest of Rainier's team. The two men shook hands.

"Hey, Paul. This is Dr. Max Ryan. She's been assigned to replace Rainier."

"Nice to meet you, Dr. Ryan," Paul said then introduced the two other members of the team, a man a bit older than Paul named Jake Pham and a young woman around Paul's age named Sarah Davidson. Jake and Sarah wheeled a stretcher over near the scene and prepared a body bag.

Maxine Ryan stood. "I understand that Dr. Rainier was called in to assist in an investigation when the coroner before him was killed."

"That's right," Paul answered.

"And then Dr. Rainier was killed."

"Yes, ma'am," Paul said as he exchanged glances with Frank.

"This isn't a job where one traditionally feels the need to be fearful for one's own life. So what happened to these two men? I'm the third coroner in less than three years. What's going on here?"

"Honestly, Dr. Ryan, I'm not the person who can answer all your questions. I was just starting my internship when Dr. Bishop was killed. I interned with Dr. Rainier, but since he's been gone, I have to wait for you to say I can continue my internship. I'm not privy to the circumstances under which Dr. Rainier died, but I can tell you Dr. Bishop had his throat torn out."

Maxine Ryan brought her hand to her throat. "Torn out?"

"Dr. Ryan," Frank interjected, "let's deal with the matter at hand, shall we? We've got a body. We need an autopsy. Detective Viveca Ambrose will be back from maternity leave in another three or so weeks. Any questions you have can be best answered by her."

"Detective Ambrose? Okay. I'll be sure to talk to her when she returns."

"And, Dr. Ryan," Frank began, "there's no reason for you to fear for your life. The circumstances, as I understand them, under which Bishop and Rainier were killed seem to indicate the men were targeted because of something they knew. There's nothing to indicate they were targeted because they were the coroner."

"I see. That does make me feel better. Well, Paul, I will need an intern, so since you know the layout of the lab and the procedures already, I see no reason why you cannot continue to intern with this office. Please make sure you submit the form to me this week, and I will sign it. Let's get the body back to the lab, and I will begin the autopsy in the morning. Detective Taylor, thank you for your time."

Frank made his way to the front entrance of the restaurant. He opened the door to see Watson exiting. "Hey, what did they say?"

"Two employees, Ben Thompson and Scott Ledoux, found the body earlier tonight when they went to dump the trash. Drake's wasn't open yesterday, so they couldn't say how long the bag had been there."

"Did they say why they opened the bag?"

"They said they went to lift it and toss it into the dumpster, but the thing was heavy. They tried to move it anyway, and that's when the bag tore."

"I see. Any reason to suspect either of them?"

"No. They're pretty badly shaken up. Thompson looked like he might burst into tears at any moment."

"Okay, let's get back to the station," Frank murmured and turned to go back to the car.

Watson followed close behind. "Want to know the weird part?"

"Okay, sure."

"There wasn't a whole lot of blood in the bag."

"What do you mean?"

"The body was cut apart, but there wasn't a lot of blood visible on the body or in the bag. Don't you find that odd?"

"Now that you mention it, yes."

"Man, this thing has vampire written all over it!"

"Oh, good grief!" Frank chuckled, hoping it was believable. If he knew nothing else, he knew the knowledge of vampires and ghouls had to be kept secret. Frank Taylor was a logical man. Perhaps too logical. In contrast, Harrison Watson was superstitious and paranoid, and the subjects of vampires, werewolves, demons, and other otherworldly folklore had often been introduced by Watson into their conversations.

"I know you think my hobby of reading about all this stuff is a waste of time, but we are living in Vampire Central, you know. There are those who truly believe they are vampires."

"I get it, Watson, but I'm not going to entertain a vampire theory unless Dr. Ryan says it's so. Now, I'm going to drive us back to the station, and then I'm going home. When the autopsy report comes out, we'll write the report and begin our investigation," Frank concluded. He saw the disappointed expression cross Watson's face.

"I know you can't wait until Viveca comes back, but could you at least pretend you like working with me until she returns?" Watson asked.

"Hey, dude, I like working with you just fine. You knew this was a temporary assignment."

"It's not that. I get passed from partner to partner like I'm the plague," Watson stated and shrugged. "I just want a permanent assignment, that's all."

"It'll happen. I went through the same thing before I got partnered with Viveca. I'm sorry if I haven't treated you like a real partner, Watson. That wasn't my intention."

"It's okay. I know that, and I appreciate working with you. I'm learning a lot."

Frank stuck his hand out. "Me too," he said, and the men shook hands. "Why don't you meet me at the coroner's office tomorrow around noon? I want to hear first-hand what Ryan has to say."

"Sounds good."

"And if she says 'vampires,' then you'll have the lead in this case."

"I will?"

"Of course! Between the two of us, you're the expert in vampires," Frank said and watched the excitement build in Watson's expression.

On the drive back to the precinct, Frank mulled over the evidence. Dismembered body, signs of mauling, heart torn out. In the folklore Watson read, vampires were evil incarnate, and the only solution was to destroy them. In Viveca's experience, vampires were humans possessed by evil but were only evil if the possessed human surrendered to the vampire spirit. Her account of Richard having been a vampire revealed that the man who refused to surrender didn't kill to feed, and he could be saved.

New Orleans was sometimes an unsafe place to live. Human crime often tarnished its carnival-bright streets. Within the past few years, a new threat had emerged. Not one that sought to spill the blood of the innocent, but one that sought to consume it. Viveca had said the vampires could be killed or prevented from returning by removing the head or the heart. She had also said that ghouls ate the dead. Recently, more than twenty citizens had gone missing. Could this man be one of those lost souls Special Victims was searching for? If so, what did the evidence tell him? *Viveca would know.*

With more questions than answers, Frank pulled into the precinct parking lot and bid Watson a good night. As he made his way to his own vehicle, his mind circled like vultures above carrion. He needed answers, and then he'd have to speak to Viveca.

∞

"Dr. Ryan?" Frank called toward the lab. Watson stood just behind him.

"I'll be right out," she called and stepped out of the lab to meet him. "Hi, Detectives. How can I help you?"

"We were coming for information. Have you had a chance to perform the autopsy?" Frank asked.

"I was just getting started," she said. "You can come inside if you want."

Frank took a deep breath. "Okay," he said, and he and Watson followed her into the lab.

She stopped at a credenza and opened a drawer to pull out smocks, surgical caps, and two pairs of goggles. At the next cabinet, she pulled two pairs of gloves from a desktop dispenser. She handed the items to the detectives. "Wear these so you don't taint the evidence."

Frank and Watson took the items and put them on. They followed her deeper into the lab. The body was arranged strategically on the autopsy table, its parts assimilated into the shape of the man it had once been. Watson threw a hand to his mouth and turned around. "I don't think I can, Frank."

"Okay. You wait outside," Frank said and turned back to Dr. Ryan.

"Your partner is easily sickened for a man working homicide, Detective."

"I guess so. Let's proceed, shall we?"

Dr. Ryan put on her goggles, adjusted her gloves, and stepped to the table. She reached up and pulled down a cord attached to a microphone. "Dr. Maxine Ryan. It is 12:32 p.m. on Monday, January 16, 2017. I am performing the autopsy on a John Doe, found dismembered inside a garbage bag behind Drake's Restaurant.

"Body parts have been arranged to account for their dismemberment. The arms and legs were removed with an unknown sharp object at the major joints. The head was removed just below the Adam's apple, severing the cervical column of the spine between the fourth and fifth vertebrae. The torso has been bisected between the thoracic and lumbar spine. The genitalia are intact. Upper torso shows significant damage to the right of the sternum at the fourth rib. The rib has been shattered, and the heart has been torn out.

"Mastication present across right arm, both legs, and at bisection and dissection points indicates the body has been partially eaten. Taking measurements and indentation scans. Preliminary evidence obtained indicate the body may have been cannibalized. Will know more when the scan results are analyzed."

Dr. Ryan looked up at Frank. Frank stared back. Whatever she was thinking, he was certain it wasn't something she thought often, if at all. She pulled her attention back to the matter at hand and took a scalpel from the surgical table. "Beginning Y incision," she said. From the left clavicle to the sternum, then from the right clavicle to the sternum, and then down along the center of the man's chest, she made incisions. Then, she began pulling open the man's chest to reveal the rib cage. The sickening *crack!* of bone accosted Frank's ears as the bone saw etched deep into the ribcage. A large pair of crescent-shaped stainless-steel clippers were used to cut the ribs away, and a chest spreader was inserted to hold the ribcage open. The cavernous hole where the man's heart used to be stared up like the fabled abyss. The lung tissue sat useless above the liver and intestines. Other organs presented themselves, but he had no idea what they were.

Dr. Ryan continued, "Blood loss is significant, as should be expected, but somehow more so. The state of the liver, pancreas, and lungs indicate a dramatic loss of blood prior to death. Dissection of the organs and additional testing must be performed to determine exact cause of visible trauma, but all indications are this man bled to death." She reached up and turned off the recording.

"So he bled to death?"

"It would seem so, Detective. I'll have to run tests on the man's tissue and organs to be sure, but you see how the lungs have paled? How the spleen is enlarged?" She pushed up the man's right eyelid. "See the yellowing of the man's eye? These are all signs of severe anemia, blood loss, or disease. Only, the organs do not look diseased. The state indicates a severe lack of oxygen stemming from deprivation of blood flow. There's nothing to indicate drowning or other cause of suffocation. If he'd been suffocated, the blood vessels in his eyes would have ruptured, and they'd appear bloodshot, not yellow."

"Could he have lost blood when he was cut apart?" Frank asked, bile rising in the back of his throat.

"Not unless he was dismembered while he was alive. The heart would have had to have been pumping for the organs to look like this. And here's another thing," she said, then used the scalpel to open up the man's vein at his right arm. "See that? This isn't normal. Even if the man bled to death, there should be more blood left in his body than this. Once a person loses so much blood, the heart ceases to pump. Even cutting him open after that wouldn't result in the kind of blood loss we're seeing here."

"So what do you think did this?"

"I'm not sure, Detective."

Dr. Maxine Ryan wasn't sure what had killed the man, but Frank was. This man was killed by a vampire. That much, he knew.

∞

"Hello?" Richard answered.

"Hey, Richard. It's Frank."

"Hi, Frank. How are you?"

"I've got to talk to Viveca. Is she there?"

Richard turned his back to the room and half-whispered into the receiver. "We're trying to bond with our son, Frank. Please don't distract her with police work."

"I'm sorry, Richard. I would never have called if it weren't important. Please."

"All right. Hold on." Frank listed as Richard called for his wife. A moment later, he could hear her speaking to him.

"Hi, Frank. What's wrong?"

"Viv, we've got a body that appears to have been drained of blood."

"Has an autopsy been performed? Has the heart been—"

"The man's heart was removed. His body dismembered. Part of him was eaten."

"Eaten?"

"Yes, that's the coroner's conclusion. I attended the autopsy."

Viveca's eyebrows rose in surprise. "You did? Wow! So what else does he have to say?"

"He who?"

"The coroner."

"Oh, no. The coroner is a woman. Max is short for Maxine."

"Ah, got it. Well, what else does she have to say?"

"Sounds a lot like the stuff you told me Bishop used to say. Body drained of blood. More so than cutting the body open would do. It's a vampire, Viv. They're feeding, but this one was a little different. There was still some blood left in the body."

"Okay, so maybe they're not killing. Maybe that's why we haven't found more victims like a couple of years ago."

"Maybe, but if I'm right, they're letting their ghouls feed on them as well."

"You think while they were alive?"

"It's possible, isn't it?"

"I don't know. I've always heard the ghouls fed on the bodies of the dead."

"Maybe the guy was dead. Dr. Ryan indicated that he would have died from exsanguination before the total amount of blood loss was accounted for. So maybe the vampire didn't want to make a vampire but did want to make food for the ghouls."

"That's not a bad theory, Frank. So where was the body found?"

"In a garbage bag behind Drake's."

"That doesn't make sense. Why would they want the body to be found?" Viveca's mind was reeling. This was a bad one.

"That's the big question, isn't it?"

"I suppose, unless they wanted the body found."

"Now, why would they want that?"

"Nana said Richard and I have three years. Maybe it's a message for us. When Malcolm left Brenda's body in her car at the Den, it was because he wanted me to find it. He wanted me on his trail because he knew Richard would follow. Maybe this is his way of keeping tabs on me again."

"Could be."

∞

"What is it, love?" Richard asked when Viveca had disconnected the call.

"A body was found dismembered and drained of blood. There aren't any obvious signs of vampire that Frank could say, but it's very suspicious. Also, the body seems to have been partially eaten."

"Eaten? Are they feeding and then letting the ghouls feast?"

"I don't know. It would seem to me that if the ghouls, plural, were to eat a body, there wouldn't be much to find. What do you think?"

"Hmm. I'm not sure. Logically, that would seem correct, but it may be a game Malcolm is playing. Maybe he's trying to draw you out, go back on his word."

"Richard, you and I both know Malcolm is true to his word. He said three years. He'll give us three years. But what will he do in those three years? Who else will he hurt? What sort of following could he acquire?"

"Now I wish I'd been turned. At least as a vampire, I would be able to protect you." Richard had held up his hands and looked at them helplessly.

"Don't say that. You're human. You're *my* Richard, and I wouldn't change that for anything."

"How can we possibly prepare for him, love?"

"Nana said something to me just before she died. She told me to prepare for the rising. Do you know what that is?"

"No, I've never heard of it before."

"We've got to be careful. Come spring, everyone who knows us is going to want to see Liam. I will have my guard up and my sight on. If I say it's time to go, you need to leave with me. Okay?"

"Okay."

"We go back to work in a couple of weeks. I feel like you'll be safe with Stan and Mike. And you'll have Liam with you when you're not staking someone out."

"Mike said he'd keep me on skip traces until we could find a daycare or nanny we can agree on."

"Great. That's a relief."

"And what about you? You going to go barreling into homicide investigations?"

"It's my job, Richard."

"What of *your* safety?"

"I'm a dream walker war—"

"I know you're a warrior, Viveca. I haven't forgotten. You forget that I know all about your constant tendency to try and prove it."

"I'm not going to look for trouble, Richard. I promise."

"Don't make promises you can't keep, love."

"I'm not. I promise I will not go out of my way to look for trouble. I will not take extreme measures to prove my mettle. Okay?"

"Okay."

∞

February 13, 2017, New Orleans, Louisiana, 7:45 a.m.

Viveca entered the station house with renewed energy. She was happy to be back to work. She'd kissed Richard and Liam goodbye earlier in the morning and had driven straight to the precinct. The desk sergeant welcomed her back. She smiled and thanked him, then swiped her ID card and entered through the secure door toward her office.

After her release from the hospital, she had begun to have video conferences with Dr. Williams twice per week. After Nana was killed, she increased those calls by an extra day. Dr. Williams sent her reports to the captain, and Viveca made her way to the captain's office to find out whether or not he was going to allow her back on full duty. She knocked.

"Come in," his deep voice announced.

She entered the office and greeted him. "Good morning, Captain."

"Ambrose, good to have you back. How are you doing?"

"You tell me, sir. I feel I'm ready to take on the world. I'm just waiting for your verdict."

"I've reviewed your doctor's reports each week. You've made progress, and so I will allow you back on duty, with the understanding that Frank will return as your partner and you both will continue to work with Watson."

"Oh?"

"Don't read too much into it, Ambrose. Watson is a good cop. He and Taylor have been working well together. I'm assigning you as a team for the next six months. The idea is that Taylor has a backup if you need to take the baby to the doctor or whatever."

"Sounds reasonable," Viveca replied, and inwardly cringed. She and Frank had become more than partners. They were friends. She'd shared her secrets with him. She wasn't sure she wanted to do the same with Watson, and if Watson was to tag along, she and Frank wouldn't be able to speak freely.

"What are your reservations regarding Watson?"

"I don't have any, sir."

"Then why is that expression on your face?"

"Which expression, sir?"

"The one that tells me you don't like this arrangement one single iota."

"I've got nothing against Watson."

"But you don't want to work with him."

"I didn't say that."

"Yes, you did. I see it all over you."

Viveca took a breath. "Captain, I am happy to work with him, and I'm glad he and Frank have worked well these past couple of months. That'll make it easier to move forward."

"Hmm. Well, I'm glad you see it that way. Go ahead and meet with your partners and get back out there."

"Thank you, sir. Do you feel I need to continue seeing Dr. Williams?"

"Not unless you do, Detective."

"Thank you. It's good to be back."

∞

"Richard! So glad to have you back. Oh, and look at this little cutie patootie!" Stan met Richard at the door and gushed over Liam.

"If you like him that much, Stan, take him. The little bugger is getting heavy," Richard teased and grinned. Stan took the baby carrier and cooed at Liam, then stepped aside to allow Richard to enter the office.

"Richard, great to have you back," Mike said from his office chair.

"It's good to be back. Thank you for allowing Liam to come into the office with me."

"It's no big deal, Rich. We love having him here."

"Yes, he's a doll, handsome," Stan said from his own office chair. He'd set Liam's carrier on his desk and was rocking it back and forth. "You're going to have fun with your Uncle Stan, aren't you, Liam?"

"Not too much fun, Stan," Richard said. "He still has to sleep tonight. Viveca will kill me if I don't get his naps right."

"No worries, Rich. He's going to be fine." Stan stood up and brought the carrier to Richard and gently placed it on his desk. Liam was asleep.

"Well, you certainly have the touch, Stan. He was fussy all the way here."

"Babies love me. What can I say?"

Mike turned in his seat. "Do you have that surveillance uploaded yet, Stan?"

"Oops! On it!"

"I need it now."

"On its way to you," Stan said, then smiled and winked at Richard.

"So do you have any skip traces or work for me to do?" Richard asked.

"Um, yes," Mike answered. "There are some skip traces here you can run. When you're done, will you please compile the last month's reports in summary?"

"Sure. On it," he mimicked Stan.

"What the hell am I going to do with the two of you?" Mike asked, smiling.

"Oh, I'm sure you can think of something tonight," Stan answered, wiggling his eyebrows. Richard laughed and went about his work.

∞

"The humans found the body! I told you to take only those who would be missed! I told you to have the ghouls dispose of it!" Malcolm paced angrily as Jazz cowered before him.

"I'm sorry, Master," Jazz said, her eyes on her feet.

"Did I not make myself clear?"

"You did, but—"

"But what? You left a dismembered body next to a dumpster in full view of anyone who might work for that restaurant!"

"It was a mistake. It was supposed to have been thrown in the dumpster."

"How is that any better? Why didn't you allow the ghouls to finish it?"

"They wouldn't eat it, Master."

"No? Why?"

"I don't know. Bain said there was something wrong with it."

"You are trying my last bit of patience, Jazz. You drained the body, yes?"

"Yes."

"So what was wrong with it?"

"Nothing."

"Make sure Bain is here promptly at nightfall."

"Yes, Master."

∞

"Master is waiting," Jazz announced as Gannon Bain stepped into the house.

"I'm growing tired of being summoned by you, little vampire."

"Master is tired of you not doing as you're told."

Bain whirled on her and took her throat in his big hand, squeezed, and lifted her off her feet. "I'm not one to be trifled with. My loyalty is to Malcolm, and I have little patience with you telling me what to do."

"Bain."

Bain turned to see the same young man he'd seen a few months before on the night after the dream walker had escaped. A few spoken memories had convinced him Malcolm resided in the body before him. "Master," Bain croaked out.

"Let her go."

Bain released her, and Jazz crumpled to the floor, then recovered and surged to her feet, ready to fight the large ghoul. "You bastard!"

"Bain, why was a dismembered body found outside a local restaurant?"

"The ghouls wouldn't eat it."

"Why?"

"Something about it turned them away."

"Did you try it?"

"No. I wasn't there at the time."

"I see. Still, why was it left where anyone could find it?"

"I instructed it to be placed inside the dumpster. My directions were not followed, Master."

"But why there?"

"I believed the body would have been carried away when the dumpster was emptied."

"Did the ghoul who failed to place it in the dumpster suffer punishment?"

"Yes, Master. He's been *dealt with*."

"You're taking too many people. Slow it down. We don't need an army, Bain. We only need a select few."

"But the dream walker …"

"Her instinct is to save the person, not destroy the ghoul. She's a nurturer. It's her curse. She'll die and so will her son. Then my brother will come to me as I predicted he would."

"You bit him and yet he didn't turn, Master. Why?"

"I am not sure, Bain."

"Still, shouldn't he have died?"

"For a time, I thought he had. What are these questions about?"

"The dream walker always has something up her sleeve. Do you really believe she will be destroyed so easily?"

"I believe that once her son is gone, her reason for existing will render her weak. She can be destroyed when she's weak."

"He has the eagle, Master. He will be very powerful."

Malcolm held up a hand. "*Will be*. Not is. We will destroy him before his rising."

∞

Fingerprints identified the victim as Arthur Brice. Viveca sat quietly while Frank broke the news to the dead man's wife. Mrs. Brice broke into tears. Frank gently laid his hand on her shoulder. "We're very sorry, Mrs. Brice."

Viveca hung on to her emotions. Now that she was a mother, the conscious thought that one day Frank would knock on her door with a message for Richard and their son filled her with dread and something very like regret, but not quite it.

When Frank was done delivering the awful message to Mrs. Brice, he stepped back toward Viveca, and she rose to join him. "We will let you know as soon as we have any information on whoever might have killed your husband."

"Thank you, Detectives."

Frank and Viveca let themselves out of the house and back to their sedan where Watson waited. More and more, Viveca believed homicide was not an area best suited to Watson. He didn't have the stomach for it—literally, and he didn't have the manners or empathy it took to deliver bad news.

"How did it go?" Watson asked timidly.

"We just told a woman her husband is dead. It's hard to deliver news like that, Watson. It's even harder to be on the receiving end of it," Viveca barely contained her temper. She wanted to slap him. *I hear someone you loved just died, but how do you feel?* She thought. *He's an idiot!*

The police radio interrupted her thoughts, and she snatched it up. "Ambrose."

"There's a disturbance on the St. Louis side of Bourbon Street near your location, Detective. Possibility of homicide."

"We're in route," Viveca said, and Frank put the car into gear and headed toward Bourbon Street.

When they pulled up, a crowd had formed around the area. Viveca, Frank, and Watson stepped forward, brandished their badges, and ordered the crowd to disperse. People stepped back and allowed them through. On the ground, a man lay bleeding. Nor far from him, another man stood. His knees were slightly bent as if he were trying to keep his balance. His arms were hanging in arches as if he were flexing his muscles. His mouth hung open. Blood stained his teeth and around his lips. His eyes were wild and searching. His hair was unkempt. "Take it easy," Viveca soothed.

The man turned his attention to her. "What's happening to me?"

"Just take it easy," Viveca repeated and stepped toward him. She held up her hand to him. When she reached the bleeding man, she had closed the distance between herself and the unkempt man by half. "What's your name?" she asked gently.

The man seemed confused. He suddenly brought his hands up to his own head and pressed his hands against his temples. He took several ragged breaths. "I don't know! I don't know! I don't know!" he screamed, his voice becoming more and more hysterical.

"It's okay. We'll figure that out. Can you take some steps back? Come on, step back." Viveca kept her voice even and smooth. He began to take steps away from her, and she stepped forward, effectively placing herself between the bleeding man and the man before her.

Frank and Watson rushed forward to move the bleeding man away. Behind them, an ambulance pulled up. The crowd parted as the paramedics brought a stretcher forward. Behind them, Viveca continued to face the apparent perpetrator down.

Viveca closed the distance between them, and the man continued to back away. The crowd was watching the paramedics. "I know what's wrong with you. If you're calm, I can help you," Viveca said calmly.

The man's hands and arms returned to their previous position. "I'm losing myself!"

"You can trust me," Viveca said softly. "I'm going to help you." She looked back briefly to ensure all eyes were on the bleeding man. If anyone were watching her, she'd have to take that chance. A moment later, she rushed toward him, took his arms in her hands, and pulled him into the dream walk.

The man, already confused and disoriented, became even more so. "What have you done to me?" He began to flail his arms. Viveca could see the ghoul crouching within him.

"I'm going to help you. Just stay you," she said and let the tigress form around her. The dream walker warrior stepped forward to place her hands on the man before her. The ghoul began to rise up around the man. She pushed her hand forward and caught the ghoul spirit and pulled it from him. The tigress burst from her to take the ghoul in its jaws. A moment later, the ghoul's heart had been removed, and it dissipated before them.

The man fell to the grass, and Viveca pulled the tigress back to become herself again. "Where am I? Who are you? *What* are you?"

She smiled down at him. "You're safe," she said and extended her hand toward him. "Let me help you up."

"What is this? Stay away!"

"I'm not going to hurt you. I do need to ask you some questions."

"What was *that*? Where am I?" The man's voice had trilled up the octaves, his eyes bulged with fear.

"What is your name?"

"Gerard Stephens."

"Mr. Stephens, my name is Viveca. I'm a homicide detective."

"Am I dead?"

"No, but you were well on your way to being dead."

"You saved me?"

"You were"—she struggled with an appropriate word—"infected," she said for lack of a better word, "with a ghoul."

"A what?"

"What do you remember, Mr. Stephens?"

∞

Watson looked up once the man had been loaded onto the stretcher. "Where's Viveca?"

Frank looked to where she had been a moment before. "Where is that other guy?" Watson began to step forward, but Frank held him back. "I'll go. Stay with this guy. If he regains consciousness, we need to know what happened."

"You got it."

Frank stepped forward. A young man from the crowd intercepted him. "You looking for that lady who was speaking to the other guy?"

"Yes. Did you see where they went?"

"They just disappeared."

"Disappeared?"

"She ran at him, and they just went poof!" He held up his version of jazz hands for a moment.

Frank resisted the urge to laugh. "Poof?"

"Yeah, man. They just disappeared into thin air."

"Okay, buddy. Go back to where you were."

"You don't believe me?"

"I didn't say that. Thank you for the information. Now, please go on back. There's nothing to see here."

"Yeah, because they disappeared!"

"Okay," Frank said and stepped away from him toward the place Viveca had undoubtedly taken the man into the dream walk. "Jesus, Viveca. What the hell are you thinking?" Frank commented under his breath. He was just about to turn back, when he spotted Viveca, and the other man step from around the corner. Frank let out a sigh of relief. "Viveca. Thank God!"

"Frank, this is Gerard Stephens," Viveca said. The man walking beside her was a changed person. He was calm. The wildness had left his eyes.

"Mr. Stephens, please come with us."

"Where is Jesse?" Gerard Stephens asked.

"Jesse? Is that the man's name?"

"Yes. Where is he? Is he okay?"

"He's being attended to by the paramedics, Mr.—"

Gerard Stephens suddenly darted out of Viveca's grasp and past Frank. "Jesse!"

Watson placed himself between the stretcher and man barreling toward him. "Stop right there, sir."

Gerard Stephens did not stop. He pushed Watson out of the way harshly and made his way to the stretcher. "Jesse! Oh my god!"

Frank rushed up behind him and pulled him away, turned him around and sent him to the ground. Watson recovered from the assault and helped Frank handcuff him. "Jesse," Stephens sobbed. "Somebody please help my brother."

∞

"Mr. Stephens, what do you remember?" Viveca asked.

Gerard Stephens sat in the interrogation room across from her. He kept his eyes on his hands. "I don't know."

"Tell us whatever you think happened."

"I don't know!" His raw outburst was full of emotion and regret.

Viveca tried a different tactic. "Gerard," she said gently. "Do you remember speaking to me earlier?"

He lifted his eyes to her. "I don't know what you did to me."

"I helped you. What do you remember about it?"

"We were in a field. The street, the people. Everything disappeared. And then *you*—"

"What do you remember?"

"It was like I was being torn apart. It hurt but didn't hurt. Something horrible was trying to get me to lash out at you."

"What did you see?"

"A tiger. You were a tiger. You pulled something out of me."

She nodded. "Now, let's work backwards. What were you feeling when you met your brother in the bar?"

"Excited to see him. I hadn't seen him in a couple of months. He works offshore."

"What about before you met him?"

Stephens thought for a minute. "I'm not sure."

"Try to think about where you were before you went to meet him. Were you home?"

"I don't think so. I was some place dark."

"What did you hear?"

Again Stephens thought. "Water, maybe. Some kind of dripping sound. It was dark. A *voice*," Stephens whispered the last word.

"A voice? What did it sound like?"

"Soft, feminine. It told me to leave."

"Where did you go?"

"I don't know. I'm not sure where I was. My cellphone rang. When I answered, it was Jesse telling me he was in town and wanted to have a beer. So I went straight to the bar."

"Did you have your cellphone on your person the whole time?"

"Yes. Um, no. Someone handed me my phone."

"What about when you left the dark place? Were you on foot the whole time?"

"Wait. No. A car was waiting for me. It drove me into the city."

"How far were you outside the city?" Viveca asked. She was getting more intrigued by the minute.

"I don't know."

"How long were you in the car? A few minutes? More than thirty? More than an hour?"

"Twenty minutes, maybe thirty."

"Could you see the driver?"

"No. There was some kind of partition between us."

"What happened when the car stopped?"

"The door opened, and I stepped out."

"Okay, going backwards again. How did you get out of the dark place?"

"There was a door."

"Do you think you would recognize where you were before you got the call from your brother?"

"No. I'm not sure where I was. It was dark. A voice said to go, and I opened a door and stepped into what seemed like a house."

"A house?"

"A big house. There was another door leading outside. Then I was on a porch, and a car was waiting for me."

"When you were let out of the car, were you given any instructions?"

"No. When I got out, I went straight to the bar."

"How long did it take you to walk to the bar?"

"Minutes, maybe ten."

Viveca took a breath. It was time for the hard questions. "Was your brother already at the bar, or did you get there first?"

"He was there waiting for me."

"Did you have a beer?"

"We ordered a beer. It took a few minutes."

"Was your brother excited to see you?"

"Yes, and so was I."

"What happened while you were sitting at the bar, Gerard?"

"We were laughing and joking around. We were having fun. Our beer finally came, and we clinked the necks of the bottles together in a toast. He was going to be home for a couple of weeks."

"When did things start to turn sour between you two?"

"They didn't. We were having fun."

"At what point did you attack him?"

"I—" he trailed off.

"Gerard? Why did you attack your brother?"

"I didn't want to hurt him."

"So why did you?"

"I don't know," he whispered. When he looked up tears were forming in his eyes. "Is he going to be okay?"

"He's been taken to the hospital. We'll know something soon. Right now, we need to figure out why this happened."

"Don't *you* know? *You* said you were going to help me. *You* said you *knew* what was wrong."

"But I need to know how it happened, Gerard. When you were in the house, were you given something to drink? Something that might've tasted awful?"

"Um … I don't know. I … I'm not sure."

"Think about it. Think about who might have handed you something to drink. Was it a woman or a man?"

"A man. A horrible and scary man."

"Do you know his name?"

"No. I don't … um … sh … she ca … called him Bain."

"She?"

"The woman with the voice."

"And she called him Bain?"

"Yeah."

"Thank you. Now going back to the bar. What were you feeling just before you attacked your brother?"

"Oh god, I don't understand."

"I know you don't, but I need you to explain to me the best you can what you were feeling just before it happened."

"Rage filled me. I was having fun, then suddenly, I wanted to rip his throat out. Something was telling me to kill him."

"What did you do?"

"I broke the beer bottle and I slashed at him. He tried to get away from me, but I was faster, and I kept stabbing at him. Oh god, why did I do that?" Stephens's lip trembled. "Why … why did I do that?" His breaths were coming in ragged, rapid gasps. "I killed my brother." The floodgate opened then, and Stephens began to weep. Viveca reached over and placed a hand on his shoulder, then left the interrogation room.

Frank and Watson met her outside. "He's a broken man," Viveca announced. "I don't think he meant to do what he did."

"Neither do I," Frank said.

"Can you please explain the part about the tiger, Viveca?" Watson asked. "He said he saw you as a tiger and that you pulled something out of him? What was all that about?"

"He was out of his mind, Watson. Whatever made him lash out at his brother was obviously still at work in him."

"How did you bring him back to his senses?" Watson eyed her carefully, and Viveca knew he wasn't going to let it go.

"I talked him down from the ledge he was on, Watson."

"Why do I feel the need to call bullshit on this one?"

"Feel what you need to feel, Watson," Viveca said. "The world will still be spinning tomorrow."

"That's a hell of a note, Viv! You know, the two of you have this little club going on, and you both are deliberately cutting me out of the loop. I'm supposed to be on this team, right? So talk to me. I have a very open mind."

Viveca and Frank exchanged glances, and Frank nodded. "Okay," Viveca began. "I know you read a lot about the supernatural. So I'm going to fill you in on some things."

"The supernatural? Okay," Watson said, his tone dripping with skepticism.

"Not here. We meet after work. Frank knows where. I'll answer whatever questions you have. All right?" Viveca asked and waited for his reply.

"All right. Tonight," Watson said and walked away.

Frank turned to Viveca. "Are you really going to share everything with him?"

"I haven't decided. He's got knowledge of the supernatural. True, he probably has most of it wrong, but he may still turn out to be helpful."

"All right. See you tonight."

∞

"Are you sure it's wise to tell this man Watson all about yourself, love?" Richard asked.

"I'm not going to tell him *everything*, but he studies this stuff, and he may be able to get us to think about things in ways we never thought of before. Plus, he's part of my team. I have to be able to trust my team. And Watson is now close to me. It's not fair for me and Frank to keep him in the dark. Malcolm could try to hurt him just for being on my team. Don't I owe him some sort of heads-up?"

"I suppose so, but what if he is part of Malcolm's team?"

"I have been watching him all day. I trust my sight. He's human. He's truthful. If he were working for Malcolm, I don't think he'd be so truthful."

"Unless the truth is how he gets close to you. You can't see everything coming, sweetheart."

"I'm only going to tell him what he needs to know. The rest is up to him."

"Okay," Richard said and handed Liam to his wife.

"Oh, my little man. Were you good for your daddy?"

"He was a good boy."

"You were? Of course you were. How did he do with the breastmilk in the bottle?"

"He did well, although I think he prefers the real thing. Frankly, I don't blame him." Richard wiggled his eyebrows and gave her a devastating smile.

"Are you saying you like my boobs?"

"I love your boobs, and everything else about you."

"I know that look. Have you forgotten I have to go out to meet Watson and Frank?"

"Nope, but I'm looking forward to when you come back home."

"Oh, are you now?"

"Yep."

"Well, I'm going to feed this kid and then I'll see you later," she said, giving him a seductive smile.

"Do not start something you can't finish, love."

"I'm not. Just can't wait to come back home."

∞

Frank and Watson were waiting for her when she arrived. The field behind Mr. Eaglefeather's house was the perfect place for both conversation and privacy. "Okay, so what's going on?" Watson asked as soon as she was within earshot of him.

"Patience, man," Frank said.

"I'm tired, Frank. Sick and tired of always being on the fringes of the truth about everything. You have some explaining to do, so get on with it."

"Watson, I know you're angry," Viveca began. "Please just take it easy. I will explain, but first, I need to know you truly have an open mind and that what you see and hear now will not go beyond the three of us."

Watson visibly relaxed. His anger dissipated. "Look, I'm not trying to give you a hard time, Viv. I'm just fed up with never—"

Viveca placed a hand on his shoulder. "I understand. You are a valuable member of this team. What's been happening is something that's hard to simply explain. You have to see it."

"Okay. Show me."

"Frank tells me you have a love for reading about the supernatural."

"Yeah, so?"

"So that's what we need to discuss."

"My love for reading about strange things?"

"No, the actual existence of those strange things."

"What?"

"Harrison," Viveca began, using his first name to ensure she had his attention. "What if I told you vampires really existed?"

"There are definitely those who believe they are."

"No, I'm not talking about those who form blood cults. I'm talking about an actual vampire."

"You're serious?"

"Yes."

"It's true," Frank interjected.

"True? Wasn't it you who laughed in my face when I said the case had vampire written all over it?"

"Yes, but it was only because I was keeping Viveca's secret."

Harrison Watson back up several steps. "You? You're a vampire? How? You walk around in the daylight! What the hell?"

"Harrison! I'm not a vampire! I'm a vampire killer of sorts."

"What? You kill vampires? Is your real name Van Helsing?"

"Ha. Ha. Funny. No. I'm a dream walker warrior. I'm a defender of the light."

"A what?"

"My grandfather was a shaman. My father his descendant. I inherited his gifts as a dream walker. My mother was a visionary."

"I don't know what the hell all that is."

"My grandfather was a shaman, a Native American healer."

"Sounds more like a witch doctor." Watson added.

"You're not exactly wrong. The dream walkers are those who can enter the dream and spirit worlds to do battle against evil in the spiritual realm, the real world, and in the dream world. We have guardian spirits that protect us and help us wage battle against evil. Our warrior selves are both physical and spiritual and can wage war on both plains."

"What the hell does that have to do with vampires?"

"Vampires are not like the ones you've read about. Vampires are like possessing spirits that cage the human soul. They drink the blood of the living to maintain their power, and they control the human like a puppet on its strings." Viveca took a breath and waited for Watson to take it all in.

"Are you just messing with me now?"

"No. Let me show you." Viveca took a few steps forward and released the tigress. The tigress burst from her and made its way around the field. When it had finally come to stand before her, Viveca reached out and stroked its head. "This is my spirit warrior, the white tigress."

Watson's eyes were big as saucers. "Is it going to attack me?"

"Why would she? I haven't commanded her to do so." Viveca turned around to face him and pulled the tigress back through herself to become the dream walker warrior. The tigress reemerged and stood at her side.

Harrison Watson took in the sight. She was extraordinary! And he concluded, whatever she was, she was on the side of the good guys. He reached out and gently touched her arm with his fingers. "Wow. Viveca, this is so cool."

Frank stepped forward. "What happened to the phoenix?"

"I lost her when I tried to save Richard," she answered, the dream walker warrior forming her words and issuing them forth with dazzling energy. In another moment, Viveca called the tigress back and was once again herself.

"Richard? Your husband?" Watson asked.

"He was almost killed by a vampire last year. I stopped the vampire from turning my husband, but it got away before I could kill it."

"So what made you decide to tell me all this?"

"You need to know so you can protect yourself, Watson. The vampire who tried to take my husband has promised revenge on me and my family. There's no reason to believe it won't try to harm those close to me in the process."

"I can't believe what I've just seen." Watson shook his head and closed his eyes for a moment.

Frank clapped him on the back a few times. "Yep. Had this moment myself, my friend."

"There's more," Viveca continued. "The vampires are feeding humans their blood. The vampires are—"

"Making ghouls," Watson finished absently.

"Yes, that's right. Is that something you read?"

"Yeah, it's practically in every book about vampires. Vamps feed humans their blood without biting them. The human does the vampire's bidding."

"That's right." Viveca turned to Frank. "See? I told you he'd be a helpful member of the team."

"Hey," Frank began, "when you're right, you're right."

Harrison Watson's face stretched into a satisfied smile. For the first time, he felt like he was in a place and among people with whom he belonged.

∞

Richard was sitting up in bed reading when Viveca returned home. She greeted him, then made her way to the shower and switched it on. She went on absently about her routine. When she emerged from the bathroom, Richard was gone from the bed. She stepped farther into the room to hear his voice rising in song from the baby monitor. A smile touched her lips, and she made her way down the hall to the nursery.

"I really love that song," she said softly as his voice trailed off at the song's end. "Will you teach it to me?"

He was sitting in the rocking chair, holding their son. He looked up at her and smiled. "I will. Come here, love."

She joined him next to the rocker. He handed Liam to her, then drew her onto his lap and placed his arms around both of them. Softly, he began to sing, never taking his eyes from hers. When he came to its end, he started again. Then again, until she had begun to join him in song. Soon, they were singing it together, their son snuggled between them.

Viveca rose from Richard's lap and placed Liam into his crib. She wound the key on the mobile, and a tinkling tune rose into the silence. "Did he eat well?" Viveca asked, looking adoringly down at her son.

"He did. Thank you for using the pump, love, and allowing me to feed him too."

She turned toward him and kissed him. "I want you to be part of everything." She smiled, took his hand, and led him from the nursery back to their bedroom.

A lazy smile spread slowly across his face. She reached up to caress the nape of his neck and draw his lips down to her own. She moved her mouth over his in a way which told him she wanted to be in control. Her hands traveled the expanse of his chest and came to rest on his shoulders. She pushed against him, moving him back toward their bed. When the backs of his legs touched the mattress, she pushed him down into a sitting position and stepped between his knees.

His hands moved to the buttons on her nightgown, but she brushed them aside and moved them back to his sides. Then she worked the buttons loose and let the nightgown slide down her body. She was magnificent. She was full of energy. The dream walker warrior within her had honed her muscles, had dissolved the weight she'd gained during pregnancy, and had made her curves more pronounced than before. Her breasts, swollen with milk, added to the effect.

She pulled the tie on his robe free and found him gloriously naked beneath. A satisfied smile touched her lips, and she pressed into him, allowing herself to graze softly against the masculine planes of his body. He lifted his hands to her arms and tenderly caressed her skin. His long fingers sought her back, then the nape of her neck, then nestled in her hair. She didn't stop him this time, allowing his hands to work magic against her body.

She moved her own hands across his skin, teasing him with her fingers, getting close to placing her hands where he wanted them, then drawing them back up his body. His hands came back down her body and smoothed around her backside, then to her most secret of places. His touch unleashed something within her. Her hands found his shoulders, and she held onto him through the wave of release he drew forth from her. Around her, energy radiated. She could feel the tigress form around her, then it surged through her to transform her into the dream walker warrior.

He looked up at her in wonder. At long last, her fingers found him and raised him up. He lifted her and drew her astride him. She guided him, and he filled her longing as he fulfilled his own. She pressed him onto his back, shadow-waltzed his hips, and their love sparked between them. The tigress's form expanded and wound around them both, entwined and bound them together until they were spent. They slept, face-to-face, arms and legs twined, Richard's lips and breath at Viveca's ear.

Down the hall, their son called someone into his dream walk.

∞

March 17, 2017, New Orleans, Louisiana, 11:25 a.m.

The hand was found at the eastside landfill. A group of young men performing community service happened upon it. When Viveca arrived,

Frank and Watson were standing at the perimeter of the site, speaking to the young men. She joined them.

"What do we have?" she asked.

"These four young men found a hand in Sector Two," Watson answered.

"I see the coroner is here," Viveca said, then looked at the four young men. "Are you all okay?"

"Yes, ma'am," one of them answered.

"Have they given their statements?"

"Yes, we have their statements," Frank answered.

"Where is their monitor?" Viveca began looking in all directions.

"He's being questioned at the front," Watson said.

"Why apart from his charges?"

"The dude freaked out," another of the young men said. "He called it in, then just lost his shit. When the officers arrived, they took him away from the scene. By that time, these two walked up, and we've been talking to them ever since."

"I'm probably going to want to talk to you all again. Please stick close to your homes for the next couple of weeks. Okay?"

"Okay," a third agreed.

Viveca addressed Watson and Frank. "Will y'all please take them to the front? Get the officers to take them home and then come back. We need to speak to the coroner."

"Okay, guys, let's get going," Frank said, and he and Watson led the young men away from the scene.

Viveca turned and stepped gingerly over the trash-littered edges of the landfill. She could see police tape cordoning off a small square in the near distance. When she approached, forensics was making their way out. Left to the scene was a woman crouching down by the tape. "Dr. Ryan?" Viveca asked as she came to stand near the woman.

"Yeah? And you are?"

"I'm Detective Viveca Ambrose."

"Oh yes, Detective. It's good to meet you."

"So what do you make of it?"

"Well, it's a hand. A woman's, from the look of it."

"How can you tell?"

"First, the hand is small, but it obviously isn't a child's hand. The nails are smartly manicured. What bothers me is that it may be chewed here at the site of the dismemberment."

Viveca leaned forward as far she dared. "Frank said the last body had chewing on it, as if someone had tried to eat it."

"Yes, that's right."

"What's the next step?"

"I'm going to take it back to the lab, gather what evidence I can from it, then get forensics to take fingerprints. Maybe she can be identified."

Viveca stood up straight as Dr. Ryan moved the hand into an evidence bag and rose beside her. "What are your thoughts, Dr. Ryan?"

"I'm hesitant to say, Detective. Once I've had a chance to examine the hand properly, I may have something to say."

"What about the previous victim? Do you have anything to say about him? I haven't seen your report yet."

"Detective, the other detectives have told me that you are the person to speak with about strange things, and that you worked closely with the last two coroners. Can we speak tomorrow in my lab?"

"Yes. Do you have a theory?"

"Not a theory, but I do have something strange." Dr. Ryan began to make her way out of the landfill. Viveca followed.

"What time do you want to meet?"

∞

"Do we have a pattern on the disappearances?" Viveca asked when she and her team had returned to the precinct.

"Not really," Frank said.

"Haven't you created a map?"

"We started one," Frank said sheepishly. "The disappearances didn't make any sense at the time. So we stopped."

"You stopped?" She shook her head. "Why did you stop? You know that what doesn't make sense could suddenly come into focus."

"Sorry, Viv. That's my fault," Watson stated. "I'm the one who convinced him to stop."

Viveca took a breath and gathered her patience. "Okay. Let's create a new one. Disappearances and bodies found. Let's go."

Frank and Watson followed her to a conference room. She pulled a map from the credenza and spread it across the table. "We need to place the disappearances on the map, in order.

One by one, the disappearances were pegged onto the map. All across the two-dimensional city, flag markers waved back at them. Twenty in all. One victim found dismembered. One found alive but with a ghoul crouching inside him. One hand found at the landfill, owner unknown.

"So here's what we know," Viveca began. "Twenty people have disappeared. No more in the past month or so. One was found dismembered, another alive. The hand may or may not belong to one of the kidnap victims. Frank, is Grant still heading up Special Victims?"

"Yes, he is."

"Let's reach out. We need to know who each of them are, where they lived, and mark those places on the map."

"What are you thinking?" Watson asked.

"Last year, the vampires and ghouls were holed up in the old, abandoned mortuary. I'm thinking they moved. Malcolm isn't stupid, but his sidekick is a new vampire. She may be the reason we found bodies. We also need to speak to Gerard Stephens again."

"His brother was okay. Jesse Stephens didn't want to press charges against his brother, so Gerard was released."

"Do we know if Jesse Stephens went back to work offshore?" Viveca asked.

"I don't know," Frank said.

"Let's find out."

"What other information are you hoping to get from him, Viv?"

"I want to know two things. One, is he suffering any ill effects from the ghoul being extracted, and two, I want to know if his brother is really well."

"Do you think Gerard passed a ghoul to his brother?" Frank asked, his eyes going wide a moment.

"I don't know, but we need to make sure they are really in the clear."

"We'll track them down," Watson said.

"Thanks. Let's reconvene tomorrow. Watch your backs. I'm almost certain we're being watched."

"Malcolm?" Frank asked.

"Who's Malcolm?" Watson asked.

"Malcolm is the vampire who tried to kill my husband. He and the female vampire he made are making ghouls. I'm almost positive they're behind the kidnappings and the reason we haven't found anyone. The coroner wants to meet with me tomorrow. I'm going to see what she has to say. In the meantime, you two stay alert."

∞

"Dr. Ryan?" Viveca called out into the relative quiet of the coroner's building.

"I'm in my office. Come in, Detective Ambrose."

Viveca entered the office. The memory of meeting Bishop for the autopsy report on Brenda rushed to the forefront of her thoughts. The arrest of Rainier. Being in this building with Richard the night she'd first learned he was a vampire. She pushed them all to the side. "Thank you for meeting with me, Dr. Ryan."

"Please have a seat." Dr. Ryan motioned toward a chair on the opposite side of the desk.

Viveca sat. "I know you're busy, so I won't take much of your time. What is it you wanted to meet with me about?"

"What do your partners know about vampires? Or you, for that matter?"

Viveca stiffened in her seat, the tigress began to gain momentum within her. "What do you mean?"

"It was a ghoul that killed Bishop, another that killed Rainier. Who is the vampire?"

"Who are you?"

"My name is Maxine Ryan. I'm the coroner brought in to replace the last two in this parish. I also volunteered for the job. I tried when Bishop was killed, but the decision to bring in Rainier kept me where I was. When Rainier died, I tried again, and here I am."

"Why did you volunteer?"

"Because you need help, Viveca. I need to know how much your partners know so that I can count them among our assets or keep them in the dark."

"I'm not sure I understand. How can you help me?"

"In the hospital, you met Dr. Battiste, right?"

"Yes."

"I, too, am a visionary. We don't have the power you do to defeat the vampires, but we can help you find and fight them."

"Is that why we haven't gotten autopsy reports? Because you're trying to use the body parts to locate the vampires?"

"Not just me, Viveca. We have a full coven working to bring light into this darkness."

"Are visionaries witches?"

"We are seers. We can locate things by touching related objects or people. You have this gift as well, though you've never been taught to use it. A gift from your mother."

"The vampire's name is Malcolm Ambrose. He was my husband's brother a long time ago."

"You pulled your husband through the blazing and now his brother wants him back?"

"Yes," Viveca answered quietly, and she visibly shuddered.

"Viveca, don't be afraid. We are working to help you."

"Nana," Viveca whispered. "She sacrificed herself to give Richard and me three years to love each other and our son. I just don't understand the significance. Why three years? Why not an eternity? What's in three years?"

"Visionaries work in powers of three. She must have known it would take three years for you to be ready."

"She said something to me just before she died," Viveca said. "She told me to prepare for the rising. Do you know what that means?"

"The rising has to do with a manifestation of power. I know someone who can help us. She's currently away, but she will be back in a few months. I'll let you know when she returns."

"Thank you. What do we do now?"

"I've run extensive tests on Arthur Brice's body. I think I know why the ghouls wouldn't eat it."

"Oh? Why?"

"Arthur Brice was a cancer survivor. I've done my fair share of study on vampires. Vampires use the natural phagocytes in human blood to carry their immortality. Arthur Brice's phagocytes had been tainted by the chemotherapy. What works to bring immortality to the vampires also does so for the ghouls. But if they ingest something that disrupts those phagocytes, it might kill them."

∞

"What did the coroner say?" Frank asked. He and Watson had joined Viveca in the conference room.

"A lot, but first, were you able to contact Gerard Stephens and his brother?"

"Yeah, they're both doing pretty well. Jesse Stephens will be heading to his offshore position soon. He's secured a position for his brother as well. Both men seemed fine. No side effects. No crazy, violent tendencies since the incident."

"Okay, a dead end."

"What did Dr. Ryan have to say?" Frank asked again.

Viveca leaned closer to the map, which now had flags for the victims' home addresses, and said, "She might know how to inflict harm on the ghouls. And if it works for them, it might also work for the vampires."

"That's amazing! What does she think will work?"

∞

June 7, 2017, New Orleans, Louisiana, 9:07 a.m.

"He's looking good, Mr. Ambrose," the pediatrician said with a smile. "Most babies tend to fuss when they get their six-month boosters."

"Thank you, Dr. Crowley," Richard replied. "Is there anything we should be doing differently or in addition to what we're doing now?"

"Not at all. Liam has a healthy growth rate. He's right on target for his age. His responses to the physical exam were as close to perfect as I've ever seen. I'd say to keep doing what you're doing, and we'll see him in another six months for his first-year boosters."

Richard shook the doctor's hand and lifted Liam off the examination table. "Did you hear that, little man? You're perfect. I knew you were. Now let's go see Mommy for lunch."

The café was nestled in a little neighborhood just off Canal Street. Richard pulled into a parking space and retrieved Liam from his car seat. Viveca was waiting just outside. "How did my little man do at the doctor?"

"He's perfect," Richard said with a smile.

Watching him hold his son, Viveca couldn't help but grin up at her husband. "Of course, he is. What else would he be?"

"Dr. Crowley gave him his six-month shots, and we'll need to go back in another six months for his first-year shots. He said Liam was healthy and right on target for his age. He said to keep doing what we're doing."

Viveca held open her arms, and Richard handed their son to her. "Are you my good boy? Yes, you are. I love you," she cooed and kissed her son on the cheek.

"Hey, what about me? Don't I get a kiss?" Richard asked with humor.

"Of course you do," she said and stood on tiptoe to kiss him.

When they were seated and had placed their orders, Richard placed his hand over Viveca's and drew her attention. She could tell he was serious. "What is it?" she asked.

"What is happening at work? Have there been any more disappearances? Any more body parts turn up?"

"Is this the right place to discuss that?"

"I need to know you're all right, Viveca. Malcolm gave us three years, but that doesn't mean Gannon Bain will follow his orders or that another ghoul put upon the public won't hurt you."

She nodded. She'd known this was coming. "I know the dangers. We're all being careful. Frank and Harrison are doing well. So far, no more disappearances and no more body parts."

"Was that hand ever identified?"

"No. Unfortunately not."

"And what of your other cases?"

"Mostly open and shut. Perp caught, crime solved, justice prevails." Her voice was beginning to edge toward sarcasm.

"I know you hate me asking these questions, Viv, but—"

She turned her hand over and laced her fingers with his. "I know why. You love me. I love you too. I'm being careful, Richard. I promise. Now, let's talk about anything but work, okay?"

He smiled and squeezed her hand. "Okay."

∞

October 23, 2017, New Orleans, Louisiana, 6:47 p.m.

It had been a long day. Skip traces aside, Liam had breezed past the crawling stage in August and had begun walking in September. Each day that passed found Liam more agile and balanced than before. "Come on, little man. Daddy has to get you home. Your mommy is going to be worried."

Liam sat abruptly down on the floor between Mike and Stan and smiled up at Richard. "Dadda," he said and reached his hands out toward his father.

"Oh my word," Stan said quietly. "Did he just call you dadda?"

Mike said nothing but stared back and forth between Liam and Richard.

Richard stood there, mesmerized. Then, slowly, a smile spread wide across his face. "I believe he did," he whispered, then he stepped to his son and scooped him up in his arms.

Liam placed his little hands upon Richard's face. "Dadda," he repeated.

Richard laughed excitedly, and tears sprang to his eyes. "That's right, Liam, I'm your daddy." He pulled his son into an embrace and kissed the top of his head. "That's right, son. That's right."

∞

"Viv?" Richard called as he entered the house.

"I'm in the kitchen," Viveca answered.

Richard stepped into the kitchen with Liam in his arms. "Honey, you won't believe this. Watch. Liam, who am I?"

Liam reached up and touched Richard's face. "Dadda."

Viveca laughed excitedly. "Oh my gosh! Liam! You said your first word. Yes, that's your daddy!" She took him from Richard's arms and hugged him. "You are so smart. Do you know who I am?"

Liam touched her face with his hands and smiled, then he let out an excited giggle that threw them all into laughter. "That's okay, my darling. You'll start saying Mommy soon. Now, how about some supper?"

∞

November 17, 2017, New Orleans, Louisiana, 2:36 p.m.

"Miller and Dawes have asked for some support," Frank said as Viveca came to sit next to him in the conference room. The map was still laid out upon the table. For all their effort, a lot of fat good it had done them. The pattern Viveca had hoped to discern didn't present itself. Victims from all across New Orleans were flagged. What was strange was the number. Twenty. No more, no less. What was Malcolm up to?

"What do they have?"

"A body. Badly decomposed. Coroner is in route."

"Where's Watson?"

"He called in sick."

"Is he okay?"

"Yeah. He said he felt like he was coming down with the flu."

"Oh geez, well, he can stay home, then. I don't want it. God knows neither of us need it."

"For sure."

"Where are we meeting them?"

"Just outside the city."

"*Outside* the city? Isn't that outside our jurisdiction?"

"FBI has been called in. They're asking for all available detectives."

"What the hell is going on, Frank?"

"I don't know, Viv. Let's go find out."

∞

It was as she had expected. FBI-issued sedans stood out like sore thumbs among the flotsam and jetsam of Louisiana State Police and local precinct vehicles. Men in dark suits walked among the local plain-clothes detectives. Viveca scanned the perimeter and finally saw someone she recognized.

Viveca led her team toward Miller. "What is the FBI doing here?" Viveca asked.

Miller sighed. "Apparently, they think the victim is the daughter of our Senator Brooks. She disappeared last year."

"Is Dr. Ryan here yet?"

"Yeah, she's down there somewhere."

Viveca stepped to the edge of the perimeter and saw the landscape sloped off into a culvert. "What time last year? How long has she been missing?"

Miller consulted his notes. "She disappeared in March of last year. She had flown home to see her mother, then went out with some friends. The reunion ended around 1:00 a.m., and the friends parted. Sydnie never made it home."

"Where does that culvert lead?" Viveca asked.

"It's a flood culvert used to redirect heavy rain and floodwaters. It starts at the other edge of town, then finds its way to the swamps. Backwater, I suspect, finds its way to the spillway. Keeps the town from flooding."

"When I was a little girl, I remember coming out here with my parents. The memory is vague, but I remember being afraid of the Cavender House. It's around here somewhere."

"Yeah, it's about a mile from here, a little farther into the woods," Miller said.

"Well, let's get this show on the road," Viveca said. "What does the FBI need from us?"

"Local support for perimeter security and assistance with door to door."

"And they wanted detectives for that?" Viveca asked impatiently.

"Yep," Miller quipped.

Miller led them to a man dressed in a dark suit and introduced Viveca and Frank. "Thank you for assisting, Detectives."

"What can you tell us about the body, Agent Vidrine?" Viveca asked.

"We believe it may be the body of Senator Brooks' daughter, Sydnie. She's been missing for about eighteen months. Her parents are divorced, her father remarried. Her mom lives out here. Sydnie had come home for a visit, met up with some friends, and never made it home."

"Were the friends questioned?"

"All but one. We weren't able to locate her, but we're still looking."

"What was the name of the friend?" Viveca asked.

"Amanda Cartwright."

Viveca froze in the place she stood. A moment later, she glanced at Frank. "Amanda Cartwright? Was she in her thirties? Married? Blond hair, green eyes?"

"I'm not sure about the married bit, but she was definitely in her thirties. I believe she was blonde, but I'd have to check her eye color in our files."

"If it's the same Amanda Cartwright, I've got some bad news. An Amanda Cartwright, matching the description I gave, went missing last year. Her body was found in an old cremator kiln on the south side. There's an old mortuary there."

"Is the Cartwright case still open?" Agent Vidrine asked.

"No. The case was closed when we arrested Charles Rainier for the crimes."

"Can we speak with Charles Rainier?"

"No. He was killed after his arrest."

Vidrine mumbled something under his breath and then sighed and placed his hands on his hips. Viveca waited for him to say something. Instead, he mumbled again.

"I'm sorry, what was that?" she asked and mimicked his stance by placing her hands on her hips.

"I said that that was awfully convenient, Detective," Vidrine remarked.

"That's funny because I didn't find it convenient at all," Viveca retorted.

"Did you file charges against the one who killed Rainier?"

"The killer couldn't be identified."

"Where was Rainier killed?"

"In the holding cell near the lower level of the precinct."

Vidrine shook his head. "So let me get this straight. You investigated several kidnap-murders last year. Had enough evidence to pin it on a man, then the man was killed after his arrest, right under your nose at your own precinct. Wouldn't you say that makes you and your team just a tad incompetent?"

"Actually, no, I wouldn't," Viveca stated, her patience evaporating.

"How else could you classify it?" Vidrine's tone had taken a few paces past condescending.

"We followed all the leads, collected all the evidence, and made an arrest. I'd say it was damn good police work."

"Really? Every time we get a case, we get stuck with you backwoods townsfolk detectives. Geez, this is ridiculous."

"Ridiculous? What I find ridiculous is an FBI agent so full of his own merit yet wholly incapable of solving his own cases that he has to call on us *backwoods townsfolk* detectives to do his job for him.

Why don't you get off your high horse and take a whiff of what you're shoveling?"

∞

"You were what?" Richard asked.

"Suspended for six weeks. With pay, thank God. I don't go back until January third."

"How did that happen?"

"I lost my patience with the FBI. Dude called my captain, and he had to do something." She remembered the anger and the humor in the captain's voice. He'd sternly told her that she was suspended for being insubordinate, then had cracked a smile. *Vidrine wouldn't know his ass from his elbow, but I've got to do something with you, Ambrose. So I'm going to suspend you for six weeks, with pay. I know it's harsh, but you'll just have to manage spending more time with your husband and son."*

"On the bright side, you'll be here, and we'll be happy to have you home," Richard said.

"You mean you won't have to worry about me."

"I mean I love you, and I'll be happy to have you home," Richard repeated, and she stepped into his embrace.

As she stood in his arms, she remembered something. "Did I tell you we have an invitation to the Spencer's next month?"

"Isn't that the couple who own the farm a couple miles from here?"

"That's them. Do you want to go?"

"That was nice of them. Yes, I think that would be great."

"I thought so too. I'll call them tomorrow and let them know we'll be there."

From the baby monitor, Liam began to cry. "He's teething again, poor baby," Viveca said. "Let me bring him down." She climbed the stairs and entered the nursery. Liam was standing up in his crib. "Oh, my sweet boy. You hurting again? Come on, baby, let's get you something to help soothe that mean old tooth." She lifted him out of the crib and carried him downstairs. "Hey, babe, will you hold him while I warm up the teething ring and get the prescription?" She handed Richard their son.

She'd taken no more than a few steps when Liam quit crying. She turned to see Richard holding their son, his forehead pressed lightly to Liam's. Richard was cooing, "Who's a good boy? You're a good boy, Liam."

"How did you do that? He always quits crying for you."

"I don't know."

"I'm feel like I'm such an absent mother."

"Come on, Viv. You're no such thing. You're here for him. He loves you. He knows you're his mother."

"But he doesn't say it. 'Dadda,' that's what he says. I'd settle for 'Ma,' I really would."

Richard walked over to his wife and handed her their son. Liam reached up and touched her face and smiled. "You see?" Richard asked. "He knows you, sweetheart. He's going to say it."

Viveca pulled the teething ring from the warm water and began soothing their son's gums. "My poor baby. I love you so much, Liam."

∞

December 15, 2017, New Orleans, Louisiana, 11:47 a.m.

Frank had kept her apprised of unfolding events. The girl had been identified as Sydnie Brooks. Both she and Amanda Cartwright had gone missing around the same time. If Rainier had taken Amanda, then who had taken Sydnie? That remained to be seen.

In the month since she'd been suspended, Viveca had spent her time taking care of her son, giving Richard a break at work, and completing some projects she'd been wanting to do at home. The longer she was away from police work, the more she felt she didn't want to do it anymore. Meeting monsters like Rollins had inspired her to want to get into the field in the first place, but now things were different. She was a wife and mother who loved spending time with her son and being there when her husband came home from work. She loved having a hot meal on the table when he walked through the door. She had forgotten just how much she loved to cook.

She let her thoughts drift to what life would be like without her job. She'd saved money her whole working life, and that wasn't all. The trust fund she'd received at the time she left the orphanage was paying out monthly, and she'd invested well, turning a few modest stock purchases into significant returns. It would support her family until she could figure out her next move.

She had almost come to the conclusion that she'd resign upon the end of her suspension, then she thought of Frank. Her partner. Her trusted friend. How could she let him down? When she'd first learned she was pregnant, she was scared and excited, and as her pregnancy had progressed, she'd convinced herself that the baby wouldn't change how she felt about her job. She'd loved her son the moment she'd met him in her dream walk. But she couldn't have guessed just how much she would love him when he'd come into the world. Everything in her life was about him. It had to be. The thought brought her back to her desire to quit. If she did quit, would Frank still be her friend? she wondered.

She pulled herself from her musings to see Liam sitting in front of the letters and numbers playset she and Richard had purchased a few weeks before. The set was a mat on one end and a series of large blocks that held letters and numbers on the other. The most widely used letters were repeated throughout the blocks, allowing parents and their children to spell almost any word. Liam was moving blocks and arranging letters around the playset mat. She approached him quietly and peered over his small shoulder. In big block letters, he'd spelled a word, and she knew it was no accident. "Eaglefeather."

She kneeled down next to him. "Eaglefeather," she pronounced.

Liam looked up at her, his inquisitive blue eyes dazzled before her. "Mama," he said very distinctly, then pointed to the blocks. "Papa."

∞

The rest of the afternoon, Viveca spent questioning Liam about how he knew about Mr. Eaglefeather, but Liam wouldn't answer. He'd called her *Mama* several times throughout the day, and that had filled her heart to bursting, but he would not communicate with her again regarding the blocks.

When Richard arrived home from work, Viveca greeted him warmly, then grabbed his hand and practically dragged him into the living room. "What's going on, sweetheart?"

She pointed. "See that?"

"What? The blocks?"

"See what they spell?"

"Eaglefeather," Richard said aloud. "Did Liam—?"

"Yes. He did that all by himself. What's more is that he seems to know who Mr. Eaglefeather was."

A few feet away in his playpen, Liam looked up to see Richard. "Dadda! Dadda! Dadda!" Liam used the side of the playpen to assist himself in standing up and continued his excited mantra.

Richard walked over to the playpen and lifted Liam into his arms. "Liam, my boy. Did you miss your daddy?"

"Dadda!"

Richard laughed and turned toward Viveca. She beamed back at him. "He called me Mama today."

"I told you he would, love."

"Bring him here. Let's see if he'll do it for you."

"Do what?" Richard asked then carried their son to where Viveca stood. "What is he supposed to do?"

"Hey, Liam. Do you know who this is? Mr. Eaglefeather?"

Liam looked back and forth between his parents, then proclaimed, "Papa!"

∞

December 16, 2017, New Orleans, Louisiana, 11:21 a.m.

"Are you guys almost ready?" Viveca asked. "We don't want to be late."

"We're coming," Richard replied. "Perfection takes time, love."

"You are perfect, my love. You know that."

"Oh, not me. Liam."

Viveca chuckled. "My two devastatingly handsome men. Now let's go. We don't want to keep the Spencer's waiting."

Viveca pulled the car in next to another and followed the parking order that had obviously been put into place. "Now, love, did you really think it was going to take ten minutes to drive two miles?"

"Ha ha."

Richard chuckled and exited the car to retrieve Liam from his car seat. "This dapper little man is party-ready."

Viveca came around the car to hold Richard's free hand. They walked to the front door together, and Viveca rang the doorbell. A moment later, Mrs. Spencer answered the door and invited them inside. "Oh my goodness! He's gorgeous, Viveca! Oh, what a beautiful family!"

"Thank you, Mrs. Spen—" Viveca began.

"Oh, nonsense. Call me Helen."

"Thank you, Helen."

"I'm sorry for the distinct absence of guests. Doug, my husband, has just gotten a new harvesting tractor, and he's out back showing it to the others. Do you want to join him? I'm here in case any other guests arrive."

"Want to see a new tractor, honey?" Viveca asked with an amused smile.

"Of course, I do," Richard answered, and Helen led them out back. In the field not far from the house, they could see a small crowd of people and the behemoth of a tractor that roared in the distance.

The tractor seemed to die suddenly, and the roaring ceased only to be replaced by a voice yelling. From the field, the figure of a man was running toward the house. "Help! Call an ambulance!"

Viveca sprang into action. "Helen, will you please hold Liam?" she asked and handed Liam to the woman without waiting for an answer. She grabbed Richard's hand. "Come on! I know first aid, and I may need your help." She and Richard ran toward the field.

When they reached the tractor, they could see another man was horribly injured. A large gash gaped over the man's upper right arm, and he was bleeding badly. "Please step back. I'm certified in first aid. I'm a police officer."

The small crowd backed away. Viveca took off the jacket she was wearing and folded the fabric over and over again to form a tourniquet. She wrapped the jacket over the wound and tied the arms together as tightly as she could to squelch the bleeding. "What's his name?" she asked.

"That's Doug Spencer. He was showing us how the harvester worked, then he shut down the engine. He slipped when he went to climb down. The harvester was still turning," a man in the crowd explained.

"Please see how Helen is doing, and please check on my son, Liam," Viveca addressed them all. "Please make sure the ambulance comes back here when it arrives."

The crowd dispersed to assist her in the task at hand. "Richard," Viveca said. "My arms are getting tired. I need you to take over holding the tourniquet as tight as you can. Now that they're gone, I'm going to call the tigress."

Richard knelt down next to her and readied himself to take the ends of the fabric from her. She had pulled the fabric tight and had brought the ends together to press down on the wound. She pulled the ends out, keeping it as tight as she could. "Grab it above my hands. When I let go, you pull and then bring the ends around and press down as hard as you can. We've got to keep him from bleeding out before the ambulance comes. Are you ready?"

"Yes," Richard said and grabbed the fabric above where her hands held it. When she let go, he pulled tight, brought the ends up and pressed down.

Viveca stood and shook out her arms. "Okay, give me a second. I'm going to call the tigress, and then I can take over again."

"Viv?" Richard said, his voice was full of wonder.

"What is it?" she asked and turned to look down at him.

Where Richard's hands pressed down, a fiery glow emanated into and around the fabric. Up and around him, fiery tendrils formed to encase his entire body. Then the tendrils surged downward into his hands and out around Doug Spencer's unconscious body. The blood that had saturated the ground around him was gone. The fabric was no longer soaked through.

"Move your hands, Richard," Viveca instructed.

"Are you sure?"

"Yes, move your hands."

Richard released the ends of the jacket, and Viveca crouched to remove the tourniquet. Beneath the makeshift tourniquet, the wound on Doug Spencer's arm was healing. Her eyes grew wide with wonder. Behind her, her husband cried out. She rose without hesitation and rushed to his side. He'd fallen to his knees, his hands clenched.

"Open your hands, baby," she said calmly.

Shakily, he unclenched his fingers. At the center of his palms were rings of light. She stared down in awe as he looked up at her. "What's happening to me?" he asked.

YEAR TWO

It made sense. All of it. From the moment she saw the rings of light, everything fell into place. The reason she couldn't feel it anymore. The reason Richard had not become a vampire. The reason he was able to calm their son when he was hurting. The phoenix had somehow been moved to Richard. She needed answers, but who could she ask?

The ambulance had come and examined Doug Spencer. The wound was still healing, and the paramedics concluded that he hadn't been hurt as badly as everyone had first thought. Doug himself had not been able to recall the accident. In the end, the paramedics dressed the wound, and Doug opted not to go to the hospital.

Considering the events of the day, the Spencers decided to reschedule their party, and the guests made their way home. Viveca retrieved Liam from Helen with her thanks, and she and Richard made their way back home as well. Neither of them said a word until they were safely inside their home.

"What is happening to me, love?"

"I think the phoenix must have somehow been moved to you, Richard."

"How?"

"I'm not sure, but it's incredible!"

"I just healed a man! How did I do that?" He flexed his fingers while holding his hands palms upward. "What is this?"

"We're going to figure this out together. On Monday, I'm going to call—"

"On Monday? I have rings of fire on my hands, Viveca!"

"Are they hurting?"

"No, but I'm scared. I'm sorry, but I am."

"It's okay to be scared. It's the phoenix, Richard. I know because that's what my palms looked like when she was with me."

"How can I even hold my son?"

"You can hold him, Richard. Take him. You'll see."

"I don't want to hurt him."

"You won't. Don't you see the intent of it is healing, not destruction?"

"You said it could be a weapon. What if I accidentally set it off?"

"You won't. Now, take him." When Richard made no effort to reach out, she held Liam out toward him. "Take him."

Liam reached out toward Richard. "Dadda!"

"What if I hurt him, Viv?"

"You won't. I promise you won't."

Richard reached out and took their son in his arms. Liam gurgled happily up at his father. Richard smiled and released a sigh of relief. "I thought I wasn't going to be able to hold you again, son."

Liam brought his hands to Richard's face. "Dadda!"

Richard chuckled. "That's right. I'm your daddy."

Viveca stepped into Richard's embrace and placed her hand on Liam's back. Liam leaned forward and let his head rest on his father's shoulder. He reached up and touched his father's face again.

The sounds of birds chirping was the first sound Viveca and Richard heard. When they opened their eyes, they were standing in a luscious green field. They held on to one another, Liam nestled between them. "Where are we?" Richard asked.

"I can't be completely sure, but I think it may be his dream walk."

"*His* dream walk?" Richard asked.

"I think so."

"He's able to—" Richard trailed off.

"You once said I pulled you into a dream walk when I was a baby. Why not him?"

Liam lifted his head from Richard's shoulder and turned his body in Richard's arms. "What are you doing, son?"

"I think he wants down," Viveca said.

Richard lowered Liam to the ground. Liam stood and walked a few paces away from them. He lifted his small arm and pointed into the distance. "Papa!"

From the edge of where the trees grew in the distance, a figure emerged. Not a child, as Viveca had often seen in her own dream walks, but that of a grown man. An elderly man. A man she knew. In an instant, she was on her knees. The man walked much more quickly than he'd done in life.

"Rise, child," the old man said when he came to stand before her.

Richard helped her to her feet. "Mr. Eaglefeather," Viveca said.

"You know better now, granddaughter."

"Yes, Grandfather. I do know."

Liam came to stand before Mr. Eaglefeather. "Papa!"

Mr. Eaglefeather reached down and took Liam's hand, then lifted the child into his arms. The old man smiled at Richard and Viveca. "The rising is upon your husband."

"What is that?"

"My time grows short. Seek me out in your own space. Call me forth," Mr. Eaglefeather said and placed Liam back onto the ground. Liam walked to his parents. Richard lifted him into his arms and placed an arm around Viveca. The distance between them grew until they were once again standing in their home.

∞

"Viveca, how did that just happen?" Richard asked.

"I don't know. Liam took us into his dream walk."

"Yes, but your grandfather was there. How in all creation?"

"I need to make a call. The coroner, Maxine Ryan, is a visionary. She said there would be someone I could speak with, but that the woman would be back later this year. Whoever she is, I think we need to speak with her." Viveca dialed the number and waited.

"Morgue. Dr. Ryan."

"Hi, Dr. Ryan. This is Viveca Ambrose. Do you remember me?"

"Of course, I do. I was going to call you this week. She has returned, and she will see you."

"Great. When?"

"December 21st at 10:00 a.m. Don't be late. You will find her above the sushi bar on Carondelet. Her name is Candida."

"Thank you," Viveca said and disconnected the call. She looked up at Richard. "We have an appointment for this Thursday at 10:00 a.m."

"Who is she?"

"I have no idea."

∞

At 9:15 a.m., Viveca and Richard dropped Liam off at Mike and Stan's. Stan was all too happy to sit him. "Don't worry about him. Uncle Stan will take good care of him."

"Thanks, you guys," Viveca said.

"Anytime, kid. We love having Liam around," Mike said with a smile.

The drive to Carondelet wasn't nearly as crowded as Viveca believed it would be, and by 9:45 a.m., she was pulling into a parking space at the rear of the sushi bar.

"Are these people just going to let us upstairs?" Richard asked.

"I presume so. Dr. Ryan said the woman would be found above this place, so she must have a residence or an office."

"Right, but we don't know who we're here to see."

"Dr. Ryan said her name is Candida."

"Candida what?"

"Oh, come on. Let's go," Viveca said and got out of the car. Richard followed hesitantly.

When they entered the restaurant, a hallway presented itself and just inside were a list of offices within the building. Viveca scanned them quickly and saw the name Candida embossed upon a small piece of paper that had been slid into the many brass slots announcing the occupants. "See here? Dr. Candida Winterhawk. This must be her," she said aloud.

"How have we suddenly been surrounded by people who knows what is happening?" Richard asked.

"So you're thinking this is weird?"

"Not that it can be weirder than our last few days, but yes, love, I do."

"Would you prefer I went by myself?" Viveca asked with a chuckle and waited by the entrance to the stairs.

"Absolutely not!"

On the second floor, Dr. Winterhawk's door was the fourth door on the left. Viveca knocked. She and Richard stood in companionable silence as they waited for an answer.

A moment later, they could hear the locks being disengaged and the door opened to reveal a lovely Native American woman of about sixty. "Good morning," she said. "I've been expecting you, Viveca and Richard. I'm glad to see you are taking matters in stride."

"I wouldn't go that far, Doctor," Richard said.

"Do come in," Dr. Winterhawk said and stood aside to allow them to enter.

The interior of the space was dimly lit. Smells of strong tea brewing and incense burning filled the room. To the right, a beaded curtain hung across a doorway. To the left, a large room was filled with various sofas and chairs. Ahead of them, another room. Dr. Winterhawk entered first, and Viveca and Richard followed. "Thank you for seeing us, Dr. Winterhawk," Viveca said.

"Yes, I've been looking forward to this for some time."

"For some time? Forgive me, but why now? Why not three years ago when I was trying to save my husband? Or last year when I was facing Malcolm on my own? Why not twenty-four years ago when I lost my parents? Why not last year when Malcolm killed my Nana? You all seem to know my grandfather, Graham Eaglefeather, and my grandmother, Enola Hampshire. Suddenly, the visionaries are coming out of the woodwork. So why now?" Viveca asked. She hadn't realized just how angry she was. She wasn't even sure if Dr. Winterhawk knew anything at all about Malcolm or the vampires or the ghouls. She wasn't even sure if she could trust the woman before her.

"Because now is when you need us, Viveca. You do not realize how strong you are."

"Well, it would have been nice for people to have jumped into the fray."

"Your struggles honed you into the warrior you are. You had to face it on your own to fully embrace your power." She turned to Richard. "Show me your hand." Richard extended his right hand to her. She grabbed it and smoothed her fingers over his palm to open his hand completely. "When did this happen?"

"On December 16th. Viveca and I were at a party where a man was injured. Viveca had created a tourniquet and had asked me to help her. When I did, I, um—"

"Healed him?" Dr. Winterhawk asked.

"Yes. When I lifted my hands, his wound was healing. It was one of the most—"

"Amazing things, yes?"

"I was going to say 'scary,'" Richard said.

"Why scary, Richard? Haven't you seen manifestations of power within your wife? Are you afraid of her?"

"No, of course I'm not afraid of her."

"Then why yourself? The phoenix has found a home within you. If you embrace her, she will complete the rising, and—"

"I'm sorry to interrupt, but what is the rising?" Viveca asked.

"The rising is a great becoming. Usually this happens to people born with power, like yourself. You are a dream walker warrior born with the tigress and the phoenix. When you arrived at the hospital, you told your doctors that you tried to keep your husband's heart going by slamming your hand down onto his chest. That's when it happened."

"What happened?" Viveca asked. "I've never understood."

"Do you remember that moment?"

"Yes."

"That was when it happened. Transference of power from yourself to your husband. You were already wielding the phoenix. When your determination to save your husband rose within you, the phoenix moved from you to him. Then she worked within him to destroy the vampire."

"How do you know about this?" Richard asked.

"I saw what was inside you the day I came to your hospital room."

"When were you there?" Viveca asked.

"Do you remember Dr. Delphi Williams?"

"Yes, why?"

"Because I was her Labrador, Shadow."

"How is that possible?" Viveca asked, astonished.

"I am a skinwalker visionary. I have the foresight of the visionaries and the revealing sight of the dream walkers. I can also shift into a variety of animals. My spirit is the wolf, but I can also shift into dogs, cats, and birds."

"A wolf?" Richard asked. "Do you change because of the vampires?"

"You've been reading too much fiction, Richard." Dr. Winterhawk said with an amused grin. "The vampires aren't catalysts, and we don't have our abilities thrust upon us suddenly. We're born with our abilities, and we are taught to use them from the moment we are born. I'm a shape-shifter. I wield magic and shift into the form I'm comfortable with in nature."

"Is Dr. Williams's dog okay?" Richard asked.

"Shadow is fine."

"Why didn't you just come to me? Why not let me know who you are?" Viveca asked.

"Because your husband's fate was uncertain. The phoenix could win, but there was just as much a chance that it wouldn't. I had to wait, and then I had to see if it would manifest itself within him."

"And now that it has?" Viveca asked.

"Richard must decide whether to embrace the phoenix or not. The phoenix is very powerful. She will only rise within one who embraces her."

"What will happen to me if I embrace her?" Richard asked and sat forward. His curiosity had grown minute by minute.

"She will rise from the ashes of defeating the vampire. The fact that you healed that man is proof that she's already coming forth within you.

When the rising is complete, she will offer her power to you. You will become a warrior, and the phoenix will become your warrior spirit."

"And if I choose not to embrace her?"

"She will die within you, and you will remain as you have been since Viveca pulled you through the blazing."

"I want to be able to protect my family," Richard stated plainly. "But I don't know how to embrace her. I don't know where I should begin."

Dr. Winterhawk brought her hand to her chest and held it over her heart. "You start here, Richard. You start with what matters most to you. Your fear of becoming will eventually cause her to leave you. You must overcome your fear and accept her. She will know when you do."

∞

January 1, 2018, New Orleans, Louisiana, 11:37 p.m.

"Richard, are you sure?" Viveca asked.

"I'm sure," Richard replied.

"I know you're freaking out about it. I think you might think embracing the phoenix will be a lot like living with the vampire. It won't. These spirits don't cage you. They delight in your freedom. They complement you."

"You know me so well, love."

"Do you remember how lost I felt without the tigress?"

"Yes, I remember."

"It's because she is a part of me. She's my strength when I have none. She's a representative of my warrior self. She embodies my confidence and my balance. I cannot do without her."

"I'm trying to accept her, love. I really am."

"I know you are. How can I help you through this?"

"I'm not sure."

Next to them, the baby monitor delivered Liam's voice. "Papa!"

Both Richard and Viveca rose and made their way to the nursery. Liam was standing in his crib. "You all right, little man?" Richard asked.

"Papa!"

Richard turned to Viveca. "Is he asking about Mr. Eaglefeather?"

"I think he must be. He's only used that word in reference to my grandfather."

"What was it that Mr. Eaglefeather told you in the dream walk? To seek him out? Call him out?"

"He wanted me to call him forth from my own dream walk. I don't know how to do that."

"Liam did it, though, love."

"Yes, and maybe he can help me do it." She reached over and lifted her son in her arms. "Come here, Richard," she beckoned, and he stepped into her embrace. In a moment, they were standing in the beautiful field of her dream walk. "Liam, can you show me how to call Papa?"

She put him down, and he walked a few paces ahead of her. A moment later, a golden light formed around him, and the eagle emerged above him. She followed his lead, allowing the tigress to form around her and surge through her to release the dream walker warrior.

"Papa?" she asked.

Liam sent forth the eagle. Up it soared then seemed to dive back down to the ground only to extend its wings to gracefully glide along the ground and return to Liam. Again, she followed his lead.

"Papa, I need you," Viveca said, and the tigress burst from her, bounding across the field and into the trees at the edge of the field. When it returned, Mr. Eaglefeather was with it. The tigress rushed forward as Viveca called it back.

To her astonishment, Mr. Eaglefeather began to run. Around him, the magnificent bear formed around him. When he came to stand in front of her, he was grinning. "Very good, child."

She smiled. "Thank you, Papa."

Mr. Eaglefeather turned to Richard. "Are you ready to begin, my son?"

Richard took a deep breath. Everything he'd witnessed had astonished him. Viveca had been right. There was no cage. The phoenix would serve to guard his freedom, not take it from him. "Yes, Papa."

Papa held out his hands, and Richard took them in his own. Like Dr. Winterhawk had done, Papa turned Richard's hands palm side up and studied the rings that had formed there. "The rising has begun. Do not fight it, my son."

Richard shook his head. "I won't."

"We must make this place a place for Richard as well, child."

"What do you mean, Papa?"

"He is not a dream walker and cannot command the walk, but he is becoming the phoenix, and he must have a safe place to learn."

"How can I do that?"

"When he is ready, your spirits will bond. When that happens, he will be able to come here at will. His presence will call me here, and our training will begin."

"How long will that take? It's already the New Year, and we are running out of time. Three years may seem like a long time, but it's not."

"The rising will take its own time, child. It cannot be rushed. Trust it."

The distance between them grew, and the three of them were once again in their home. Liam yawned, and Viveca placed him back into his crib. Viveca and Richard returned to their bedroom. "When our spirits bond?" Richard reflected.

"Your guess is as good as mine. I believe we will just have to wait and see."

"Tonight, something was on your mind. What was it, love?"

"Oh, it's nothing."

"Tell me."

"I was thinking of quitting my job as a homicide detective and make an attempt to become a police consultant."

"Is that something you really want to do?"

"I've thought it through, and no. Besides letting Frank down, I'd lose the access I have to the very information I need to try to figure out where the vampires are."

"Plus, you love your job, Viveca. It's your life, love."

"You and Liam are my life, Richard. I became a homicide detective because I thought I could do some good. I think I have, but lately, it's been about paperwork and going along to get along. I'm thirty years old. I don't want to get stuck in a job that causes me to miss my son growing up. I feel like I'm missing everything lately, and these past six weeks have been so wonderful being home with Liam and being here when you get home from work. I want to be your wife in all the ways that matter and count."

"You are my wife, love, in all the ways that matter and count. We wouldn't be the first parents to select a daycare or nanny for their child during work. You aren't letting anyone down doing what you do, love."

"I started to feel that I should slow down. Time is passing so quickly. Liam is already a year old. How did that happen? I don't want to miss anything anymore. The three years will have gone by, and I will have missed it all."

"Sweetheart, you've been here. You haven't missed anything. Now, let's get some sleep. We have one more day together, and then it's back to work for both of us."

∞

January 3, 2018, New Orleans, Louisiana, 7:45 a.m.

Viveca entered the precinct building and made her way to her desk. Neither Frank nor Watson had made it in yet. She walked down the hall to the conference room. The map they had flagged had been pushed to the other end of the table to make room for current case discussions. She took a seat in front of the map and began to study it. She knew the answer must be staring her in the face.

A small desk at the other end of the room held a cup containing whiteboard markers, permanent markers in various colors, and several ink pens. Viveca selected several of the permanent markers and made her way back to the map. Reseated, she used different colors for different areas of New Orleans, first linking each victim with their residence, then began to link people in the order they went missing. When she was done, she stood and stepped back from it.

"Hey, Viv," Frank greeted her.

"Hey, Frank. Come look at this."

He came to her side and looked down at the map. "What's all this?"

"It's always bothered me that there wasn't any discernable pattern to the disappearances. So I linked them to their addresses, then to each other by date missing. This is what I get."

"Okay. What do you make of it?" Frank asked.

"You see this area here?" Viveca pointed to a spot on the map where all the lines drawn cordoned off an area in the center. It wasn't a perfect circle, but it was still a theory.

"Yeah."

"Well, I think that wherever they are, they're somewhere in this area. This looks like a spider's web. The spider usually sits in the middle of web, just waiting."

"That's a fairly big area, Viv."

"It is because they've taken people from all over the city. Now, we might have a way to find them. And you see how the area is outside the city limits? New Orleans is a fishbowl within the city limits. Heavy rain can cause flooding, so there aren't any underground structures, but outside those limits, there may be places where underground structures could survive."

"Where do you suppose we start?"

"With Ferguson. He can provide us maps of the area and tell us what's there. We check any place where there's underground access first. Then we move on."

"Sounds like a plan to me."

"Let's fill Watson in, and we can get going."

∞

Ferguson provided the map and helped Viveca overlay his map onto hers. "Can you tell us if there are any structures in this area that have underground access?" Viveca asked.

"There are two. It looks like they're both old apartment complexes. Both have underground parking garages."

"Great. Anything else?"

"Not that I can tell. If you want, I can start identifying the major buildings and structures."

"That would be fantastic! Thank you, Ferguson," Viveca said.

"I'll email you the information once I've got it."

"Thanks again!"

∞

"This building is abandoned. Has probably been abandoned for years. Do you really think we're going to find something out here in the middle of the day?" Frank asked.

"We're looking for vampires. The best time is during the day. They would be asleep. Do you want to try to find them after nightfall?"

Frank chuckled. "No, thanks."

"What about you, Watson?" Viveca asked. "You want to wait until after dark?"

"Not me."

"Okay, then. Now it is. You two stick close. And check your targets, please. Our mission is not to shoot up a bunch of homeless people."

"What about that idea Dr. Ryan had?"

"She knows it works on ghouls, but she has to synthesize it before it can be used. It's going to take some time."

"It'd be really nice to have right about now," Watson muttered.

"If we run into any ghouls, remember to shoot them in the head. It won't kill them, but it will slow them down for a few minutes."

"Jesus, Viv. How do we know who's who?"

"Trust me. You'll know, Watson."

"Okay, now focus. Here we go."

The building stunk of mildew and rot. All the signs of a man-made structure left to the elements. In single file, with Viveca at the lead, the three detectives made their way down the hall. An aging sign held up by two rusty hooks pointed to the stairwell.

Viveca opened the door. Darkness peered up at her. She quietly called the tigress, and her vision became acute. She looked back at Frank and Watson and placed a finger to her lips. Frank turned on his flashlight and held it between himself and Watson. They descended the steps, Viveca leading the way.

All around them, the sound of water dripping echoed. What seemed a stairwell now seemed as cavernous as hell itself. Underneath the dripping water, another sound arose. A sound of friction. A scraping that could have been anything, but which felt to Viveca the sound of claws being drawn across the concrete pillars of the structure.

They came to one landing and descended another to emerge on the floor below where they started. Viveca moved her vision across the expanse before her like a spotlight. Whatever might be lurking there was unseen and unknowable.

Frank and Watson used their flashlight to unveil the darkness behind them. Light revealed dank walls and pillars, signs of extreme age and water damage, but nothing supernatural.

Viveca turned toward them. "Let's keep moving," she whispered and walked ahead.

Frank and Watson followed her across the concrete expanse. Ahead of them, Viveca's vision illuminated another stairwell sign and its accompanying door. The three of them stood in front of the door as though they were Dorothy waiting to see the wizard in a demented Oz. Viveca reached out and pressed against the door's release bar and swung it open. More darkness, deeper than the level above, yawned up at them. Moving forward as before, they descended the stairs.

∞

The doorbell rang. Richard rose from his chair with Liam in his arms. Careful not to wake him, he placed Liam gently down onto the playmat and made his way to the door. No one was at the door, but a small package addressed to Richard had been left for him. He picked it up and turned it over in his hands. No return address had been listed.

He stepped back inside and shut the door then peeked into the living room from the foyer to find Liam still asleep on the mat. In the kitchen, he used a knife to sever the tape and unfolded the flaps of the small box. Richard lifted the envelope from the box and removed the paper within it.

It was a letter, neatly written. Malcolm's handwriting looped elegantly across the page:

Brother,

> *I give you this choice out of respect for your family. Come to me now and allow the healing between us to begin. We are brothers, and neither time nor space can change it.*
>
> *I chose you for this gift. It is a gift, Richard. How can you not believe it? Without it, you would have never met your wife nor had your child. Without me, none of the joy you have would have been possible. Do you not see it? We are bound by blood. Wherever you go, I go. Wherever you are, I am. In the places you call home, I exist. Time moves on swift wings. Life and death swirl around us, yet we go on unchanged. We live in a shadowy place where time lives. Undetected, yet as evident as man's face in a mirror. We are eternal.*
>
> *Come to me before the third year is spent, and I will spare your wife and child. Choose them over me and I will take them from you as surely as the moon controls the tide. I wait for you, brother.*

Malcolm

Richard dropped the letter to the counter and stepped back from it. He moved from the kitchen and returned to the living room. His son was sitting up on the mat. When Liam saw Richard, he smiled and held his arms up. Richard scooped him up and hugged him close. "I love you, Liam," Richard said and returned to his chair.

Close to Richard's ear, Liam announced, "Wuv you."

Richard loosened his hug and sat Liam on his lap. He smiled broadly. "You love me, Liam?"

"Wuv Dadda!"

"You are so smart," Richard said.

"Dadda 'fraid?" Liam asked suddenly.

"What makes you say that Liam?"

Liam brought his hands up and pressed them onto Richard's chest, just over his heart. "'Fraid," Liam said. "Dadda 'fraid."

"Between you and me, son, I am afraid. Afraid I'm going to lose you and Mommy."

Liam turned on Richard's lap and took one of his hands and held it palm up. "Dadda, no 'fraid."

"What?"

Again, Liam held up Richard's hand. "Dadda, no 'fraid."

"Are you saying I don't need to be afraid?"

Liam turned again in Richard's lap and wrapped his arms around Richard's neck. Richard hugged his son. Malcolm had given him a way to protect his family, and he knew if he took it, he would die. He could not live without them. Yet if it meant his wife and son were safe …

Liam broke the hug and placed his hands on his father's face. Richard peered into his son's eyes. A vast understanding and wisdom peered back at him. Gently but quite deliberately, Liam spoke two words, "No, Dadda."

"No? No what, Liam?"

Words seemed to escape Liam, and Richard could see him getting frustrated. All the wisdom of the universe might lie within his son, but Liam was unable to express it in a way Richard could understand. Richard pulled Liam back into a hug. "It's okay, son. It's okay. Daddy is going to protect you."

Liam struggled out of the hug. "No, Dadda! No!"

Even though it felt impossible, Richard was suddenly sure Liam was reading his thoughts. "You can't know what I'm thinking, Liam."

Liam once again pulled his father into a hug. Richard held his son, the wonder of the experience overwhelming him. "You do know, don't you?" Richard asked.

"Dadda," Liam said softly, yet his tone seemed more an affirmative than him simply addressing Richard.

"Don't worry. I'm not going anywhere."

Liam pulled his arms tighter around his father's neck a moment, then settled onto Richard's lap. He took Richard's right hand and turned it palm up and ran his small fingers across the ring of light.

Within him, Richard felt a warmth began to spread throughout his body. Richard held his hands out. The rings on his palms darkened for a moment, then brightened vividly. At the center of each ring, flames rose. His hands began to shake.

Liam let out a delighted giggle at the sight of the flames rising from his father's palms. Around him, a golden light began to radiate. Liam reached out and took Richard's hand again. The golden light mingled with the flames. Richard watched in wonder, at first fearful that the flames might harm his son. The golden light and the flame complemented each other, swirling around like two friends at play. A vast peace settled around Richard's heart. He'd seen the spirit warriors at work, had witnessed their awesome power. He was not afraid. Not anymore. It was time to learn to accept the phoenix.

∞

Nothing but darkness.

They'd swept each level of the parking structure and had found nothing. Viveca swept her vision across the lowest level while Frank and Watson used the flashlight in the opposite direction.

"Okay, guys, let's go. There's nothing here," Viveca said.

Frank and Watson joined her. They began to make their way back to the stairwell when the first sounds rose behind them. Viveca whirled, and the tigress surged through her to bring forth the dream walker warrior. Ahead of her, a whispering rose, and the darkness began to move.

"Stay behind me," Viveca advised. She released the tigress, and it stepped ahead of her. She projected her vision and began looking through the tigress's eyes. There was more movement not far ahead.

The tigress crept forward. Then a figure came into focus. A woman. She froze under the scrutiny of the tigress's gaze.

"Please don't hurt us," she said frailly.

"Who are you? What are you doing here?" Viveca asked, halting the tigress and drawing her back to become herself again.

"We were brought here early this morning," the woman said.

"What is your name?"

"Jennifer Simpson."

Viveca knew that name. Jennifer Simpson was among those who had gone missing in the past few months. "Ms. Simpson, my name is Viveca Ambrose. I'm a police detective. If you'll come with us, we can help you."

"What was that? What are you?"

Viveca thought a moment. She'd not been prepared to explain herself. "She's a friend, and so am I. You can trust us." Behind her, Frank and Watson used their flashlights to further illuminate the area. Several people were gathered together near a wall. The woman, Jennifer, was standing not very far from them.

"It looked like a tiger."

"Yes, that's what she is. We will not hurt you. Can you tell me who brought you here or why?"

"None of us are sure, but if you're here to help us, one of the men is hurt. We haven't been able to wake him."

Viveca turned to Frank and Watson. "Please check him out." Watson moved toward the people still huddled beside the wall while Frank remained near Viveca with his flashlight.

Viveca turned back to Jennifer Simpson. "Where were you before you were brought here?"

"I think we were in a house. There were rooms we were kept in, and there were bathrooms."

"How did you get there? Can you tell me what happened to you?"

"I was in my kitchen, preparing supper for my family. I remember a knock on the door. I answered, and I'm sure someone was there, but I cannot remember who it was. The next thing I remember, I was in that other place."

"Did you get a good look at the person or people who took you?"

"Not really. He kept to the shadows, and it was pretty dark."

"So you're sure it was a man?"

"Yes. He spoke a few times."

"What did he say to you?"

"He brought food and water. He gave me orders like when to stand and where to go when he moved us."

"Did your room have any windows?"

"Yes, but they were blacked out with paint or something."

Ahead of her, Watson's voice rose in the near darkness. "Viv, I think you need to see this."

"Frank, stay with her. I'll be right back." Viveca made her way to Watson's side.

Watson's flashlight illuminated a man who seemed to be asleep. Viveca could see the wounds on his neck had clotted and were beginning to disappear. "You see that?" Watson asked.

"These people are in danger," she said and addressed them all. "All of you, please step away from this man."

"We can't," Jennifer's voice rose behind her. "We're all bound together. See? We can't get more than a few feet away from each other."

"Okay, I need everyone's attention. I have a special ability, and I can help you. Do not be afraid. I'm not going to hurt any of you."

"What is happening?" A man nearby asked.

"I will explain later, but right now, I need you to be still and quiet." Viveca stepped back and called the tigress again. The tigress formed around her, surged through her to reveal the dream walker warrior, then burst from her.

The men and women on the floor before her scuttled back against the wall as far as they could. Viveca stepped toward them. "Don't be afraid. We're not going to hurt you. Trust me." She approached the first person, a woman, and crouched before her. She reached out to inspect the binding at her ankle. "Stay still. We're not going to hurt you."

The tigress bent its head toward the binding and opened its mouth. The woman tried to back away farther. The tigress stopped and turned its head and rubbed it gently against the woman's knee. Then turned its head the other way and rubbed again. "You see?" Viveca said. "She's not going to hurt you."

The woman relaxed, and the tigress bent its head again toward the binding and opened its mouth. One razor-sharp tooth hooked between the binding and the woman's ankle and pulled gently. A moment later, the binding snapped, and the woman was freed. "Go stand near Jennifer," Viveca ordered, and she made her way to the next person.

When she'd freed them all, she and the tigress joined them along with Watson. "Frank, Harrison, take them up."

"What is happening to him?" a man asked.

"He's infected," Viveca said calmly.

"Infected with what?" Jennifer asked. "Are we going to catch whatever he has?"

"No. You all are going to be okay. He has to be awake to infect you."

"What is it he has?" another woman asked.

"It's nothing you need to worry about. Now, follow Frank and Harrison to safety. I'll be right behind you."

"Is he going to die?" another man asked.

"I hope not," Viveca stated.

"So you can help him?" Jennifer asked.

"I'm going to try. Now, go. All of you. Now!" She kept her eyes on the sleeping man, but she could hear the others behind her leaving the room. Now she understood why these people had been placed in utter darkness. Had Malcolm intended for this vampire to feed once it awakened? Or had he intended it to turn the others?

She tuned into her vision. She could see the vampire cage forming. The man was unconscious. She could not communicate with him. Unless ...

She reached out and took hold of the man's arm and pulled him into the dream walk. The man opened his eyes and looked up at her. "What is your name?" she asked.

"Harold Patterson."

"Harold, my name is Viveca, and—"

"Where am I?"

"It doesn't matter. What matters is—"

"Am I dead?"

"No. Not yet. I need you to listen. You've been infected with a vampire."

"A vampire?"

"Do you remember being bitten?"

"No. I remember leaving work and heading to my car."

"What do you remember after that?"

"I woke up in a dark room. A man was speaking to me, but I couldn't understand what he was saying. He had a strange accent, and I couldn't make out his words."

"Harold, I'm not going to lie to you. Once you wake up, the vampire will take hold of you. Do you have the will to fight it?"

"I'm not awake?"

"No. I've pulled you into a special place where I can speak to you."

"Are you an angel?"

"No, but I do want to help you."

"How?"

"Fight it, Harold. Take hold of the cage and fight it. Don't let it rule you. You can live a life of peace with what you are. You don't have to kill."

"And if I don't or can't?"

"I'll have to destroy you."

"My wife. My daughter," he said sadly.

"I'm sorry. When we leave this place, you'll awaken. Please try to hold on to who you are, Harold."

∞

In the lower level of the parking structure, Harold Patterson opened his eyes. He knew a moment's peace and a memory of speaking to a beautiful unearthly woman. He drew his vision through the darkness and noticed his vision sharpening. He felt a growing constriction inside himself and an awful feeling of being held against his will. Almost as if he had been locked in a cage. The thought reminded him of his conversation with the beautiful woman. *Hold on to who you are, Harold!*

He willed his hands forward to take hold of the cage, but his hands would not obey. Around him, a whispering rose. *"You are mine,"* it said inside his mind.

Harold Patterson thought of his wife, Audrey, and their daughter, Abigail. He thought of the woman with the ivory hair and golden eyes. *I'll have to destroy you.* He was sure she'd meant what she said. She had tried to give him a way to live with the thing inside him, but he had not been fast enough. While he was still himself, he made the last conscious decision he would ever make. Deep inside the cage, he closed his eyes and surrendered. He would become a monster, but he would not be one for long. He would die, but perhaps that was for the best. It was the last gift he would give his family. They would mourn him, but they would not be burdened by the thing he was becoming.

Viveca watched the cage constrict and the determination in Harold Patterson's eyes. She could see he would not be able to control it, and so he had done the only thing he could do. She called upon the tigress, and it began to build momentum inside her. She watched as the vampire systematically took control of his body. In the next moment, the thing stood up, wearing Harold Patterson like a suit, tailored to fit with threads of evil.

Finally, it turned in her direction and revealed its elongated canines. It hissed at her and prepared to attack. The tigress burst from her, driven forward with the warrior's power. One claw slashed across the vampire's chest and pulled its heart from its body. The vampire imploded into dust.

∞

Viveca made her way out of the parking structure to join the others in the sunlight. She had tried to keep a composed expression, but Frank could see she was upset. Being a defender of the light sometimes came with a terrible, taxing price.

"You okay?" Frank asked when she'd come to stand next to him.

She nodded, then addressed the others. "Harold Patterson didn't make it. I'm so sorry."

"What was he infected with?" Jennifer asked.

"It's mostly a fatal condition," Viveca answered.

"Are we going to be infected as well?" a man asked.

"No. We were able to get you to safety before he could infect you. You all are going to be okay."

"What about you? Will you be infected?" Jennifer asked.

"No. I will be fine."

"So you're just going to leave his body down there?" another woman asked.

"No. We'll call in the coroner. You all were moved to this place in the early morning. Was it daylight yet?"

"No," Jennifer said. "It was still dark."

"And you were all in separate rooms before you were brought here?"

"There were times when we all were allowed in a large room. There were people who seemed unwell, but those were taken away. I remember speaking to one of them before he was taken. He seemed injured, and then the next day, he was gone," Jennifer explained.

"Do you remember his name?"

"His name was Gerard, I think. I don't know his last name."

"How many of you were there?"

"I'm not sure how many there were to start, but when it was just us five, that's when they moved us here."

Viveca drew her cellphone from her pocket and made the call. Soon, the place would be crawling with police, forensics, and the coroner, but first, there was something she had to do. Quietly, she called the tigress and focused her vision on each person. The man, Gerard, Jennifer had mentioned was most likely Gerard Stephens. She had to make sure there were no more ghouls among them.

Each of them was human. The vampire Harold Patterson had become would have been strong enough to break the ties that bound them while leaving the humans too weak and disoriented to escape. If they were meant as food for Harold, they would have been easy prey. Inwardly, she shuddered.

Sirens sounded in the distance, and before long, emergency vehicles and police cars were pulling into the parking lot. Dr. Ryan pulled in behind them and made her way to Viveca. "Where is the body?"

"I'll show you," Viveca answered and led her into the building. When they were inside, she turned to Dr. Ryan. "The man was a vampire. I destroyed it. There's nothing left but ash."

"Don't worry. There are ways to cover that up."

Down below, Viveca illuminated the spot with her flashlight. Dr. Ryan stepped forward and drew a body bag out of the large case she carried. She spread it across the floor near the ash and unzipped it. She pulled a device from the case that turned out to be a small vacuum. Once she'd cleaned up the ash, she deposited it in the body bag, then poured a chemical over the ash. Viveca watched in amazement as the chemical expanded like a foam, absorbed the ash, and weighed down the body bag. Dr. Ryan zipped the bag and waited for her team.

"That was incredible," Viveca said.

"Yes, well, the existence of the supernatural is mostly a secret from ordinary society."

"And if ordinary people knew?"

"Some would think it a joke, others would seek us out."

"Seek us out? For what?"

"Healing, mainly. The magic we carry comes from nature. Nature is the ultimate provider and healer. It's why you hear the whispering when you're in the dream walk. Nature is speaking to you and working through you."

Viveca smiled. "I see. Thank you."

"Why don't you join us in a few weeks? The visionaries meet each month. We'd like your input on the vampires and ghouls."

"I'd be happy to."

"I'll text you the date, time, and address," Dr. Ryan said, and the sound of voices rose behind them. The door to the lower level had been propped open, and they could see light illuminating the landing just outside it. A moment later, Paul and another man Viveca recognized as one of Dr. Ryan's assistants enter the room with a spinal board.

"Hey, Doc," Paul said.

"Detective Ambrose, you remember my interns Paul and Jake?"

"Yes, I do," Viveca said. "It's good to see you both again."

"Already have him bagged up?" Paul observed. "Great. We'll get him out of here and take him back to the lab."

"Thank you," Dr. Ryan said. "Place the body, bag and all, on the autopsy table. The body is in bad shape. Keep the bag closed. I'm going to have to start the autopsy at the closed bag for evidence purposes, and I cannot have anything contaminate it."

"You got it," Jake said, and he and Jake loaded the body bag onto the spinal board and strapped it down. They lifted the board and started back up the stairs.

From the first flight of steps, the sounds of two young men making effort to carry an awkward object echoed down to Viveca and Dr. Ryan. Then Jake's voice followed. "Man, this dude is heavy."

Viveca turned to Dr. Ryan. "Do you think they'll keep the bag closed?"

"Yes. They're good interns, and they go by the book. They know the importance of maintaining the integrity of the evidence."

"What will you actually do?"

"I have another chemical at the lab. It will dissolve the foam, and I'll bag the ash for his family."

"How will you explain it to his family?"

"Same as I explained it to Jake and Paul. The body was in bad shape, and there was no other alternative than to cremate."

"I feel terrible," Viveca said.

Dr. Ryan stepped forward and placed a hand on Viveca's shoulder. "It wasn't your fault, Viveca. You tried. That's all you could do. You did save four people today. That's definitely something."

"I'm glad for that, but—"

"No. No buts. You did all you could do. You cannot save everyone. If you want to someone to blame, blame the vampire. The blame belongs with the thing that did this. Not with you. Okay?"

Viveca nodded. "He was so scared, and he was worried about his family."

"And he did what he had to do to make sure he couldn't hurt them. He was brave and selfless when he surrendered. He knew he would die. He earned that. Don't take it away from him."

Viveca nodded again and took a deep breath. "You're right. He died a hero's death, and that's what I'll tell his family."

"Now we need to discuss how we'll handle those four who saw the tigress."

"We won't hurt them, will we?"

Dr. Ryan smiled patiently. "Of course not." She pulled her cellphone from her pocket and made a call. When she'd completed the call and returned the phone to her pocket, she once again gave Viveca her attention. "He's on his way. He'll meet us at the station."

"Who is on his way?"

"A friend who can help us wipe their memory."

"Is that safe?"

"He's very good at it. I know you're concerned about their safety. He's not going to hurt them. He'll only remove their memory of you as the warrior and the tigress."

∞

A day off had done him good. While the job he had wasn't all that stressful, Richard was enjoying watching his son play. Liam arranged toys around himself as if he were at a party and babbled and giggled along to them as though they were his best friends. Richard sat in his chair, contented to watch.

Liam suddenly stopped chattering, and a golden glow surrounded him. He stood up and awkwardly turned in a circle. When he faced his toys again, he looked up at Richard and held his arms out. Richard rose and lifted his son into his arms. "Dadda," Liam said quietly.

Following his son's lead, Richard whispered, "What is it, Liam?"

Liam's eyes seemed unfocused and his head lolled slightly. The golden light grew around them, and Liam reached up and touched

Richard's face. Liam whispered one word that threw a band of ice down Richard's spine. "Bain."

∞

The two men and two women Viveca and her team had rescued from the parking structure were exhausted and anxious to be reunited with their families. Viveca apologized to each of them but explained that making their statements now was an important step in ensuring the most accurate information could be gathered in the attempt to identify their kidnappers. Each was escorted to a separate interrogation room and offered food and drink while they waited.

Dr. Ryan introduced her to Daniel Windsong. He was a tall man. Handsome. She guessed him to be in his midthirties, but she couldn't be sure. He nodded congenially in her direction, but politely refused a handshake. She carried on unoffended and led him to the first interrogation room. She introduced herself again and then introduced Mr. Windsong. Mr. Windsong stepped forward and extended his hand to Jennifer.

Viveca switched on her vision, but she was unable to see whatever magic worked within Mr. Windsong. She sat quietly and took note of their facial expressions. Jennifer, upon touching Mr. Windsong's hand, seemed to become mesmerized. Mr. Windsong stood tranquilly, holding her hand. He closed his eyes and whispered under his breath. His eyes moved under his lids as though he were asleep. Several minutes passed. When he opened his eyes, he moved his hand, and Jennifer once again became fully aware and yet did not seem to notice that any time had gone by. Then they sat across from one another, and Viveca began the debriefing.

∞

Richard grabbed his keys and carried Liam to his truck. He quickly loaded Liam into his car seat, then slipped behind the wheel. He turned the key, and the truck cranked to life. He shifted into reverse and peeled backward down the driveway, turning out onto their quiet street. He threw it into drive and slammed his foot onto the accelerator. The truck lurched forward, and he sped out of the tranquil little neighborhood. At the main highway, he turned right and made his way east, hoping he was making the right decision.

He reached around the seatbelt and pulled his cellphone from his pocket and slipped it in the holder attached to the air vent. He gave a command to his digital assistant. "Call Viveca."

"Calling Viveca," the automated voice announced, and the phone began to ring. A moment later, her voicemail greeting announced she was unable to come to the phone and requested he leave a message. He reached up and tapped the disconnect button and ended the call. He'd try again in a few minutes.

Ahead of him, the light changed from green to yellow. He slowed down and then stopped when the light shone red. He tapped the steering wheel impatiently. He watched cars moving through the intersection. An eternity went by. Finally, their light flicked from green to yellow, then the flood of vehicles came to a stop. A moment after, their light turned red, his light turned green, and he moved his foot to the accelerator once more.

From behind him, Liam announced, "Papa!"

"Mr. Eaglefeather," Richard said absently. "That's right, Liam. Papa. Are you talking to Papa right now?"

"Dadda say Papa!"

"I don't know what you mean, sweetheart," Richard replied.

"Eenx!" Liam exclaimed.

"Eenx? What does that mean, Liam?"

"Dadda eenx!"

"Okay, son," Richard said, then tried to dial Viveca again. Again, he got her voicemail. When the beep sounded, he spoke. "Viv, please call me when you get this message. It's important. Love you." He disconnected the call and focused on the last word his son said. *Eenx. What the hell was Eenx?*

From the back seat. "Bain. Dadda eenx ire."

"Eenx ire? Son, what are you trying to say?" Richard asked and accelerated, focusing on the road but rolling the mashup of words around in his mind. "Ire," he whispered under his breath. Ire meant anger, he knew, but he felt that wasn't what Liam was trying to say. He rolled the word around in his head. *Ire. Bire. Cire. Dire. Eire. Fire.* "Fire?" Richard said aloud. "Eenx fire?" Then it hit him. "Phoenix fire!"

Liam exclaimed from his car seat. "Eenx ire! Dadda eenx ire."

"Yes, Daddy is working on phoenix fire, love."

"Say Papa!"

"Papa!" Richard obeyed.

"No, Dadda say Papa!"

"Say Papa?" Richard inquired.

"Say Papa!"

Richard pushed a hand through his hair. Whatever Liam was trying to tell him was important, he knew. Liam wanted him to say something regarding Mr. Eaglefeather, but whatever Liam wanted him to say eluded him. He tried a different tack. "Where is Papa, Liam?"

"Papa schars."

"Papa schars? Do you mean 'stars'?"

"Papa schars."

"If only you could just say it, love. I'm trying. Papa stars. Is Papa in the stars? You mean he's in heaven?"

"Papa schars," Liam repeated.

Richard commanded his phone again. "Call Frank."

"Calling Frank Taylor," his cellular assistant announced, and the phone began to ring.

"Detective Taylor," Frank answered.

"Frank! It's Richard."

"Hey, Richard, what's—?"

"I'm sorry, but I don't have time. Do you know where Viv is?"

"She's in interrogation with some witnesses. Are you and Liam okay?"

"I don't know. I need to talk to her now. Is there a way she can come to the phone?"

"Okay, just hang on. I'll go and get her." Frank set the phone down. The urgency in Richard's voice alarmed him. He stepped to the interrogation room door and knocked softly. A moment later, Viveca opened the door and stepped outside.

"What is it?" she asked.

"It's Richard. He's on the phone, and he sounds frantic," Frank began, but couldn't finish because she suddenly darted past him. He followed. "He's on my cell," Frank said when he caught up.

She snatched it up from his desk and pressed it to her ear. "Richard?"

"Oh, thank God! Viv, Liam has been saying things that don't make sense, and he's been talking about Mr. Eaglefeather and the phoenix and Bain."

Her eyes went wide. "Bain? You mean Gannon Bain? Are you *sure* he said that?"

"Yes. It was so clear. He was playing and then he stood up and turned in a circle. Golden light surrounded him, then he reached out for me. I lifted him in my arms, and he touched my face. He looked right at me. He said, 'Bain.' And now he's babbling about 'Papa' and schars."

"Schars?"

"I think he means stars, but I can't be sure. He keeps telling me to say Papa. I say it, but I'm certain that's not what he wants me to do because he keeps telling me."

"He tells you to 'say Papa?'"

"Yes."

"He wants you to call him."

"Call him?"

"He held his toy phone up a couple of days ago and told me to say Dadda."

"I said 'Dadda,' but he handed me the phone and told me to say again. I realized he meant for me to call you."

"Okay, so how do I call Papa?"

"Where are you?"

"When he said 'Bain,' I put him in the truck and left the house. I'm headed to Mike and Stan's."

"When you get there, don't leave. I'll be there soon," Viveca said. "I love you."

"I love you too," he said, and she disconnected the call.

∞

She handed Frank his phone and took a deep breath.

"Is everything okay?" Frank asked.

"I don't think so," she said.

"What can I do?"

"I need to finish the debriefing. It won't take long. If Richard calls again, let him know I'll be on my way in just a few minutes."

"You're on the last witness?"

"Yes."

"And who is that guy in there with you? What's he doing?"

"I'll explain later, I promise." She stepped away from him and made her way back to interrogation. She composed her face, then opened the door. "I'm so sorry about that. Let's see. Where were we?"

∞

She drove like a madwoman and mulled the interrogations over in her mind.

When she questioned them about their rescue, each recalled that she had identified herself as a police officer, but none could remember the tigress or having seen her as the dream walker warrior. Each of them assumed they had been freed by Viveca and her team. Each of them remembered Harold Patterson, but none of them remembered her staying behind.

All four of them remembered where they had been prior to being kidnapped and all of them remembered being kept in a room with darkened windows. Each had access to a bathroom. They all remembered being allowed to mingle among one another. They remembered being frightened, and they remembered their numbers dwindling until there were but five of them remaining.

Before daybreak, they were awakened and taken to the parking structure. "Do you remember how you got there? Did you walk? Were you driven?" Viveca had asked. All answered the same. They had been driven, then led down into the bowels of the place and left in the darkness.

∞

Richard pulled into the driveway, relieved to see Stan's vehicle parked at the side of the house. He switched the engine off and moved quickly to retrieve Liam from the car seat.

The front door opened, and Stan stepped out onto the porch. "Hi, handsome! I thought you were off today."

Richard rushed forward with Liam in his arms. The expression on Richard's face sobered Stan into seriousness. Stan moved to open the door and held it as Richard passed inside. "I'm sorry to barge in like this, Stan," he began. "I didn't know where else to go."

"Hey, calm down, Richard. What's happened?" Stan asked, as he followed Richard inside and shut the door behind him.

"Viv is on her way. Liam said something today that scared the shit out of me, and I had to take him out of there."

Stan placed a hand on Richard's shoulder. "Come on. Let's go sit in the other room. I'll make some tea, and we'll have a chat."

Richard carried Liam into the living room. He remembered sitting in the room with Viveca a few years ago when he was still a vampire. Her cat, Ebony—he thought that had been the cat's name—had just been killed. The room had not changed. He took a seat on the sofa and sat Liam on his lap.

Stan came in a moment later with tea. He passed a cup to Richard, then sat in the chair adjacent to the sofa. "Tell me, Richard. What's happened?"

"He was playing and then suddenly he said a name. Bain."

"Who is Bain?" Stan asked.

"Viveca told me she shared her secret—and mine—with you. Bain is Gannon Bain. He's Malcolm's ghoul. I received a note from Malcolm. He's given me an alternative. Return to him now. Become a vampire again and he'll spare my family. Refuse and he'll kill them."

"Have you told Viveca about the letter?" Stan asked.

"No. She's freaking out as it is. The three years are passing so quickly. Liam is already a year old. He'll be two before we know it, and then three, and then …" Richard trailed off.

Liam reached over and grasped Richard's forearm. "Dadda, no 'fraid."

"I'm trying not to be scared, Liam. I'm trying."

"Dadda eenx ire."

"Did Viveca tell you why I didn't become a vampire again?" Richard asked.

Stan shook his head slowly. "No."

"When Viveca tried to save my life, she transferred the phoenix to me. I'm becoming something else. A warrior, like her, but not like her. I'm afraid that I won't … that I will be too late." Richard took a sip of tea.

"Dadda eenx ire!" Liam grasped Richard's free hand and turned it palm up, then he drew a hand over the ring on Richard's palm. The ring darkened, then brightened. Flames sparked upward from the center of the ring. Liam clapped his hands together. "Dadda eenx ire!"

Stan stared in wonder. "What exactly is it, Richard?" Stan asked.

"It's the phoenix fire."

"Eenx ire!" Liam exclaimed.

"You can make fire with your hands," Stan uttered.

"Yes, but something called the rising has to be completed for me to truly control it. I don't know how to explain it."

"Oh, that's okay, honey," Stan said, still awestruck. "I've never seen anything like it. Not since Viveca showed us the—" Stan paused and thought a moment. "When Viveca took us into her dream walk, she showed us a tiger, not a phoenix. How could she have transferred a phoenix to you?"

"Viveca had two spirit warriors. One at the forefront, the tigress, and another that remained hidden. When she pulled me through the blazing, she sacrificed the tigress to save me, and then the phoenix revealed herself. She commanded the phoenix after that. Malcolm took me away, and when she came to find me, she fell into labor. She told me she stood halfway into the dream walk. That's where she saw Liam, and that's where he gave the tigress back to her. When she emerged, she was the tigress warrior again, but now able to wield both spirits. When we arrived at hospital, she tried to keep my heart beating. She had already commanded the phoenix to try and heal me. She slammed her hand down onto my chest, and that's when the phoenix transferred to me. That's why I didn't become a vampire. The phoenix destroyed it inside me, and now the phoenix is rising from its ashes again."

"Say Papa!" Liam squirmed on Richard's lap, and Richard placed him on the floor where he walked awkwardly around the small coffee table that separated the sofa from the rest of the room.

"Liam, where are you going, love?" Richard asked, watching his son carefully.

"Don't worry about him, hon. He'll be fine," Stan replied.

"Liam?" Richard said, then stood to make sure his son did not leave the room. The house wasn't overly big, but there were still plenty of things he might get into that he shouldn't. "Stay with Daddy."

"Say Papa!"

"Later, son. Come on. Come sit with Daddy." Richard held his hand out to his son, but Liam refused to take his father's hand. Richard was just about to lift Liam into his arms when he heard a vehicle pull up. "That must be Viveca."

"Say Papa! Say Papa! Say Papa!" Liam wailed, his voice getting higher with each utterance.

"Liam, calm down son!"

"And here we thought the rising meant your son," Stan said, his voice wavering between his usual light tone and something more sinister.

"Stan?" Richard asked, and put his hand on Liam's shoulder to walk him back, away from whoever it was standing in front of them.

Liam turned away from Richard and faced Stan. He opened his arms wide. "Say Papa!"

Behind them, Viveca entered the room. "Richard?"

A golden light formed around Liam. The great eagle formed around him and rose into the room. "Say Papa!" From above him, another light descended. This one was electric blue. At the center of Liam's chest, a bear formed, and the great eagle settled down to peer over Liam's head.

Stan stood and stepped closer to Richard. Viveca, who had been gaping at her son, moved her vision from Liam to Stan. In an instant, the tigress surged through her, and the dream walker warrior stepped fully into the room. She grabbed Richard by the shoulder and shoved him behind her, then she joined her son. "What have you done with him?" she demanded.

The tigress stood at her side, ready for her command. It snarled. On her other side, Liam projected the bear and the eagle. Together, they moved, effectively blocking Stan's path. Behind them, Richard stood confused. "What is happening? Why are you doing this, Viv?"

She didn't answer him. She kept her focus forward. "Where is he?" she asked.

"I don't know what you mean, Viv," Stan said, but it wasn't Stan who stood before her, she knew. What stood before her was a very clever impersonation. "Take it easy, Viv," it said.

"I would, except you're not Stan. Where is he?"

At last all pretense was dropped, and so was Stan. The shell of one of Viveca's best friends folded in on itself and fluttered to the floor. The great eagle took flight after the spirit now attempting escape. One talon seized it. Liam called to his father. "Dadda!"

Richard stepped forward. "Liam!"

Liam turned his attention briefly to Richard. "Eenx ire!"

Richard felt his hands grow hot. He opened his hands to see the rings glowing bright red. Before him, Liam drew fire from his palms. The phoenix in its post ash phase joined the eagle and the bear. The eagle still held the spirit, its sharp beak now tearing through it. The rebirth fire branded across them. Below, the eagle tossed one mangled and scorched half to the tigress and the other half to the bear. Jaws snapped and teeth rent the halves apart.

The bear gently faded. The great eagle returned. The rebirth fire extinguished. The tigress retreated. Richard's hands ceased to singe his palms. Viveca fell to her knees and wept. Behind her, Richard approached and knelt to fold his son and wife into his arms. "What was that, Viv?"

"Skinwalker," she sobbed.

He looked at the graying and decomposing pile before them. "You mean—?"

She sniffled. "Stan is dead."

"Is this all that's left of him?" Richard asked, horrified.

She said nothing, but she nodded.

"But wasn't Candida Winterhawk a skinwalker? Wasn't that woman's dog okay?"

She nodded again then took a deep breath. "Dr. Winterhawk is a skinwalker visionary. She's on the side of the light. She's a shapeshifter. I read about them when we got home that day. The skinwalker visionaries do not harm others. The dark spirit skinwalkers kill their hosts, devour them, and use their skins to impersonate them." Then she sobbed harder. Richard pulled her close, then he turned his attention to their son.

"Liam, what just happened? Where did the bear come from?"

"Papa," Liam replied.

"The bear was Papa?" Liam smiled and snuggled against Richard. He reached out a hand to Viveca, and she took his hand in hers. Richard looked between his wife and son. "He was trying to tell me. He kept saying 'Say Papa.' I don't understand how he could have wielded his eagle *and* his grandfather's bear *and* the phoenix. How did he do that?"

"I don't know," Viveca replied. "We do need to find out, though. There is a meeting of the visionaries coming up. I've been invited, but I want to take you and Liam with me. We have to get answers, Richard."

Liam leaned against Richard. "He's exhausted," Richard observed.

"I guess so. He's waged battle. He's seemingly borrowed energy from you and Papa. It's no wonder he's tired."

Richard took a breath. "I have to tell you something, love."

"I'm afraid to ask."

"I received a letter from Malcolm."

"What did it say?

"He gave me a choice to join him now. If I surrender before the three years are over, he will let you and Liam live. If not—"

"Let me guess. He'll kill us. He'll take you away from me. He'll take us away from you."

"Basically."

"Malcolm needs some new lines," Viveca said.

Richard shared a small smile with his wife. "This is serious."

"I know. I'm sorry."

"And what about Liam mentioning Gannon Bain?"

"I don't know. The meeting is in a few weeks. We have to stay on guard until then."

Behind them, Mike entered the room with a grocery bag in his hands. He looked from the threesome hugging at the center of his living room and then to the heap of hollowed out skin before them. Even from the doorway, he could see the heart tattoo Stan had gotten placed on his wrist the day they were married. He dropped the bag. "Viveca?" he asked as he stepped farther into the room, tears welling in his eyes. "What's happened?"

∞

February 13, 2018, New Orleans, Louisiana, 5:17 p.m.

"This building looks as though it should be condemned," Richard said as he and Viveca approached the entrance.

Viveca carried Liam, and Richard held the door as she passed through the entrance. He followed behind her, and a kind-looking woman with wire-rimmed glasses greeted them. She was sitting at a table not far off the entrance. "Good evening," she said. "Can I get your names, please?"

"Good evening," Viveca replied. "I'm Viveca Ambrose, and this is my husband, Richard, and our son, Liam."

"I see your name here, Mrs. Ambrose, but I do not see your husband or son. Let me check with someone, and I'll be right back." The woman rose from her seat and made her way down the hallway that stretched behind where she'd been sitting. A moment later, she returned with Dr. Maxine Ryan.

"Hi, Viveca. Thank you for coming," Dr. Ryan said. "I've spoken with some of the other members, and your husband and son have been approved to join us." She turned to the woman behind the desk. "Rosalie, will you please pencil in Richard and Liam Ambrose?"

"Of course," Rosalie said and made the notations.

Viveca and Richard followed Dr. Ryan to a modest circular room near the end of the hallway. A fire burned brightly at the center of the room. Around it, people sat on stone benches, some in full Native American regalia. Others dressed more casually. Above them, inset into the ceiling, a large circular aperture drew the smoke and allowed the moon and stars to peek in. The floor was covered in colorful stone tile. To the north, the stone tile gleamed onyx black. Depictions of meadows and mountains swept across the stone. To the east, the tile was an ivory white. Depictions of the sun, the moon, and the stars graced the stone. Swirls of light blue almost seemed to blow across the two-dimensional sky. To the west, the tile was a golden yellow. Depictions of rivers flowed to the sea where tidal breaks kissed the shore. To the south, the tile was red. Depictions of flames burned brightly. The visionaries stood, faced north, then turned to face south, then east, then west. At each turn, they called upon the elements to strengthen them and for their elders to bless them with wisdom. At last, they called upon a fifth element: the spirit. The smoke, Viveca noticed, seemed charged, almost as though it had a life of its own, as if it were a living part of their collective wisdom.

Viveca sat with Liam on her lap and Richard at her side on the stone bench where Dr. Ryan led them. She looked around the small room once everyone had taken their seats. She recognized Samantha Vaughn, Candida Winterhawk, Delphi Williams, and Kent Battiste among those who sat nearest the fire. Turning her gaze before and behind her, other people from the community presented themselves. She recognized several of the ladies who had so often joined Nana for lunch. The visionaries hadn't just suddenly come upon her and Richard. They had always been here, quietly waiting for this very moment.

An elderly woman dressed in full Native American regalia rose and introduced herself as Chief Moonshadow. She spoke low and steady. "We all feel it. A great evil is once again at work. This evil has been thwarted twice now by a great warrior. She sits among us now with her family. She has been invited here so that she may help us understand the vampire and its motives."

All eyes turned to Viveca, Richard, and Liam. Candida Winterhawk stood. "Viveca Ambrose is a powerful dream walker warrior, descendant from Graham Eaglefeather and Enola Hampshire. Our brother and sister have joined our star elders, but their wisdom remains among us."

Samantha stood. "My visionary sister, Trudy, was murdered by the vampire's ghoul."

Viveca stood. "No, there's no evidence of that."

"Excuse me? I could smell the ghoul inside the house," Samantha argued.

"Yes, Gannon Bain did accompany the murderer, but it was the coroner, Charles Rainier, who murdered your sister, Samantha," Viveca confirmed and retook her seat.

Chief Moonshadow spoke again. "Do tell us about this vampire, Viveca."

Viveca moved to stand and Richard placed a hand on her shoulder. He stood instead. "My name is Richard Ambrose. You may or may not already know, but I was once a vampire. Viveca, my wife, saved my life. The vampire you want to know about is my brother, Malcolm. At least, he was my brother long ago.

"I was born on August 22, 1791. I was six years old when Malcolm became my brother. His parents lived on a farm not far from my parents' own farmland. Plague had taken his parents, and my father and mother took him in and raised him as my brother. We were the same age, though Malcolm was older by a few months. On my twenty-eighth birthday, Malcolm led me to an estate not far from London where I met a woman who took my life and made me a vampire. Malcolm was already a vampire by then. The woman, Alyssa, had had enough of life and gave him the choice to either wander the world a lone vampire or select someone to walk the world with him. He chose me, his best friend, his brother. I trusted him, but when I woke a vampire, I could not abide by what I'd become. I held on to that cage and never let go of it.

"Nearly two centuries later, I met Viveca. I was told of the dream walker legend and how a dream walker would be the person who could undo the curse set upon me. But when I met her, even as a baby, I knew I would never ask her to perform the blazing. The importance of her life—*her* life—I could see, was more precious than my own, and I vowed to protect her. Her parents caught me with her in my arms. I waited for them to destroy me, but they could see that I meant her no harm, and for the first time in a long time, I felt what it was like to be trusted again.

"The vampire you seek is my brother, Malcolm. His motivation is to bring me back across and make me a vampire once again. He is angry, and he feels betrayed. He will not stop, and he will do anything necessary. He does not care about human life, and he will kill anyone who gets in his way.

"When Viveca pulled me through the blazing, she destroyed him, but two years ago, he was brought back in the body of a young man who had tragically died in an accident. The young man's father injected his dead son with Malcolm's blood. Vampires are made from living souls that the possessing vampire spirit cages and controls. Without that soul, the vampire is free to do as it pleases. Its power is seductive, and I can understand why Malcolm gave in to it so readily, but it is not the life for me.

"Something is happening to me that I am trying to accept and understand," Richard paused, taking a deep breath before continuing. "You now know about Malcolm and what his motivation is, but that's not why I'm here. I am asking for your help for the sake of my wife and son. Your absence all this time has honed Viveca into a powerful warrior, but please do not leave it up to her again. Malcolm is creating ghouls, and last month, we defeated a skinwalker."

At the mention of a skinwalker, the visionaries began chatting nervously among themselves. Chief Moonshadow rose and spoke above them. "Sisters and brothers, we know evil has no limits because it operates outside nature and is not bound by its rules. The presence of a skinwalker is indication that the vampire is escalating its efforts. Candida Winterhawk understands the skinwalker. She will tell us."

Chief Moonshadow sat, and Dr. Winterhawk stood. "There are two types of skinwalker. I am a defender of the light. A visionary and a shapeshifter. I take on many skins, but I do not shape into other people. My power lives in nature, and the animals lend their strength to me. The skinwalker Richard and Viveca encountered works outside of nature, taking human lives and using their skins in disguise. It is evil absolute."

Stephanie stood. "How? How did Viveca and Richard defeat this skinwalker? How could they defeat such evil?"

"It was our son," Viveca said quietly. "It was Liam who defeated it. We're not sure how he did it, but he called upon his great-grandfather's spirit, his own, and the phoenix, which is now rising within Richard. He commanded my tigress and his grandfather's bear to work in unison, but outside himself. The rest, he took and was wielded within himself."

"Your son created a chimera?" Chief Moonshadow asked.

"I don't know what that is," Viveca admitted.

"Your son commands the great golden eagle."

"That is correct," Viveca said, and again the visionaries erupted into conversation.

Chief Moonshadow held up her hand and spoke. "The great eagle is the spirit of *Wakan Tanka*. All spirits can be wielded through him. Your son will become a great leader for our people, Viveca, and a powerful dream walker warrior."

"I know. My grandfather told me this before Liam was born."

"Graham Eaglefeather was a very wise man. Shaman, dream walker warrior, and commander of the mighty bear. He taught you well, child."

"So what is a chimera?" Viveca asked.

"It is a combining of spirits wielded as one. The warrior who can command a chimera is most powerful. How old is Liam?"

"He's fourteen months old," Viveca answered.

"His rising hasn't completed and yet he was able to command a chimera. How was he after?"

"He was exhausted. He wouldn't eat that night. He slept through."

"Yes, the rising is exhausting, especially in one so young."

"I don't remember going through that," Viveca said.

"Because you were born of the phoenix and the tigress. Both are spirits of stealth. Didn't you always feel protected as you grew up?"

"Yes, but I thought that was because of Richard watching over me."

"I'm sure it was in some way, but it was mainly because of who and what you are, Viveca. You felt protected because you were protected."

"Why, then, when I was being attacked, didn't the phoenix and tigress present themselves?"

"Where was Richard, Viveca? Was Richard not there to thwart those who sought to harm you?"

"I suppose he was," she reflected.

"The spirits present themselves when they are needed. I feel confident that had Richard not been there, those who tried to harm you would have met a vastly different fate," Chief Moonshadow said, then turned her attention to Richard. "Richard, Viveca has said you possess the phoenix. Do you know how it happened?" Chief Moonshadow asked.

"I was told Viveca transferred the phoenix to me when she tried to save my life. The phoenix defeated the vampire within me and is now rising again from its ashes."

"So the vampire did bite you?"

"Yes, but I don't remember much after that before I woke up in the hospital."

"Perhaps that's why we felt the surge and then the relief," Chief Moonshadow said quietly.

"What do you mean?" Viveca asked.

"About a year ago, we all felt a surge of evil, as if a new evil were being born. Then it abated as though it had been wiped away."

"I see," Viveca said.

"I can show you," Richard said. "Liam helps me bring it forth." Richard held his palm out to Liam, and Liam ran a finger over the ring. The ring brightened, and the rebirth fire leapt from the center of the ring to flicker in Richard's hand. "I wielded it by accident a few months ago when I placed my hands on an injured man."

"You healed him?" Chief Moonshadow asked.

"Yes."

"How did that make you feel?"

"Scared."

"And now that you know it is the phoenix that works within you?"

"Still scared, but for different reasons."

"And what are those reasons?"

"That the rising won't complete before Malcolm comes for me. That I won't be able to protect my family. That I'll lose them."

"Come here, Richard, and bring your son," Chief Moonshadow requested.

Richard rose and approached the elderly woman with Liam in his arms. Chief Moonshadow placed a hand at the center of Richard's chest. With her other hand, she turned Richard's right hand over to reveal the still blazing ring on Richard's palm. "You are a good man with a good heart. The phoenix is rising, Richard. She is rising because she has found a home within you. The expression on your face tells me you've heard this before at least in some variation. Don't be afraid. The phoenix is a warrior of stealth. She will present herself when least expected."

"What did you want of my son?"

"Your son has a message for us," Chief Moonshadow said.

"Really?"

"Yes. Liam, please tell us," the elderly woman said. "It's okay, Richard. You can put him down."

Richard put his son down in front of Chief Moonshadow. The elderly woman reached forward and took Liam's hand. "Bring her forth, Liam."

Emanating from Liam, Enola Hampshire's voice rose into the smoke. "My dear friends, I have made my journey, and I wait for you patiently at the great council fire of our people. The enemy is powerful, but a new warrior is being born among us. The phoenix rises from the ashes of her great deeds so that she may do greater ones. The prophecy has come to pass. The great golden eagle is among us again. Please watch over my granddaughter and her family. My great-grandson will be the next shaman. Guard him well."

Enola Hampshire's voice faded into the smoke, and Liam stood smiling and watching it rise out of the ceiling. Richard watched as well. He glanced down at Viveca to see her crying.

Chief Moonshadow touched Richard's arm, and he sat blinking at her. "Go now. Rejoin your family."

Richard retook his seat next to Viveca, and Liam reached over for Viveca to pull him onto her lap. Liam cuddled close to his mother and closed his eyes. Richard and his family drew the visionaries' stares. He felt placed under a microscope.

"I have a question," Viveca said suddenly.

"Ask it," Chief Moonshadow said.

"When Trudy Vaughn died, I was the first detective on the scene. I didn't recognize her. She looked much, much older than she had when I'd known her. In the hospital, Dr. Battiste made mention that the visionaries age slower. Her son identified her, and still I can't explain why I saw her in such a state."

"You must remember that you see things and people for what they truly are, Viveca," Stephanie explained. "You saw my sister as her true age. In death, she could no longer hide it from you. The visionaries wield their magic to hide within society. Evil can rarely see us, but it senses us. Trudy was ninety-seven years old. I am eighty-nine. Your Nana was over one hundred years old. Visionaries are what modern-day folk refer to as witches. We cast, we find, and we can fight. Our sister, Maxine, is working on a weapon to defeat the ghouls."

Viveca nodded. "I know," she said and turned her attention to Dr. Ryan. "Can you give us an update on its effectiveness?"

"The body that was masticated but not devoured was that of a cancer survivor. Research has revealed that the man's cancer was a rare form of leukemia. He had undergone an experimental chemotherapy, and the phagocytes within his body had to adapt—mutate, if you will—to rid his body of the dead cancer cells. This mutation may be the reason the ghouls didn't eat it. Ingesting phagocytes that are different in nature to those within their maker's blood might cause a breakdown in physiological functionality. It could kill them. As for the vampire that drank the blood containing those mutated phagocytes, I might have a theory."

"Why the ghoul and not the vampire?" Viveca asked.

"The ghoul ultimately is human. The ghoul doesn't take hold until the human kills. That act of evil secures the ghoul within the human host, and then it can transform. The human would be lost. It's kind of like what Richard was talking about earlier. The differences between himself and his brother, Malcolm. Richard didn't give in, but Malcolm did. That's why the blazing worked for Richard. Once the soul is welded to the possessing spirit, it cannot be undone. This is why you were able to separate Gerard Stephens from the ghoul, but not Jack Price."

"How do you know all this?" Viveca demanded.

"We have been watching, Viveca."

"Okay, so what is your theory regarding the mutated phagocytes in vampires?" Viveca asked.

"It might not have any effect at all."

"Or maybe some effect?" Viveca led.

"Maybe. It would probably be a transformative effect, especially if the vampire is one who surrendered to the cage."

"Transformative? What do you mean?"

"The mutated phagocytes could alter the vampire's DNA."

"What would it become?"

"Now that's a good question, isn't it? I don't know."

"And if that mutated vampire creates ghouls?" Viveca drew in a deep breath.

"If it does have a mutating effect on the vampire, it may create something we've never seen before."

∞

April 28, 2018, New Orleans, Louisiana, 11:21 a.m.

"We're going to be late, babe," Viveca said. She was standing just outside the downstairs bathroom door. She knocked. "Richard?"

"I can't go," he said breathlessly behind the door.

"Why not? What's going on? Are you okay?"

"I don't know." Now, he sounded like he was struggling for composure.

"Open the door, honey," she said softly.

"It's not locked," he replied but made no effort to open the door.

"I'm coming in," she said and turned the knob; the door swung open.

Richard was naked and sitting on the shower floor. The showerhead sprayed stinging needles at the back of his neck. On the bathroom vanity, a pair of his boxer shorts awaited. He held his hands out in front of himself and stared at the bright red rings on his palms. He looked over at her when she entered the room. "It's hurting me," he said. "My skin feels like it's going to cook away."

"Dr. Winterhawk said it would be difficult for you," she said and reached out to take his hand.

He jerked his hands out of her reach and scooted closer to the shower wall. "I might hurt you, love."

She drew her hand back and ran her fingers through his hair instead. "When did it start hurting?"

"Last night, after we made love."

"Why didn't you wake me? Have you been here all morning?"

"Most of the morning."

"Stephanie is here. She's sitting in the living room with Liam. Why don't you go on upstairs and change and then come down to talk to us? Maybe she can help."

He nodded and stood and switched off the shower. She handed him a bath towel, and he accepted it gingerly, suddenly afraid the terry cloth might burst into flame. When it remained unsinged, he dried his hair then wrapped the towel around his middle. "I'm sorry, love," he said.

She stood on her tip toes and kissed him. "I'm not afraid, Richard. The phoenix isn't going to hurt me. *You* aren't going to hurt me. It's going to be okay. I promise. Take the back way up, and we'll see you in the living room."

Viveca joined Stephanie and Liam in the living room and plopped into a plush armchair. "Everything okay?" Stephanie asked.

"Richard is having a hard time with the rising. The phoenix is starting to burn his skin. It's hurting him."

"I see. Dr. Winterhawk may have something that may help. Would you like me to ask?"

"Yes, please. We'd really appreciate it."

"I'll make the call today."

"Thank you," Viveca said and turned her attention to Liam, who was sitting on his playmat and drawing on a piece of paper with a large red crayon. A collection of other crayons laid in odd angles around him. "He's getting so big so fast."

"He's a doll, Viv."

From his playmat, Liam looked up and held up the crayon. "See Mommy!"

"I see, sweetheart. What are you drawing?"

"Daddy."

"Daddy? Let's see," she said, and Liam rose from the mat to carry his drawing to her.

He held it up to her. "See, Mommy?"

Viveca took the piece of paper and turned it over to view what Liam had drawn. One figure was dressed all in black, its mouth yawned wide, and jagged teeth protruded from within. The figure's eyes were large *X*s. Above that figure was another, again dressed all in black, but with tendrils of fire surrounding it. Liam pointed to the figure with the fiery tendrils around it. "Daddy!"

Viveca placed a finger on the figure. "Daddy," she said, then moved her finger to the other figure. "Who's this, Liam?"

"Mayco!"

"Mayco?" she questioned, but she knew very well who he meant. How did Liam know about Malcolm?

Stephanie rose from the sofa. "I better get going, Viv. Are you all still coming to the picnic?"

"I think so, but we may be a little late. Would you mind taking the potato salad I made just in case?"

"I'd be happy to. If I don't see you in an hour or so, I'll make your excuses, and I'll make sure you get your bowl back."

"Thank you so much, Stephanie," Viveca said, then stood to embrace her. "I just wanted to say how happy I am that you decided to stay and run the bakery. Trudy would be so proud of you, and we all would have missed you so much."

Stephanie smiled. "I'm glad I stayed too." She gave Viveca a squeeze, then broke the hug and started for the kitchen. "Is the potato salad in the fridge?"

"Oh, sorry. Let me get it for you," Viveca said, and the two women stepped into the kitchen.

From the kitchen, Viveca heard Richard address their son. "Hey, little man. What do you have there?"

Liam's excited voice echoed to her. "Daddy!"

Richard turned his head and addressed Viveca. "Hey, when did he start saying 'Daddy?'"

Viveca smiled and answered, "Actually, I think today, when I asked him what he had drawn." She slipped the potato salad bowl into a large bag with handles for easier carrying and handed it to Stephanie, and the two women returned to the living room.

"Hi, Stephanie," Richard greeted.

"Hi, Richard," Stephanie said with a smile. "I'm going to go on ahead. I hope to see y'all there."

"Thanks again," Viveca said and saw her to the door. "We should be along soon."

∞

"Where did you learn this name, Liam?" Richard asked as he peered down into Liam's drawing.

"Papa!"

"You saw Papa again?"

"Deem wok."

Viveca translated. "Dream walk. He's still having trouble with *R*s and *L*s."

"Oh, I understood what he said. Why would Papa teach him about Malcolm?"

"To prepare him? I don't know."

"Can we ask him?"

"Okay," Viveca said. She grasped Richard's hand and pulled Liam into her embrace. A moment later, they were standing in her field. She passed Liam to Richard and let go of Richard's hand. "Papa!" she exclaimed and released the tigress. It surged around her, bringing forth the warrior and then burst from her with tremendous speed. Across the field, toward the trees, the tigress raced.

When the tigress returned, Mr. Eaglefeather came with it. "Child, you are mastering the Elder Call very well. I'm very proud of you."

"Thank you, Papa. We need to ask you about something. How often does Liam call you into his dream walks?"

"Most every night, child."

"You're teaching him about the vampires?"

Upon hearing the word, Liam looped his fingers inside his mouth, pulled wide and bared his teeth, then he growled, "Rawr! Rawr!" Then he giggled and laid his head on Richard's shoulder.

"He must be taught, child. You cannot protect him from this knowledge."

"He's so young, though."

"Liam's rising will happen soon, just as yours did."

"Mine? I don't remember."

"You were very young. Not more than four. Your mother thought to protect you from the knowledge, but it's not something which can be hidden from those who can truly see the world. Like you. Like Liam."

"He commanded a chimera a few months ago, Papa. His rising is coming quickly."

"His spirit is strong, child. Our collective memories live in our cells. Liam acted on instinct. He did not so much command as much as he drew upon this instinctive knowledge. Once the rising is complete, he will learn to control it, wield it, and respect it. His destiny is greater than any of us can imagine."

"He drew a picture of Richard as the phoenix and Malcolm defeated. Is he seeing the future?"

"Liam draws what he wants to happen, not necessarily what is *going* to happen."

Viveca nodded. "I understand."

Mr. Eaglefeather focused his attention on Richard. "Are you working to accept the phoenix?"

"I'm trying, Papa. She's hurting me. My palms are burning."

"Ah. Do not fight the burning, my son. Relax against it, and it will not be so terrible. It's like removing a splinter. When you fight against pulling it from your flesh, it hurts worse. Relax, and your skin will make way for its removal."

Richard nodded. "I think I understand, Papa."

"I know you do, my son." Mr. Eaglefeather turned and made his way back toward the trees. The distance grew between them, and Viveca and her family returned from the dream walk.

∞

"Dr. Winterhawk said to tell Richard not to fight it. The pain will subside," Stephanie said when they arrived at the picnic. "So glad you could make it."

"We are too," Viveca said, and they walked toward the others who were gathered closer to the picnic tables.

"This is really nice," Richard said, balancing Liam on his hip and picking up a plate. "What do you want to eat, son?" Liam pointed mainly to the pies and cakes, which sat among the proteins and vegetables spread across the various tables. "Okay, lunch first, dessert last." Richard chuckled and looked over at Viveca. "Your son takes after his father," Richard teased.

Viveca nodded and smiled. "I can see that. I remember you telling me how your mother used to chase you out of the kitchen for putting your fingers in her pies to draw out the filling. Now, me? I would have eaten all the crust."

Richard laughed. "You're a crust thief? Ha! That was my brother, Christopher. My mother used to say that between the two of us, our father was lucky to have a slice. When Malcolm came, my mother had to get creative in hiding the desserts. We always found them, though." Richard trailed off, the beautiful memory of his brothers tugged at his heart and warred within him for a moment.

Viveca placed a hand on his arm. "It's okay to remember him fondly, Richard. He was truly your brother once." She gave him a kind smile, and they made their way around the tables to complete their plates. Then they made their way to the grass not far from the tables, spread a square of fabric and sat to enjoy their meal.

∞

June 5, 2018, New Orleans, Louisiana, 8:37 p.m.

The day had been as hot as the seventh circle of hell, and the setting sun did nothing to relieve the sweltering heat left over from the day. Viveca sat in the front passenger side of the sedan. Frank sat behind the wheel. Watson sat with Miller in another sedan not far away. "Can we at least turn on the air conditioner?" Viveca asked. Her window was down, but it still felt like an oven inside the car.

"Not yet. We're supposed to be incognito and lights out. Don't want to tip this asshole off."

Viveca rolled her eyes. "Anyone who comes out of the club is going to freaking smell us, Frank. We're rank in here, dude. I think we've been sweating since eight this morning. If we were staking out a landfill, we'd fit right in."

"It's uncomfortable, I know. Relief in twenty minutes."

"My clothes are sticking to the seat, Frank. It's going to sound like Velcro when I get out of this car."

Frank brought a hand to his mouth to prevent the laughter from escaping his lips. "You're killing me, Viv."

She was about to remark when the door to the club opened and a tall weasel of a man stepped out into the blistering night. The light above the door threw his frame into a spotlight. "That's Fontaine," she said under her breath. "Where's Bourque? I want to get that piece of shit."

"Patience," Frank muttered softly. David Fontaine was a low-level dirtbag with handy computer skills and even handier fake ID skills. Shane Bourque was a man in need of those skills. He was wanted in connection with a series of attacks, but his money had, so far, bought his freedom from prosecution. His young female victims had described him as a torturer, each sustaining physical trauma ranging from scratches and bruises to deep gashes and surgical incisions. Each girl had been abandoned at the entrance to one of several hospitals spanning the area. Usually, Special Victims handled such cases, but the latest victim, a fifteen-year-old girl, had died after being stabbed and burned. DNA recovered from under her fingernails had matched Bourque's extensive criminal record, and Special Victims extended an invitation to Homicide.

Viveca and Frank were parked along the street, filed in among other nondescript vehicles. From behind them, a car rolled slowly up toward the club. Viveca inched toward Frank so she could subtly turn her head and keep watch. The door closest to them opened. Viveca quickly turned her head away and locked eyes with Frank. He kept one eye on Viveca and the other eye on the door. Behind her, she heard a man exclaim, "Damned cops!" She could hear footsteps approaching. She heard the sound of metal against leather and the slide of the gun rollback then snap into place, sending a bullet into the chamber.

Viveca took a breath and grabbed Frank, threw her arms around him, and planted her lips firmly against his. Frank did not hesitate to follow her lead. He turned his head, drew one arm around her, and planted his other hand in her hair. The kiss escalated. She leaned into him, her eyes firmly shut. He pulled her closer, all but moving her onto his lap. His hand moved under her shirt and touched the bare skin of her back. Their mouths opened to take in breath. Frank's tongue touched hers briefly, then withdrew, then sought her mouth again.

A sound of metal tapping against the frame of the car drew them apart, and they stared blankly at the man who stood at the passenger window. He gave them a wide, toothy grin and showed them his gun. "You two, get a freaking room."

Viveca smoothed her hands through her hair and did her best to straighten her shirt. She looked up at him with what she hoped were innocent doe eyes. "Sorry, Officer. We just got carried away. We'll be leaving now."

"Yeah, you do that."

Frank started the car and switched the air conditioner on then pulled out of the space. "I'll round the block. That was Bourque's bodyguard. He's here."

"Okay," Viveca said and finished straightening her clothing. When Frank rounded the block, Bourque's vehicle still blocked the street. He pulled the sedan in behind another parked vehicle and shut off the engine. Viveca was immediately sorry to lose the air conditioning.

"Sorry about your shirt," Frank said carefully.

"That's okay. He bought it."

Frank took a breath and blew it out slowly. "Yeah."

"You okay?" Viveca asked.

"Yeah, I'm fine. Why?"

"I don't know. You sounded a little *off* for a minute."

"I just want to get this bastard," Frank said.

"I know. Me too." Viveca's cell vibrated, and she answered. "Ambrose." She listened to Miller as he let her know where to wait. When she hung up, she turned to Frank. "Let's go, partner. We're taking the rear exit."

∞

The deal had gone down in the men's room, in the last stall. David Fontaine sat on the john with an open briefcase on his lap. New passport, new ID, new birth certificate, new Social Security Number, new credit cards. Bourque collected the items and reviewed them to his satisfaction. He'd slipped the items into his jeans pocket, then pulled the gun from his jeans at the small of his back and shot Fontaine once between the eyes. The silencer snuffed the muzzle flare and the gun's report. Fontaine had died too quickly; the open briefcase still sat perfectly on his lap. Bourque closed the briefcase and hefted it in his free hand. Easy-peasy. Shane Bourque had a new life to start living. He couldn't afford to leave witnesses.

He closed the stall door behind him. It stood slightly ajar, but anyone entering the restroom would think it was closed and occupied. He stopped at the sinks to make sure he hadn't gotten any blood on his clothes, then quietly stepped out of the restroom and removed the *Closed for Cleaning* sign he'd placed on the door when they'd first entered. His bodyguard joined him and took the briefcase. They headed out of the club through the rear exit.

"Stop! Police!" Frank exclaimed when Bourque and his bodyguard stepped outside.

"I knew you was cops," the bodyguard growled.

"You should trust your instincts, jackass," Viveca said and turned the man around, relieved him of the gun she'd seen him brandish earlier, and placed handcuffs on him. Then she sat him down against the alley wall.

"Lady! Watch the suit, will ya?"

"I'm Detective Ambrose, not Lady, and you're under arrest for accessory to murder. You have the right to remain silent. Anything you say can and will be held against you—"

"Yeah, yeah," the bodyguard said unpleasantly.

Viveca turned to Bourque. Frank had turned him around and was patting him down and reading him his rights. Frank confiscated the silencer-enabled handgun and the counterfeit paperwork. "Shane Bourque, you are under arrest for the murder of Tilly McArthur."

"Was that her name?" Bourque asked dismissively. "Never got that far. She was a sweet kitten, though."

Viveca could see anger flare across Frank's face, but he held his tongue and retrieved his handcuffs. He slipped one cuff onto Bourque's left wrist and made to grasp Bourque's right wrist. A flurry of movement. Bourque's right hand was free. Bourque swung his hand back and caught Frank in the side. Frank fell to the left, and Bourque made a run for it.

"Frank!" Viveca was at his side. "Are you okay?"

Frank moved his hand from his side. His palm was smeared with bright red blood. "I think I've been stabbed, Viv."

She dialed Miller and had him call for an ambulance. She looked down at Frank. "They're coming, Frank. You just hang on."

He was losing consciousness, he could feel that, and he welcomed it. He would soon be free of the pain. One thought surfaced, and he used the last of his strength to convey it to her. "Go get that bastard."

Sirens rose in the distance. She nodded. "You hang in there, partner." Then she stood and ran after Bourque. Inwardly, she called the tigress, and it began to build momentum inside her. In the distance, she heard a car start and tires peel friction against pavement. She sped on foot around the building to see Bourque's car speed away. Too much in the open, too many witnesses. Miller's car was close. Watson emerged from the vehicle as she approached.

"Viv? How's Fr—?" Watson began.

"Keys in it?" she asked between breaths and not slowing her pace.

"Yeah, but—"

She climbed in, started the car, and raced behind Bourque, leaving Watson on the curb. Slamming her foot onto the accelerator, the sedan picked up speed exponentially. Ahead of her, Bourque's car weaved between lanes, narrowly missing other vehicles.

Viveca purposefully switched off the siren. If Bourque knew she was following, he might begin to create obstacles, and that would place the public in danger. He was about a block ahead. At the next traffic light, he took a wild left turn. The rear tires fishtailed a moment, and then the car righted itself and sped forward. He was heading toward the riverfront. If he made the ferry, she would lose him. She made the next U-turn and doubled back toward Canal. He was heading through the French Quarter. She would go around. She just might beat him there.

∞

Shane Bourque pulled the car into a dark alley. He waited, and he listened for sirens. He had thought at first a car was giving chase, but it had made a U-turn as he had made a left. *Stupid cops.*

He was back to square one, but there were others who dealt in counterfeit paperwork. They were arresting him for the murder of that girl? If they only knew. He chuckled inwardly and opened his car door. He'd take the ferry on foot. His bodyguard had been arrested, but he'd find another. He locked the car door and tossed the keys in a nearby dumpster as he passed it.

"Going somewhere?" A voice rose behind him, low and almost feral. The hair on the back of his neck stood on end. He turned to see the source of the voice. A beautiful woman with long ivory-white hair, porcelain skin, and golden eyes leaned against the side of the dumpster.

"Who are you?" he demanded. "What are you?"

"I'm here for you, Shane."

He turned to run, but the warrior was much faster. Like a cat playing with a mouse, she outpaced him and brought her leg up to drive a foot into his abdomen. The breath was knocked out of him, and he fell backward. He scrambled to his feet but did not try to run away again. "What do you want?"

"I can see you're nothing more than human. I was hoping you'd make things more interesting for me. You brutally tortured those teenage girls, but that wasn't good enough for you, was it? No, no. You had to kill one of them too, right? Come on, Shane, impress me with what you've done."

"You want a confession? Who the hell are you?" he asked, backing away from her and moving toward his car parked near the alley's dead end.

The warrior smiled and stepped forward. A few quick paces brought her directly in front of him. "I want to hear all about it, Shane," she whispered into his face.

"You want to hear how I spent time with those girls? They were just nameless, faceless kittens. Fun way to pass the time. What do you care?"

"Why did you kill this last one?"

"Felt like it."

"Wasn't your first time killing, though, was it?"

"What do you know about it?"

"You took her life too easily, Shane. Surely you'd done it before."

Shane dropped the facade and shrugged. "It's not hard to kill, you know. But getting the job done and how is where being creative comes in handy. Getting close enough to see the light leave their eyes. Now that's fun. Here one moment, gone the next. Bullet to the brain does that nicely. But if you really want to see it in slow motion, I recommend you render them helpless and spent first. To declare control over another, to hold their very life at your fingertips, is the ultimate pleasure. That moment when I've got a young girl pinned down to my specimen board and I make that cut or I put my hands around her neck is heaven. The look of pain on a young girl's face is exquisite. It's something she's never felt before. Pain sparks across her face, tears spring up in her eyes, her pupils spread wide to take me in. Then my hands are on her throat, or my knife is drawing red lines. Those fleeting moments when she thinks I might let her go and then the realization that she isn't going anywhere, at least not until I'm done with her. And this last one was wonderful. The knife went in, and she gave me that look of surprise like it couldn't be happening to her. Then she sees the blade painted with her blood, and she starts to struggle, but I know I've got to draw the full expression from her, so I pick up the torch. Her eyes bulged and then that incredible expression of fear just before her eyes went flat and unseeing." Bourque took a deep, sensual breath. "Is that what you wanted to hear, honey?"

The warrior's smile unnerved him, and he took another step backward instinctively. She said nothing but matched his movements step for step. She walked him all the way to end of the alley where he could go no further. The warrior matched steps with him. He pressed himself against the alley wall and shut his eyes. "Who are you?" he asked again.

"I'm karma, Shane," she said with more satisfaction than she thought she'd have.

∞

"How did you catch him?" Miller asked when Viveca drove the sedan back to the club with Shane Bourque in the back. He'd laid on his side and drew his knees to his chest.

"I went around the French Quarter and beat him to the ferry. How's Frank? Is he going to be okay?"

"Yeah, the knife missed all major organs. Frank bled pretty good, but the paramedics said he should be okay. They took him to New Orleans General. This shithead isn't any better at stabbing than he is at being a criminal. The DNA taken from Tilly McArthur's fingernails now links Bourque to more murders in Mississippi and Texas. She wasn't his first rodeo, poor kid."

"Thanks, Miller," Viveca said.

"So what did you do to him?" Miller asked.

"What do you mean?"

"He's lying in a fetal position, Viv. He looks like if his hands weren't handcuffed behind his back, he'd be sucking his thumb."

"Well, let's just say he met a side of me he didn't like too much. I caught him by surprise and caught him off-guard. I didn't hesitate to kick his ass into submission before I cuffed him. I identified myself, and I read him his rights the whole time. What's that line from *The Karate Kid*? 'Strike first, strike hard, no mercy'? Well, that's what I did." And that was the truth. She left out the part where she had taken him into the dream walk and unleashed the tigress on him. *Paws. No claws. Them's the rules.* She chuckled to herself.

"That's going to take some paperwork, Viv."

"What? He doesn't have a mark on him, Miller." And that was true too. "I made a clean arrest. Just ask that jackass."

"Okay, but make yourself available when I call."

"Okay. *If* you call, I will. Now, if you'll excuse me, I want to go see my partner and then I want to go home and see my husband and son. Have a great night, Miller," she said as she walked down the street to where Frank had parked the sedan.

She climbed behind the wheel, started it, and made her way to the hospital. When she pulled into a parking space, she switched off the engine and gripped the steering wheel tightly. She leaned forward and pressed her forehead against it. She took in a deep breath. Then she let her emotions wash over her. Tears flowed and stained her jeans. *All those girls.* She cried for them, for the ordeal some of them still lived with and for the parents whose children never made it home. She sobbed for what she'd done. She'd worked Bourque over with a tenaciousness that wore him down to the bottom of his putrefied human soul. He would be a shell of the man he'd once been. And she remembered the words she'd spoken just before she'd carried them both from the dream walk: *"You're right. Holding your life in my fingertips* does *feel good. This really is the ultimate pleasure. Thanks."*

∞

Frank was lying on his left side on the hospital bed. A pillow had been wedged behind him to prevent him from rolling onto his stitches. "Hey, partner," Viv said as cheerfully as she could. "I'm told you're going to live."

Frank gave her a smile. "Yeah, I heard that too. Weird, huh?"

Viveca laughed lightly. "How do you feel?"

"Like I've been stabbed."

"Okay, smart guy. Really, how are you feeling?"

"I feel okay. Painkillers are wearing off. I'm seesawing between hitting the nurse call button and taking it like a man."

"You did good. You know that?"

"I screwed up, Viv. I shouldn't have let him keep that hand up like that."

"We still got him."

"We got him, or *we* got him?"

"*We* got him."

"Make him pay?"

"Yep, big time. I'll be surprised if he ever gets out of jail, but if he ever does, I'll be surprised if he doesn't become a wandering spokesman for the word of the Lord."

Frank laughed, then winced. "Don't make me laugh."

"Sorry."

Frank pressed the nurse call button. Viveca smiled at him. "What can I say? I'm a pussy."

Viveca laughed. "I don't think so, but pain is painful, and that's why God created morphine."

Frank laughed again. "Oh geez! You trying to kill me?"

"No, but it is good to see you smile."

"How're Richard and Liam?"

"They're doing good. Richard is learning to relax, and Liam is getting smarter every day. I don't know exactly when it happened, but he's suddenly calling me Mommy and Richard Daddy, and his vocabulary is growing. Pretty soon, he'll be reciting Shakespeare."

"Did Mike pick the business back up?"

"No. He left the city and moved up to Baton Rouge to be closer to his sister. We chat over text, but he doesn't want to talk to anyone right now. I'm hoping we can go for a visit soon."

"I hope so too."

"Well, I suppose I should let you get your rest. It was good to work with just you today, Frank. Felt like old times."

"Yeah, it did," Frank said and smiled. She was just about to open the door when he said, "Viveca, I think we should talk about that kiss."

She turned to face him and then came to take her seat across from him again. "Okay, let's talk."

"I know why you kissed me. We were in danger of being made. I want you to know that I know that."

"Why are you telling me this? What are you trying to say, Frank?"

"I feel like I might have taken things too far, you know, with my hand up the back of your shirt and, well, the whole tongue thing."

"Honestly, I think that's *why* it worked, Frank," she stated, but she saw a nervousness in his eyes. "Is there something else?"

"No, I just wanted to clear the air between us. Hit the reset button. Whatever it's called. I know you tell Richard everything, and I wanted to make sure I hadn't upset you or compromised you in some way. I'd never do anything to hurt you, Viv. I value our friendship and partnership so much."

She smiled at him. "I know you wouldn't, Frank. And I value our friendship and partnership so much too. While we're on the subject, though, do you think I crossed a line when I kissed you, Frank?"

"No. Not at all. You did what you had to do to keep us in the game. You got that asshole. I couldn't be prouder to be your partner and friend."

"Me too, partner. Thank you, my friend."

"Time to go home to see Richard and Liam."

"Can I bring you anything tomorrow?"

"No, I'm pretty sure they're going to discharge me."

"Can we pick you up? Take you to lunch or take you home or take you to lunch and then home?"

"You sure you'll have time?"

"I'm sure. Plus Liam adores you. I know he'll want to see his Uncle Frank."

Frank grinned. "Sounds good. I'll give you a call when I'm told I can go."

"Okay. See you tomorrow. Get some rest and get to healing. These next few weeks are going to be crazy without you."

"You got it."

∞

Richard was asleep in his recliner. Liam was draped across his chest, asleep as well. She stood there, content to watch them for a moment. She took a deep breath and ran her fingers through her hair. The night had been long and not just a little insane.

Richard opened his eyes and smiled up at her. "Glad you're home, love. I was worried."

"No need to worry. I'm fine."

"You don't look like you're fine. What happened?"

"Let's get Liam to bed and let's get you to bed. Then we can talk."

"Okay. You go on ahead, and I'll be up in just a minute," Richard said.

"I think I'll have a shower. Wash this day off me."

"Okay, love. Be there soon."

∞

"Did he wake up?" Viveca asked as Richard stepped into the shower with her.

"No. He was a good little boy."

"He was? And how about my big boy? Have you been good today?" She turned around and drew her arms around him.

"I've been extra good, but I hate not having a job."

"Take your time, baby. If you loved private investigator work, I know you have enough hours and training to take the license exam. Would you want to pursue that?"

"The best part of being a private investigator was working with Mike and Stan. I don't think it would be any fun without them." He leaned in and kissed her.

"Okay, well, like I said. Take your time. Figure out what you want to do, and we'll work out how to make it happen."

"Turn around, love. I'm going to wash your hair."

"Pulling out all the stops tonight, are you?"

"I love having my hands in your hair."

Viveca thought about the kiss between she and Frank. She turned around again to look up at her husband. "I need to tell you something. A few somethings, actually."

"Okay. What?" Richard smiled serenely, and his eyes searched hers. The expression on his face was one she'd seen many times directed at her, and she was certain she'd never grow tired of seeing it.

"When you look at me like that, it's hard to concentrate."

"Well, I am trying to distract you, my love." He leaned down and kissed her and drew his arms around her, pulling her as close as he could. He moved his lips from hers to her neck, then to her collarbone. Then back to her lips again.

"It's important, honey," she said between breaths.

He drew back to give her a more serious expression. "Okay, sweetheart. What is it? Are you okay?"

"I'm okay. Let's finish this shower, and we'll talk in a minute."

"Wow, it must be really serious."

They washed their bodies quickly, but she still allowed him to wash her hair. There was no denying his hands worked their magic. They dried themselves and slipped into their usual night attire. When they had settled into bed, Viveca's head on her husband's chest, she said, "Something happened tonight that was necessary, and something happened that wasn't necessary. I feel okay about one and not so okay about the other. I need to tell you."

Richard wrapped his arms around her. "You can tell me anything, love. There's nothing you could say that would stop me loving you. You know that, right?"

"I know that, but I think you might be disappointed in me."

"I can't imagine that sweetheart. Tell me. What could be so bad?"

"We were on stakeout for that serial torturer. He had murdered his last victim. Remember?"

"Yes, I believe so."

"We were parked almost directly across from the club so we could see all the comings and goings. The guy, Shane Bourque, his car pulls up right beside us and his bodyguard steps out. I had been sitting close to Frank so I could see without being overly obvious. When the bodyguard got out, I turned toward Frank. I could hear him. He muttered something about cops and then he drew his weapon and loaded a round. I had to do something, anything, to get the guy to lose interest in us."

"What did you do?"

"I grabbed Frank and I kissed him like we were two crazy lovers making out in a car."

Richard gave her an amused grin. "And you thought I'd be disappointed in you or angry? What did Frank do?"

"Frank kissed me back. We sold the guy on it, and he left us alone. Told us to go get a room."

Richard laughed. "You thought I'd be angry with you or Frank? Sounds like you had to do that. Is there some awkwardness between you and Frank now?"

"No. We talked it over. We're both cool about it."

"Well then, that's all that matters, love. I like Frank. He's a good friend to us. I don't think he'd do anything to hurt us."

"No, he wouldn't."

"Viveca, what aren't you saying? Did something else happen?"

"Not between me and Frank."

"Between you and someone else?"

"Not like you're implying."

"But?"

"But I don't feel okay about it."

"What happened?"

"I used the tigress to exact revenge on a serial torturer and murderer."

"I'm sorry. What?"

"I knew you'd be upset."

"I'm not upset. I'm confused. How do you mean?"

"The guy, Shane Bourque, he stabbed Frank and made a run for it."

"Frank got stabbed? Is he okay?" The alarm in Richard's voice made her sit up.

"I'm sorry. I should have led with that. Yes, Frank is okay. He's going to be fine. We will pick him up from the hospital tomorrow and take him to lunch and home."

"Okay. Now that that is settled, back to the Bourque guy and your revenge."

"I was angry. I chased after him and beat him to the ferry. He parked in a dead-end alley, and I waited for him there. When he passed me, I spoke to him as the warrior."

"Did you kill this man?"

"No. I played into his ego about the murders he had committed."

"I thought he'd killed one girl. There were others?"

"Yes, in Mississippi and Texas. He's a predator. So I asked him to tell me about what made it fun for him, then I dragged him into the dream walk and released the tigress on him."

"Viveca."

"Just paws, no claws. I didn't leave a mark on him, but he felt every blow. He knew I could kill him at any moment. What he said to me was disgusting and inhuman. I used his words against him and destroyed all the pleasure he'd ever gotten from it. When I brought him back, and tossed him in the back of the sedan, he was done. All curled up in a fetal position, sucking on vinyl."

"How did you feel once you'd brought him back?"

"Satisfied. When we were arresting him before Frank was stabbed, we gave him the name of the girl he murdered. 'Oh, was that her name?' he asked, all high and mighty."

"What happened to change how you felt?"

"I calmed down. I reflected on the situation. Honestly, I thought I might kill him. All those girls, Richard. All those girls," Viveca trailed off, and a few angry tears stained her cheeks. She composed herself and continued. "I kept telling myself that I'd done the world a favor, but really all I did was exact a revenge that wasn't mine to make."

"You feel like what you did was wrong, so you feel badly about it."

"Do you hate me for what I did? Do you think I was wrong?"

"Of course I don't hate you. I think what you did falls into a gray area. On the one hand, this man will never get pleasure out of hurting people again. On the other hand, you took justice into your own hands."

"Are you disappointed in me?"

"No. Are you disappointed in yourself?"

"Somewhat. Yes. I know it wasn't my place to punish him, and using the tigress wasn't the right thing to do. I only wanted to make him feel like those girls he hurt. I wanted him to understand what it was like to be at the mercy of someone who might decide to kill him at any moment! I wanted him to know what it was like to be his own victim!"

"And now that he knows?"

"I feel bad for any small part of him that might've been good, no matter how small it is or how deeply inside him it lived."

Richard drew her down into his arms again and held her close. "It's going to be okay, love."

"What if I've somehow corrupted the tigress?"

"What do you mean?"

"There's a part of me that still feels satisfied. The tigress was never meant for revenge. Protection, yes. Defense, yes. But not revenge."

"So you think *she's* disappointed in you." It was a statement, not a question.

Viveca nodded.

"Do you think she would have done this just because you commanded her to do it?"

"I don't know."

"The tigress is a defeater of darkness. She's a defender of the light. You didn't kill that man, Viveca. You destroyed the darkness within him. That sounds to me like what the tigress was meant for."

"It's not like I turned him into a good person, though."

"Maybe you made room for goodness."

Viveca chuckled without humor. "You believe in redemption?"

"Of course I do. How could I be here otherwise?"

"But you're a good man, Richard."

"I wasn't strong enough to resist Alyssa. Maybe there was a part of me that sought the darkness. I was sorry in the aftermath, but I always kept in mind that had I been strong enough to resist her from the beginning, then maybe I wouldn't have become a vampire."

"Then I never would have met you, and Liam would never have been born. You've told me about what she did to you, how you felt through that process. You did resist her, Richard, because how else could you have held on to yourself the way you did?"

"I suppose that's one way to look at it."

She brought her lips to his. "It's the only way I see it."

"I feel the phoenix now, just as you described her. There's a warmth over my heart. She's making her home here," he said, placing a finger at the center of his chest.

"The rising will complete soon, and you'll begin your training. Just remember to listen to what Papa says. He will guide you through it."

∞

July 23, 2018, New Orleans, Louisiana, 1:23 p.m.

So much could happen in six weeks. Dawes retired after twenty years on the force. Watson was partnered with Miller. Shane Bourque was admitted to a psychiatric facility for evaluation. And Frank returned to work.

"Now you know how I felt when you were out on maternity leave," Frank teased.

"I am *so sorry*," Viveca said with a smile. "It was literally hell without you, but the good news is that Watson has how found himself a partner, and we are once again the dynamic duo."

"Well, at least that's one good thing to come out of being stabbed." Frank laughed.

"Bourque got himself committed. Lost his mind, poor fellow," she mocked Richard's accent.

"Couldn't be because you scared the bejesus out of him, could it?"

"Maybe, but I can't say I'm entirely sorry."

"That's one less bad guy on the streets. I say we chalk one up on the side of the good guys."

"So how do you feel?"

"I feel good. Side is still a little tender, but otherwise good to go. Doc said it'd be that way for a while. Stab wounds take time, but as long as I don't go getting myself stabbed again, I should be okay."

"You going to wear a vest now, right?"

"Going to have to for a while."

Her phone rang. "Ambrose." She listened a moment. "Send them back."

"What's up?" Frank asked, intrigued.

"Just someone here to see us." She kept her eyes on the hallway and soon saw their visitors. Frank looked and saw Richard coming down the hall with Liam in his arms. When Richard reached the desks, he put Liam down.

"Unca Fwank!" Liam walked to Frank, and Frank lifted Liam onto his lap.

"Liam! How are you, kid? Uncle Frank has missed you." Liam snuggled close to Frank's shoulder.

"He missed you a lot, Frank," Richard said and shook Frank's free hand. "How are you feeling? Are you glad to be back?"

"I'm feeling good. Very glad to be back. I don't think I could have taken even another day of forced vacation."

Richard turned his attention to Viveca. "I brought someone with me. Hope that was okay."

"You brought someone with you? Who? You don't know anybody." Viveca laughed.

"I'll be right back," Richard said and walked back down the hall. When he returned, a man trailed after him, and when Richard stepped aside, Viveca was up on her feet and rushing into the man's arms.

"Mike!"

"Hey, kid," Mike said and wrapped his arms around her.

"When did you get back?"

"Today. Went by your house to find Richard and Liam. My goodness, Liam has grown!"

"Yeah, he's getting big," she said and paused. "Are you back for good?"

Mike nodded. "My sister let me cry on her shoulder for a few months, then she kicked my ass to the curb and told me I was letting people down by quitting."

"Oh, Mike, that's not true. We understood. We miss Stan too."

"I know. We all loved him. So tomorrow, I'm going to rehire your husband, prepare him to get his license, and make him a partner in the business."

"Really?"

"Really. I called my clients, and they're all too happy to have me back. Besides, Stan would have wanted me to."

"I'm so proud of you, Mike. Why don't you come by tonight for supper? Richard is making lasagna he learned to make from some show on the Food Network, and I'm picking up French bread and wine on the way home."

"Sounds great. I'll see you tonight." He turned and shook Richard's hand and then Frank's.

"Good to have you back, brother," Richard said.

∞

October 4, 2018, New Orleans, Louisiana, 2:46 p.m.

A package was waiting at the front door when Richard arrived home. Addressed to Viveca, Richard picked it up and set it on the kitchen counter. "Diana?" he called as he entered the living room.

Diana Lawson came quietly down the stairs to greet him. "Good afternoon, Mr. Ambrose," she said kindly. "Liam has just gone down for a nap." Diana Lawson was an elderly woman of about seventy. Referred to Viveca and Richard by Stephanie Vaughn, the woman came with an impeccable résumé, a fine list of references, a kind smile, and a sweet disposition. Viveca had thoroughly studied her, and Liam had taken to her immediately.

"Thank you. Was he a good boy today?"

"He was. He's such a sweet child," she said as she grabbed her jacket and purse from the coat rack. "I'll be back in the morning, sir."

"Diana, please call me Richard."

"I keep forgetting, Mr. Ambr … Richard. I was a nanny for the Carlisle's for such a long time, and they always insisted on proper address."

"I understand, but Viveca and I want you to be comfortable here, and I find that a relaxed address between people makes for a relaxed atmosphere."

"You're quite right, Richard. Thank you."

"See you in the morning." Richard showed her out and then set about to start supper.

∞

Something was happening to her. For nearly a year, the changes had begun to set in. First, a series of unattractive nodes had formed along her cheekbones, then more appeared between her eyes. Next, her skin had begun to pebble. Malcolm took every frustration out on her, and Jazz had begun to wonder if he wasn't to blame.

At nightfall, she awakened thirsty for blood. She felt about her face to find the nodes had gone, now replaced by rough, calloused skin. A check of her hair found it thinner than the night before and more strands had been left behind on the slab where she slept. What was happening to her?

"Master?" She gingerly approached him.

"What is it?" he asked, impatiently.

"Something is happening to me," she said, her voice quavering.

"What is it now?" Malcolm stood and turned to face her. He reached out a hand but withdrew it quickly. "First the horrible lumps, and now this. My beautiful Jazz, have you been feeding enough?"

"I feed every night, Master. I wake each night with new changes. What is happening to me?" Her voice echoed in the dark chamber.

"Why don't you stay here tonight? I'll send Bain out for food."

"Thank you, Master."

∞

"I'm home!" Viveca entered the house and called to her family. She placed her keys in the ornate bowl that decorated the small table and deposited her gun in the table's top drawer.

"I'm here," Richard said and pulled the baked chicken from the oven. A pleasant aroma filled the kitchen and the little foyer where she stood. From the living room, Liam came trotting up to her.

"Mommy!"

She scooped him up in her arms and hugged him. "How's my little man?"

"Good. Daddy make chicken."

"He did? Daddy is a good cook, isn't he?" Liam giggled, and she put him down. She stepped into the kitchen to greet her husband. "Hi, Daddy," she said and kissed him.

"Hi, Mommy," Richard answered. "How was your day?"

"It was fine. Uneventful. Pretty much sat at the desk all day, typing up reports."

"Exciting!" Richard laughed lightly.

Viveca noticed the package. "What's this?"

"Oh, that came for you. Found it on the porch when I got home."

"And how's Diana?"

"She's doing well. I finally got her to call me Richard."

"Oh, progress! Good job." Viveca extended her fist, and he bumped it with his own. She stepped into the kitchen and retrieved a utility knife and began cutting the seal from the package. She unfolded the flaps and peered inside. She remained calm. "Richard, take Liam upstairs."

"What is it?"

"Take him now," she said and pulled her cellphone from her pocket. Richard didn't question her further. He turned off the oven, turned off the burner where the vegetables were heating, and made his way to the living room where Liam had returned to play. From the corner of her eye, she saw him carrying their son upstairs. She dialed the number and waited. When the call was answered, she didn't wait for the greeting. "Frank, I need you to get to my house now."

∞

The tone of her voice told him not to question anything but to grab his keys and go. Something was wrong. When he arrived, the forensics van was pulling up, and the coroner's van pulled in just behind. Frank switched off the engine but didn't pull the keys from the ignition. He bolted from the car, raced up the steps to the porch, and swung the door open. "Viv!"

She came into the foyer from the kitchen. She looked ill. "It's in here."

He followed her into the kitchen and to the counter where a very innocuous box sat, its seal broken but perfect in every other way. "What is it?"

"I think it's Stan's. There's a piece of paper under it, but I thought it best to wait for forensics."

Frank stepped to the box and used a pen to unfold the flaps. The hand lay in the bottom of the box, set in velvet, palm up, fingers curled in like a claw. Flesh had begun to rot away from the bone. Nothing about it could identify the hand as Stan's except for the golden band on the hand's ring finger. "Shit," Frank whispered, then looked around a moment. "Where's Richard and Liam?"

"Upstairs. I thought it best to keep Liam away from it."

Frank nodded and opened his mouth to say something more, but forensics stepped into the room followed by Dr. Ryan. Viveca and Frank stepped back to allow the evidence to be collected. Once the box had been swabbed for fingerprints and after taking note that Viveca had touched the box, they took photographs and then made way for the coroner.

Dr. Ryan stepped forward and pressed the flaps open. "When did the box arrive?"

"Richard said he picked it up off the porch when he got home. He's usually home between 2:45 p.m. and 3:00 p.m."

"Is Richard here?"

"Yeah. I'll get him." She turned to head toward the stairs, but Frank stopped her.

"I'll go get him and stay with Liam while he comes down."

"Thanks, Frank."

Frank nodded and headed toward the stairs. A few moments later, Richard joined her in the kitchen. "What is happening?"

"The package has a severed hand in it. I think it's Stan's."

His eyes went wide a moment. "Are you sure?"

"Not a hundred percent, but the ring on its finger looks like Stan's."

Richard brought a hand to his mouth. "This is going to kill Mike."

Viveca shook her head. "I'm not going to tell him. There's nothing he can do."

"Shouldn't he get his husband's ring back?"

"*If* the hand turns out to be Stan's, I will make sure Mike gets the ring. I promise. But there's no sense in telling him about this."

"You're right," Richard said and pulled his wife into his embrace. "Who would want to send that to you?"

"Who do you think? If Malcolm can't get to you, then he'll try to get to me. Otherwise, I don't think he'd bother getting a skinwalker to do his bidding."

Dr. Ryan carefully lifted the hand, velvet and all from the box, and placed it in an evidence bag. Richard turned his head and let his chin rest on the top of Viveca's head. It was more awful than he had imagined. Dr. Ryan sealed the bag and turned to them. "I know this is difficult. Do either of you know if Stan's fingerprints or DNA would be in the system?"

Richard answered. "It should be. He was a private investigator. We have to go through background checks and fingerprinting when we sit for our licenses."

"The hand doesn't have any skin on it, Dr. Ryan," Viveca stated. "How can you pull fingerprints?"

"We collected the skin from the scene in January. I immediately removed the soles of the feet so it couldn't be used again."

Richard pulled Viveca closer. "Dr. Ryan, please," Richard said.

"I'm sorry. I know it's difficult, and I understand he was a very close friend of your family. We will be able to compare the DNA from the skin we have with the DNA from the hand. If it matches, we will know it belongs to Stan. The ring will have to remain in evidence for a time, but I promise I will release it to you as soon as I can so you can return it to his husband."

"Thank you," Viveca said. "What about the piece of paper inside the box?"

Dr. Ryan looked down into the box to see a piece of paper, which had been tri-folded. Viveca's name had been elegantly written across it. With a gloved hand, Dr. Ryan picked up the piece of paper and unfolded it to read it. Then without a word, she refolded the paper. "It's Stan's hand," she said quietly.

"What is that? What did it say?"

"It says, 'I thought you'd want some of your friend back.' It's signed with a large *M* at the bottom."

∞

November 27, 2018, New Orleans, Louisiana, 3:37 a.m.

"It's getting worse, Master!"

"Let me see, my precious," Malcolm stepped over to her and took her face in his hands. The callouses that had formed on her cheekbones and between her eyebrows had darkened and become more pebbled, and smooth like stone to the touch. Her milk-chocolate skin had taken on a cool, almost reptilian texture. Her eyes, once dark hazel, were becoming brighter. Less golden brown, more yellowish green. Her pupils had become elliptical, and her teeth had each sharpened into points.

"What's happening to me?"

"You're going through a metamorphosis, my love. You said this started happening a year ago? On whom did you feed?"

"Just a man I felt wouldn't be missed."

"Did his blood taste different?"

"Maybe, but I was so hungry I didn't pay close attention. Do you think his blood did this to me?"

"I remember you said the ghouls wouldn't eat the body."

"That's right," Jazz reflected.

"Whatever was in his blood must be causing this. The phagocytes in your system must have mutated. New blood must fuel it."

"I was so beautiful once. Now look at me!" Jazz lamented.

"You are still beautiful, my love. Just think of the vampire you'll become, Jazz. How wondrous you are! How incredible!"

"You still want me?"

"Of course I do, love," Malcolm said and pulled her into his embrace then lowered his lips to hers. "Now, you stay here with me. Bain will see to your needs."

"He hates me," she said quietly.

"He's loyal to me. He doesn't have to like you. He only needs to do as I say."

"What if he rebels?"

"He won't," Malcolm reached out a hand and caressed Jazz's chin. "Eat well, love. I have plans for you."

∞

December 22, 2018, New Orleans, Louisiana, 9:37 p.m.

"Our son is two years old. Time is moving so quickly, Richard," Viveca said, and she climbed into bed with her husband. The day had been busy in the afternoon with the birthday party they'd thrown.

Liam's birthday had fallen on a Wednesday, and they'd had a small celebration a few days before but reserved the gifts for the party itself.

"Pretty soon, he'll be going off to college," Richard teased her.

"You're so funny," Viveca said and mock slapped him on the arm.

"What do you think about having another baby?" Richard asked.

"Now? What about Malcolm's three years?"

"I love you. I want to build our family."

"And we will, but not before Malcolm is gone for good. The solstice is one year from today. Having an infant to protect as well as a three-year-old will split our concentration too much, honey. I want more than anything to have another child with you, but we must think of the family we have right now. You do understand, right?"

"Of course I do, love. You're right." He leaned his head down to kiss her.

"I still want to make love to you."

"Me too."

She reached up, caressed the nape of his neck, and drew his lips down to her own. She moved back, pulling him on top of her. She moved her hands to his chest and then moved to caress the broad expanse of his muscular back.

He wrapped his arms around her, moved into a kneeling position, and pulled her onto his lap. His hands moved to the hem of her nightgown and pulled it up. She raised her hands above her head to allow him to strip her of it. His T-shirt followed, and she leaned back in to press her breasts against his bare chest.

Her lips found his collarbone, and his fingers nestled into her hair. She felt his temperature rise, and she could feel her own climbing. A rise of his hips and a few jerks of fabric freed him of his boxers. He hooked his hand into the delicate lace of her panties and tore them free. A satisfied smile touched her lips, and she pressed into him, allowing herself to graze softly against him. Her hands explored the masculine planes of his body. His arms went around her again and lowered her back onto the bed.

His hands came back down her body and smoothed around her backside. He pulled her toward him; their bodies became one. She reached up and pulled him down to kiss him. His kiss seared her slips deliciously, his touch was hot and electric. Their passion became palpable and surged from and around them. She closed her eyes.

He increased the ardor of their rhythm, and she matched it, clung to him, and called his name. She opened her eyes to look at him. Fiery tendrils of rebirth fire entangled between them. Richard returned to his kneeling position and pulled her up. In the next instant, the tigress surged from her. The two spirits rose above them, encircling one another, almost seeming to war between themselves until all at once, they fused into a circle of power. Hot fire, cold cunning. Death, life. Today, tomorrow. Forever.

They looked up in wonder. A moment later, their warrior spirits formed around them. Tigress and phoenix, two halves of an ancient yen and yang.

YEAR THREE

January 5, 2019, New Orleans, Louisiana, 7:46 a.m.

Richard relaxed his mind and slipped into the dream walk. When he opened his eyes, he stood in the luscious green field. From the trees that stood in the distance, Mr. Eaglefeather approached. The bear, which had always eluded Richard, now presented itself around Mr. Eaglefeather in electric blue.

"Are you ready, my son?" Mr. Eaglefeather asked.

"Yes, Papa."

"Then let us begin. Close your eyes and focus all your senses on your surroundings. Tell me what you hear."

"But I'm not a dream walker."

"That does not matter. The spirit of the phoenix has chosen you. You have accepted her. You are a warrior. Now, close your eyes."

Richard closed his eyes and listened. He felt his doubt fall away. In its place, a whispering rose around him. Below the whispering, other sounds presented themselves. Somewhere not far away, water flowed. Animals scurried among the grass and trees. He conveyed these to Mr. Eaglefeather.

"Very good. Open your eyes, Richard."

Richard opened his eyes and looked over at Mr. Eaglefeather. "Is that how the phoenix looks? Does it surround me as your bear surrounds you?"

Mr. Eaglefeather smiled. "That you can see her is proof of your becoming. Now, you must learn to control her."

"How?"

"The phoenix is a spirit of rebirth. Life. She is also a spirit of fire and energy. She can heal, but she can also be wielded in battle. You must show her you trust her. The rising is nearly complete."

"How can I show her I trust her?"

"Believe in yourself. You are a force for good, Richard. You always have been. Even as a vampire, you warred against the darkness within yourself. The phoenix recognizes this. She would never attempt to rise within one who was not worthy of her. Think of your family. Let their love fill you. Accept the phoenix and rise with her."

Richard closed his eyes and concentrated on Viveca and Liam. Love filled him. He thought of his brother, Christopher, and how he'd longed for the day when he, too, would marry and have a family of his own. He thought of the moment in the alley so long ago, when he'd first spoken to Viveca outside her dream walk. He thought of the moment Viveca had first kissed him and the unhinging of his heart as he realized his affection for her. He thought of the vampire that had caged him and guarded him with a viciousness only love could conquer. And he thought of the moment Viveca told him she was pregnant, the moment he met his son in the dream walk, and the moment he first held Liam.

The first sensation he felt was a warmth that began to spread across his entire body. He bent his elbows and held open his hands, palms upward. The rings grew bright. At the center of his chest, a great flame rose and grew around him. The power was immense, and he thought for a moment it might rip him apart. His muscles struggled to withstand the pressure building within him. His triceps and biceps stretched and were enhanced, his abdominal muscles honed. Pain seared through his body. A cry of anguish escaped him as he continued to struggle.

The pain began to subside. In its wake, Richard was transformed. His body was strengthened, more muscular. Whereas he had always been fit, the phoenix had improved his physique. He felt strong and powerful. The flames still surrounded him, but now he held an unfettered confidence. From his chest, the phoenix soared upward and formed around him.

"Very good, my son," Mr. Eaglefeather said.

"This power is incredible. I feel invincible."

"Power of any kind is deceptive, Richard. Always remember this. The phoenix rises from the ashes, but this also means she can—"

"What? Die?"

"In a manner. Her power surges within you. Do you not grow tired? Do you not need rest?"

"I think I understand. She is powerful, but her energy must regenerate."

"When you grow weary, when you rest, so shall she. You must learn to command her well. This I will teach you. You have seen how the tigress and the phoenix are two halves of a circle of power. Together, they will defeat darkness. Your son possesses the great golden eagle. He will be a great leader for our people and a bright spark of hope for this ever-darkening world."

"I see the goodness in Liam already."

"Yes, he is very special. Your training begins tomorrow, my son. Rest now."

"Thank you, Papa," Richard said and felt the distance between them grow.

∞

"How did it go?" Viveca asked. She was at the kitchen sink, her back to him.

"It went well," Richard answered. "But you tell me."

She turned around. He stood at the cusp of the foyer and the kitchen. He was shirtless and wearing a pair of sweatpants over boxers. The sweatpants hung low on his hips. A dark spattering of hair rose from the band of his boxers. She raised her eyes to a trim waist, a well-defined set of abs, strong biceps, and built pectoral muscles. Her eyes took in every inch of him. "The rising did that?"

"Mmm-hmm. Do you hate it?"

"Um, nope. Don't hate it."

"It's such a drastic change."

"It's not *that* drastic. Honey, you are beautiful. You have always been beautiful. I loved you before the rising, and I love you after. You were perfect before the rising and you're perfect after." She closed the distance between them and wrapped her arms around him. "So what did Papa say?"

"He said that I can use up the phoenix's energy. That she will regenerate her power when I rest. That I can expect to become tired easily at first."

"Follow his advice. You'll need your strength when the time comes."

"I know. What if—?"

"No. No what-ifs, Richard. You're going to learn to control your power, and when the time comes, you're going to understand the phoenix and how to wield her, when to draw her back, and when to rest." She leaned up and kissed him tenderly.

"Where's Liam?"

"He's in the living room, playing."

Richard peeked around into the living room. Liam was sitting on his playmat and linking large interlocking blocks together. "Hey, Liam," he said.

Liam turned and rose from the mat and rushed to Richard. "Daddy!"

Richard scooped his son up into his arms and kissed Liam's forehead. "What are you building, son?"

"A house."

"That's a good start. Want me to help you?"

"Yes!"

Richard lowered Liam back to the floor and sat down next to him. Liam began passing him blocks, then told Richard where to place them. "Oh, you're the foreman, I see," Richard chuckled.

Viveca watched them. Father and son having a beautiful moment. She'd tried to capture every moment she could. She pulled her phone from her pocket and opened the camera app. She took several shots then returned to the kitchen. Time was a blessing and a thief.

At one o'clock, she called for Liam and Richard to have lunch. They joined her at the dining table. She lifted Liam into his highchair and placed a sectioned plate before him. Small cubes of chicken breast were flanked by tender string beans and thin apple slices. For Richard, a large, sliced chicken breast, string beans, and apple wedges.

After lunch, Liam returned to the mat, and Richard helped Viveca clean the kitchen. She washed; he dried and put away. They could hear their son chatting happily away at play in the next room. Contentment filled Viveca's heart. She reached up, took her husband's face in her wet hands, and stood on her tip toes to kiss him. "I love you, Richard."

He grinned down at her. "I love you too."

From the living room, "Daddy! Blocks!"

"Duty calls, love," Richard said with a grin and turned to join their son.

Viveca took her phone from her pocket again and opened the camera app. "Wait!"

Richard stopped and turned to face her again. His grin was still spread across his handsome face. She captured the moment. "Now, wait a minute," he said and made his way back to her. "Give me that phone." She handed it to him. The camera app was still active. He pressed the reverse button to turn the shutter toward them. He pulled Viveca back into his arms. "Smile, love," he said, held the phone out, and pressed the shutter button with his thumb. He kissed her cheek, returned her phone, and joined their son in the living room.

Viveca pressed the picture icon and the selfie presented itself on the screen. A perfect moment captured. Two happy, content people in love, smiling for an impromptu shot. She had begun to categorize the photos on her phone. She'd had printed several shots on photo paper, framed them, and hung them around the house—Liam over the past two years, she and Richard at their wedding, photos of them standing on the porch. All the little instants, the amazing moments, and the intimate quiet moments. She knew the moment Richard had just captured would be framed and placed on the nightstand next to her side of the bed.

Richard's voice pulled her from her reverie. "Hey, babe, I'm taking him up for a nap."

She smiled. "Okay."

"You have to work tonight?"

"Yeah, but we'll be relieved at eight. I should be home by nine. What about you? You and Mike staking anyone out?"

"No. We completed the last job on Thursday, so I have a rare weekend off. Want to fool around tonight?"

"Sounds naughty, Mr. Ambrose."

"Oh, I promise it will be, Mrs. Ambrose."

∞

March 3, 2019, New Orleans, Louisiana, 8:31 p.m.

"Just when you think it's safe to go back to French Quarter alleys," Frank said sarcastically. "God, is it Easter yet?"

"Come on, Frank, you know Mardi Gras throws people together in a way no other time of year does," Viveca replied.

"Mardi Gras is in two days, Viv. This shit is going to get worse before it gets better. And it pisses me off! People don't have better things to do than shoot each other?"

The body was lying in an alley off Bourbon Street between Toulouse and Saint Peter. The young man had been shot several times in the torso. Forensics had completed their sweep of the area, and she and Frank walked the scene while waiting for Dr. Ryan. A few moments later, she arrived and approached the scene with Paul and Jake in tow.

Maxine Ryan looked between Viveca and Frank. Viveca was standing in reverent silence while Frank was pacing angrily along the alley wall. Finally, Viveca turned to him. "Frank, why don't you help the officers gauge the crowd?"

"What? Go see if anyone saw something?" he scoffed. "You kidding? No one saw anything, Viv. They never do, and here's one more young person dead with nothing for us to go on. This murder won't ever get solved. Why? Because people don't matter here!"

"He matters to you, Frank, and he matters to me. So let's get it done so we can at least say we did everything we could. Okay?" Her voice remained kind and calm.

Frank took a deep breath and let it out slowly. "Okay," he said and made his way out of the alley.

"What was that all about?" Dr. Ryan asked.

"His cousin was killed a month ago. Of course, *he* couldn't investigate. No witnesses. He's angry and he's sad. He's working through it. He's trying to, anyway."

"I see. Well, let's do all we can for this one."

Viveca nodded.

∞

May 2, 2019, New Orleans, Louisiana, 7:31 a.m.

The phoenix formed around him, and Richard held up his hands and gazed at his palms. His body was surrounded by bands of fiery energy. At the center of his palms, the circular rings appeared. A blazing electricity formed within each ring. "Trust yourself. Trust the phoenix," Mr. Eaglefeather's voice echoed around him and melded with the glorious whispering of nature, which spoke to him from every direction.

Instinct grew within him. In the next instant, he catapulted himself into the field. The phoenix was a spirit of fire. She carried him within herself. She lent him her wings, and he sped across the field, soaring with the warrior spirit's power. Moving back toward Mr. Eaglefeather, he threw his palms down toward the grass. Energy burst from his palms and ignited the field before him. A wall of fire rose before him and obliterated the field in a line that split the space in half.

In the next instant, the whispering changed. From within himself, he felt the phoenix bend to his will. *Thank you*, he thought. *I won't let you down.* Now in full control, he pulled the energy back and propelled himself back to Mr. Eaglefeather's side. "Did you see that?" Richard asked.

"She gave you her power, my son."

"She spoke to me," Richard said.

"Then she has, indeed, found her home in you, Richard."

Richard looked back at the field and at the line of scorched earth. "I'm so sorry, Mr. Eaglefeather."

"Not to worry. Viveca did the same thing. This field will heal."

"The phoenix's power is awesome."

"Practice. Like all things which must be mastered, the more you hone your ability to call her, the more control you will have."

"You know Malcolm is coming, don't you?"

"Even now, you feel it. A great battle will be fought. It was foretold long ago, and now all the elements are aligning. You and your family are defenders of the light. The enemy is strong, but it can still be defeated. Defend the light, my son. When it makes itself known, you must be ready."

"I will be ready, Papa."

"Come here and practice. There is safety here. Listen to the phoenix and let her spirit guide you. She is more powerful than anyone has seen. Trust her and trust yourself. Call me when you have need of me and I shall come."

"Thank you."

"When Viveca pulled you from the blazing, we knew that a day of reckoning would come. The darkness will come for you, my son. If it cannot have you, it will try to take away those you love."

"I will not let anyone hurt my family, Papa."

∞

June 7, 2019, New Orleans, Louisiana, 3:26 p.m.

Viveca and Frank joined the others in a large debriefing room. The captain stood at the front of the room with several other high-ranking officers, including a man Viveca recognized as the commissioner. Officers and detectives from surrounding precincts joined them. The commissioner waited for the room to settle, then began to speak. "In the past month, there have been several reports of people being attacked by an animal. Injuries range from nips to deep gashes. Ultimately, Animal Control is in charge, but we've been asked to assist as the summer drags on and more tourists make New Orleans their temporary home."

"What kind of animal is it?" Frank asked.

"Reports say the animal is reptilian."

"So like a lizard or snake?" Frank asked.

"Yes, Detective. Exactly like a large lizard or snake. None of the victims have gotten a good look at it, but it seems to be spread across and around the city. We've received reports as far away as Saint Tammany and Saint Bernard Parishes and then widespread across the city."

"Do we have an incident map yet?" Viveca asked.

"We're working on it, Detective."

"Have there been any pet shop robberies lately or anyone we know who specializes in exotic reptiles?" a detective by the name of Minden asked.

"There are no reports about pet shop robberies. We have called in a consultant. He should be joining us this afternoon. His name is Colton Jarreau, and I expect you all to cooperate with him should he have need to consult with you. In a moment, we will break out into separate rooms where each precinct captain will address their individual teams. Are there any other questions?"

Viveca stood. "Sir, if this thing is as widespread as it seems, then could it be a mistake to break us up by precinct? Would forming a taskforce comprised of members of each affected precinct be more efficient in making sure we all remain on the same page?"

The Commissioner stepped away from his microphone and consulted with her captain for a moment, then returned. "Detective Ambrose, I think that's a great idea. Thank you for volunteering to lead it. I expect each captain to consult with their individual teams and nominate two members to serve on Detective Ambrose's taskforce. Dismissed."

Within two hours, members of each affected precinct had joined Viveca in the large debriefing room. She stepped to the microphone. "Thank you for volunteering for this assignment. The first thing we need to do is create an incident map to—"

"Excuse me, but isn't that an outdated approach?" a man at the back of the room asked. She recognized him as Detective Minden.

"It might seem outdated, but it's effective. It's how my partners and I found several kidnapping victims. It creates a web-pattern. Usually, what you're looking for is within the center of the web."

"Still, I think it is a waste of time, ma'am."

"Which precinct are you from?"

"The second precinct in Saint Bernard Parish."

"Okay, Detective Minden, I'm all ears. What is your idea? If you've got a better approach, tell me. In fact, if anyone has a better idea about how to determine where the animal is coming from, I'd like to hear it."

Detective Minden sat down and crossed his arms. No one in the room spoke. Viveca waited. She looked over at Frank, who nodded. "Okay, now that that is settled, each precinct will gather a list of victims and locations where they were attacked. Each precinct will use a separate flag color. Decide among yourselves which color you will use and stick to it. Once all known attacks are flagged, we will begin linking them together. The map will be placed on the table at the back of this room. We will reconvene at 10:00 a.m. tomorrow. Let's get started. Thank you."

∞

"Me and my big damn mouth!"

"Oh, don't kick yourself, Viv," Frank said. "This is a great opportunity."

"A great opportunity to what? Share ideas with Animal Control?"

"You are now leading a multi-agency op. You get to tell that jerk, Minden, and the others what to do. You the woman! Think about it like that."

She smiled and shook her head in good humor. "Okay, Mr. Sunnyside-of-the-Situation. Let's go home. Tomorrow is going to be a bitch, and already I have dissension in the ranks. There's mutiny ahead!"

"Give them a minute to adjust to being led by a woman. Once they get over being from Neanderthal South, it'll be fine, partner. Look at me. I'm evolved. I've got no issues taking orders from you."

"Because you trained under me, Frank."

"Yes, and I know how good you are. They don't know it yet. Come in prepared and show them your smarts. You'll have their respect in no time."

"Thanks, Frank. Hey, you want to join us tonight for dinner?"

"I'd love to."

"Great. Richard is making spaghetti, and it's really good."

"Can I bring anything?"

"Nah. We have everything we need."

"Well, I'm going to bring something anyway. I never show up empty-handed."

"Okay. See you at the house around six?"

"Perfect. See you there." Viveca exited the room and drew her phone from her pocket. Richard answered on the second ring. "Hey, honey. I'm bringing Frank home for dinner."

"Great. It'll be good to have him over."

"Be home in about an hour. Love you."

"Love you too. See you soon."

∞

June 10, 2019, New Orleans, Louisiana, 4:57 p.m.

More sightings. All at night. The map was filling up fast. Viveca drew lines between the flags in a circular motion, almost as though she were creating a spirograph. The lines were drawn across city and county lines, across parishes, and across precincts.

Colton Jarreau watched over her shoulder. She hated that. The feeling of being watched disrupted her concentration. Slowly, the pattern emerged. When she finally stepped back, two blips sat at the center of the graph.

"So what are those buildings?" Jarreau asked.

"That's what we're going to find out," Viveca replied. She drew her cellphone from her pocket and dialed Ferguson. "Hi, Brian, it's Viv. Can you please get us a map of the area between New Orleans and

Chalmette, east of the interstate?" She listened and disconnected the call. "We'll have the answer in about an hour."

"It's five o'clock, you know, Detective," Minden said. "I'd love to stick around, but I'm expected home. It was fun to watch you play connect the dots, though."

"Minden, it might emasculate you to be led by a woman, but I don't really care. Something is out there hurting our citizens. Ours. Yours. Who knows, maybe someone you do care about will be next. So maybe it's in your best interest to start giving a crap about what's happening. Odds are the animal is coming from this area. You might want to know because the area is closer to Saint Bernard Parish than to Jefferson, but that would just be my guess. So you can go if you wish, but I'm going to stay and find out."

"Detective Ambrose, I don't need a map. I already know what's there." He pointed to the first blip at the center of Viveca's drawn graph. "This whole area is one big property. The blip here is a barn set off from the main. And this," he pointed to the other blip. "This is Cavender House. It's been abandoned forever. Goodnight. I'll see you tomorrow."

"Cavender House? Are you certain?"

"Yeah. I have to go around it every day when I go home. What? You think what we're looking for is there?"

"I think it's worth checking out. Don't you?"

"You want to go tonight?"

"No. Tomorrow morning. Just because the animal attacks at night doesn't mean it's strictly a nocturnal creature."

"Okay. That works for me. Call Animal Control. See you there at what time?"

"Let's meet at 7:00 a.m."

"Not for nothing, but good work, Detective." Minden made his way out of the room and the rest of them followed, leaving Frank and Viveca alone.

"See? You now have his respect," Frank said with a smile.

"You're coming home with me again, Frank."

"I am?"

"Yes. We need to question Richard about Cavender House."

"Okay. Why?"

"Because he used to own it. We need to know who he sold it to."

∞

"I can't believe I didn't see it before!" Viveca ran a hand through her hair in frustration. "Everything we heard from the witnesses pointed to it. The house with rooms and bathrooms. The blacked-out windows!"

"It's not your fault, Viv," Frank said.

"Yes, it is!" She turned her attention to Richard. "Babe, who did you sell Cavender House to?"

"It was a company specializing in vampire tours."

"Vampire tours? Or vampires? I think this is where Malcolm is."

"Oh my god. You may be right. Hang on," Richard said and left the room. A moment later, he returned with an envelope. "This is the letter Malcolm sent me last year." He handed the envelope to Viveca.

She removed the letter and unfolded it. She read silently, then came to a part she felt was significant. "*Wherever you are, I am. In the places you call home, I exist.*" She read it aloud and looked between Frank and Richard. "I think this means he is the one who bought Cavender House."

"If he bought Cavender House, then what do you think the animal is that's attacking people all over the tri-parish area?" Frank asked.

"I don't think it's an animal at all. I think it's a ghoul."

"Viv, ghouls don't usually have reptilian traits," Richard said.

"Maybe they do, now."

"What do you mean by that?" Richard asked.

"When I was on maternity leave, Frank and Watson caught a case regarding a body found in a trash bag behind a restaurant. The body was dismembered, the heart was removed. Remember? Frank called me about it?"

"I do remember."

"The autopsy report contained statements saying that the body, apart from being cut to pieces, had also been cannibalized. As it turns out, the body belonged to a man who was a cancer survivor. Dr. Ryan theorized that the ghouls hadn't eaten the body because the phagocytes had been mutated and that it would probably be lethal to them."

"Okay? I'm sorry. I'm lost," Richard said.

"She also theorized that the vampire who fed on the body might go through some kind of metamorphosis. So, what if that vampire metamorphosized into something else because of that man's mutated blood? And what if it is creating ghouls? If it is, those ghouls should take on the traits of the vampire, right?"

Richard brought a hand to his mouth and closed his eyes. A moment later, he nodded. "So what do you think it's become?" Richard asked quietly.

"I don't know, but there are reports that whatever it is, it's reptilian in nature, like a lizard or snake. We need to get in touch with the visionaries again. The solstice is going to be here before we know it."

∞

"This is insane, Viveca," Richard said.

She lay next to him on the bed and moved closer to him. "I know, but all my instincts tell me I'm on the right track."

"You're planning to go there, aren't you?"

"In the morning, Frank and I are meeting Minden."

"Don't go out there, Viv. We need more information first."

"I have to go. I need to confirm a few things, and I have to make a plan to throw all the others off the trail."

"You're going to tell them you made a mistake?"

"Yes, if only to keep them safe."

"How?"

"I don't know yet, but I'll have a plan by the time I get there. The good thing is that Cavender House sits in the middle of nowhere. Everything from miles around it is abandoned. That's where we can fight them without the public being in danger."

"You don't know that place, Viv."

"But *you* do. You can teach us."

"Us?"

"Me and Frank."

"You're dragging Frank into this?"

"We need him to stay with Liam, Richard. If Liam uses his power, it will drain him. And I need you to be careful as well. If you need rest and recharge, you're going to have to get behind me."

"I'm not going to cower behind my wife, Viveca."

"It's not cowering. It's recharging, and it'll happen fairly quickly."

"I'll try to remember."

"Don't *try. Remember.* Got it?"

"Got it, love."

"How is your training going?"

"My training is complete, love. I'm just going in there to practice now."

Viveca took a deep breath. "That's great news."

Richard smiled. "Don't worry, love. I'm going to be ready for them."

Viveca leaned in and kissed him. "I know you will be."

∞

The property was much vaster than Viveca had imagined. Minden told her about the history of the property and how it had once been a thriving farm owned by a gentleman whose name he couldn't recall, but who managed the land with a number of hired hands.

"That's interesting," Viveca said.

"What's interesting is that the man later opened the doors to the community and took in people who had fallen on hard times, who needed a safe place to stay, and who needed a place where they could get back on their feet. Cavender House, which means 'emotional woman' in old English, was a place of great sympathy and heart. I imagine how sad the community was when they'd learned about his death."

"How did he die?"

"It's said he got sick and died of disease. But no one really knows."

"Thanks for the history lesson, Minden. And I mean that sincerely."

"So you ready for the tour? Do you want to split up and search the grounds, or what?"

"I think we should stick together as much as we can."

"Okay. That'll take longer, but okay."

They fanned out the search area and then reconvened at the driveway. The day was growing hot, and it would be impossible to search the entire grounds without help. Viveca called it a day two hours later. "I guess I was wrong. There's nothing here," she observed.

"There're still plenty of places to search. You sure you want to give up your theory now?"

"Yes. I guess you were right."

"What about the house?" Minden asked.

"It's abandoned and left to ruin. I doubt anything lives there except spiders and other insects. Certainly not some huge lizard. I'm thinking whatever it is belongs to someone, and it keeps escaping. People bring exotic animals into their homes all the time. Sometimes they get out, but the owners don't say anything because they know Animal Control will confiscate it and potentially destroy it," Viveca concluded effectively.

"I think you're right, Viv. Minden is right," Frank said.

"Well, okay," Minden said. "If you're sure, I can accept that. And there won't be any I-told-you-so coming from me. It was a good theory."

"Thanks. Let's get to the precinct and brief the others. We need to come up with a different angle," Viveca said and followed Frank to the sedan.

∞

Night fell. Jazz woke and slithered from the slab. Malcolm woke on the slab next to her. "She's been here, Master," Jazz hissed.

"I know. Let her come. Your ghouls will destroy them, and you will be rewarded sweetly for your loyalty, Jazz."

"Thank you, Master."

∞

September 14, 2019, New Orleans, Louisiana, 12:46 p.m.

Viveca reflected on the last few months. Her plan had worked. After meeting with Minden at Cavender House, he had returned to the precinct the next day and made the move to take over the role of taskforce leader. She explained that Minden was a born leader, and his insight would surely lead to a quick resolution. She'd been questioned closely by her captain regarding her desire to step down as team leader, and she dismissed his claim by explaining that she didn't *want* to step down, but that her recognition of Minden's instincts were such that she felt it best for the team overall.

The captain had accepted her explanation and set about to convince the commissioner. Minden's reputation as an egomaniac and sexist was tamped down under the guise that he was simply that good at his job. He exuded confidence in all areas of his professional life because he had reason to be confident. Once approval had been received from the commissioner, she'd quietly slipped into the background. Frank had joined her, and they'd begun their own preparations.

Minden led the taskforce away from Cavender House. He moved the investigation in conjunction with Animal Control back to the perimeter boundaries of the city. The unfortunate owner of an exotic pet shop had been taken into custody. Numerous large lizards and several pythons had been found in the back of the shop. Release of keystone species was illegal, and selling them on the black market was even more illegal. The pet shop owner had been charged, the case closed, and the taskforce had disbanded. Viveca sensed Minden had already had his eye on the pet shop owner; perhaps he'd even been investigating him prior to the attacks, but she said nothing and allowed Minden's swift closure of the case to prove her correct with regard to his skills as a detective.

The bill of sale for Cavender House listed a vampire tour company. A thorough investigation into the origins of the company led Viveca to conclude that the company itself did not exist. She remained convinced that Richard had not sold Cavender House to a vampire tour company but to a vampire. Malcolm had said that he existed in all the places Richard lived. It made sense that Malcolm would want to purchase his brother's house. It had been Richard's vampire sanctuary, and Malcolm was sentimental enough, she thought, to desire that walk in Richard's path. He'd been doing it for centuries now.

Richard practiced in the dream walk every day. Viveca sensed the phoenix rising within her husband in a way it had never done within her. And how could it have? Her tigress had been returned to her before she had allowed the phoenix to fully rise within herself. She sensed a power within Richard upon which she had only grazed the surface. His confidence in controlling his power grew more evident with each passing day. And then it had happened. Richard had returned from the dream walk a week ago excited about something he'd learned. She'd listened as he'd enthusiastically explained how he felt he and the phoenix had bonded in all aspects of his life. His mind. His body. His spirit. She'd quietly switched on her vision, and she could see it was true. The phoenix enveloped him; she draped around Richard like a majestic and powerful coat of armor. The transformation was complete. He would continue to hone his skills, but Viveca knew Richard was ready.

Now, she sat among the visionaries around the circle of fire. She stood and addressed Chief Moonshadow and the others. "Thank you for meeting with me," she said.

"You are our visionary sister," Kent Battiste said and extended her a kind smile.

"You need only call upon us," Stephanie said.

"How can we help you?" Chief Moonshadow asked.

"I believe that Dr. Ryan is correct. I believe we may be dealing with a mutation of the vampires and ghouls, and I know where they are."

Conversation erupted around her. Chief Moonshadow held up her hand and stood. "Where?"

"Cavender House."

"We have known and fought this enemy across generations. This enemy has been among us for over a century. We know its motivation. And now we know where it lives."

Chief Moonshadow took her seat, and Maxine Ryan stood. "The synthetization is complete. We must be prepared for it to work on the ghouls who have not undergone the mutation. It likely will not affect the mutated ghouls."

"The rising is complete," Viveca shared. "Richard commands the phoenix."

Chief Moonshadow stood again. "All our warriors are gathered. Prepare your blades and arrows. Hone your bows. Prepare for battle. The solstice draws near."

∞

November 23, 2019, New Orleans, Louisiana, 11:29 p.m.

The list of names was long. Viveca and Frank had gathered the list of those who'd been attacked and had, over the past month, systematically interviewed them. The wounds inflicted had healed and so far, no one had suffered after-effects from the bites, scratches, and gashes. A few had lasting scars, but none had felt ill or had developed infections.

Viveca had used her vision in each interview to scan for any signs of vampire or ghoul. None of the victims presented either creature. Outside the final interviewee's home, Viveca sat quietly next to Frank in their sedan.

"Penny for your thoughts," Frank said.

"I don't get it," Viveca said quietly.

"Isn't it a good thing that none of these people will turn?"

"Of course it is, but what the hell were they doing?"

"Practicing?"

She looked over at him with a surprised expression. "Of course. They weren't trying to kill anyone. Not trying to turn anyone. They were honing their skills of attack. Oh my god."

"So now what?"

"We're dealing with an even bigger threat. These ghouls are stealthier. They'll be looking to catch us off guard."

"So what do we do?"

"We need to look again at where the attacks took place. What sort of cover were they using before they attacked? How did they get away without being seen by people other than their victims? It's a month to the solstice, Frank. We need to learn and learn fast."

∞

December 21, 2019, New Orleans, Louisiana, 12:49 a.m.

Frank slept in the guest room. At dawn they would meet the visionaries and make their move on Cavender House. The battle would soon begin.

Viveca lay quietly next to Richard. He lay on his side facing her. He had draped his arm over her and wrapped his fingers around her arm. She watched him sleep. Everything hinged on what would happen tomorrow. She closed her eyes and leaned her head toward him. In sleep, he brought his lips to her hair and kissed her softly. She tilted her head up and brought her lips to his. "I love you so much," she whispered. A small smile touched his lips, but he did not wake.

It was quiet. Too quiet. The usual sounds of crickets and other nocturnal creatures had fallen away. Viveca tensed, held her breath, and listened. Below the white noise of silence a scraping sound entered her senses. She projected the tigress and sent it forth throughout the house, first checking Liam, then Frank, then heading downstairs to investigate. The tigress crept throughout the rooms, staying low and quiet. The scraping sound was coming from the living room window that looked out onto the side porch. Then the scraping stopped and the unmistakable sliding of the window within its track reached the tigress's ears. It crouched low and prepared.

The first sight of the creature was a scaly and clawed foot. The curtain covering the window billowed under the creature's entry and dramatically revealed it like a mask being slowly removed. The muscled leg and thigh followed by taut muscular torso, clawed hands, and a fierce face. It was a ghoul, but unlike anything seen before. Reptilian in nature, the flattened nostrils flared wide when it took a breath. Its mouth opened in a soft hiss to reveal rows of sharp, angular teeth. Its eyes were elliptical, a thin film crossed over them momentarily to replenish moisture as it blinked. It stood like a man and seemed to sniff the air, then it crouched on all fours and slinked along the wall. As it made its way to the large space between the sofa and the stairs, the tigress stepped into view.

It hissed and reared back into a standing position to tower over the tigress. One clawed hand swept the air, and the tigress evaded. It pulled back its scaly lips and bared its teeth. The tigress reared to its full height. The ghoul charged, and the tigress caught it in the shoulder. Claws ripped through scaly flesh. The tigress didn't hesitate to double back and take the ghoul by the neck and crush it between its massive jaws. The ghoul fell to the floor and lay still. The tigress stepped back and waited for it to rise up again. The ghoul's raspy breathing told the tigress it was down but not out.

Viveca peered through the tigress's vision at the horrific creature lying at the bottom of her stairs. The ghoul moved. The dislocated and torn shoulder righted itself and healed. The vertebrae in the neck popped back into position. The ghoul began to push itself off the floor. The tigress waited. When it turned, the tigress swept a massive claw forward and tore through the ghoul's chest, but the heart did not come with it. The tigress stepped back and watched the gaping hole close.

Research she conducted when compiling her theories came flooding back to her. In a human being, the heart was near the center of the chest, just to the left of the sternum. But in reptiles, the heart was located higher up on its torso, just beneath where the neck transitioned into the torso.

The ghoul hissed and approached the tigress. It positioned its claws in preparation for attack. The tigress crouched and growled. The ghoul sprang forward, using its muscular legs and spry balance to propel itself forward toward the waiting warrior spirit. The tigress launched itself forward. The ghoul grazed the tigress along the left shoulder. The tigress's claws knocked the claw aside, crouched again and brought a massive hind leg up to strike the ghoul in the lower torso.

The ghoul flew backward into the space between the foyer and the kitchen. The tigress sprang and pinned the ghoul to the floor, its claws digging viciously into its arms and legs. A twist of the tigress's body rent the ghoul apart. The ghoul screeched. Even now, tendrils of flesh reached out between the ghoul's torso and its hewn limbs. The tigress sprang again, vaulting upward and bringing a massive claw down upon the upper part of the ghoul's chest between its neck and ribcage. The claw dug deep and with one mighty jerk, cleaved the ghoul's heart from its body.

The ghoul lay still. The tendrils of flesh stopped the regeneration process where it was. In the silent aftermath, crickets began to sing again.

∞

"Wake up!" Viveca shook Richard, and he opened his eyes with a jolt.

"What is it?"

"Get up. Get dressed. That bastard is going down now."

"Viv, what is happening?"

"Malcolm sent a reptilian ghoul here tonight."

"Liam!" Richard began to make his way toward their son's room.

"It's dead. I destroyed it."

"Why didn't you wake me? I could have helped you."

"There was no time. It was coming in. Get dressed. Go wake up Frank and Liam. I've got to call the visionaries. We were wrong on how to destroy them."

"What do you mean?"

"They regenerate. We have to take out their hearts and even that's in a different place."

"Shit!"

Richard dressed in record time. He pulled on his shoes and quickly made his way to Liam's room, then went to wake Frank.

Viveca dialed Maxine Ryan. She answered on the second ring. "We have to move now," Viveca said urgently.

"What's happened?"

"Gather the others and meet us at the council fire. We have to do this tonight. If we wait until dawn, it'll be too late. The son of a bitch isn't waiting for the solstice!"

"I'm on it. See you there." Dr. Ryan disconnected the call.

Viveca dressed quickly and made her way downstairs. The destroyed ghoul lay in pieces to the right of the stairs. Frank and Richard descended the stairs. Frank let out a cry of surprise when he saw the ghoul. "What the f—hell is that?"

"I'll explain on the way. Let's go." Viveca had had most of the preparations made before going to bed. She grabbed her keys, and the four of them stepped around the dead ghoul and made their way to the car.

PART THREE

THE RISING

CHAPTER 1

December 21, 2019, New Orleans, Louisiana, 2:34 a.m.

Viveca pulled the car haphazardly into a parking space. The four of them raced inside and made their way to the council room. Dr. Winterhawk, Dr. Ryan, Dr. Battiste, Chief Moonshadow, and Stephanie Vaughn were waiting.

"We were wrong!" Viveca panted, trying to catch her breath. "We have to move now!"

"Tell us, child. What has happened tonight?" Chief Moonshadow asked.

"A reptilian ghoul came to my house. They're harder to kill than we imagined. They regenerate, and they do it quickly. The only way to kill them is to take out their hearts. They look humanoid, but their hearts are positioned as though within a reptile. At the base of the throat between the throat and the top of the ribcage."

"We will get the word out to the others. When do you want to attack?" Dr. Battiste asked.

"Now. We don't have time to waste. If we let them come to us, innocent lives will be in danger." Viveca stepped close to Richard, and he put his free hand around her shoulders.

"I saw the ghoul," Frank said. "It's horrific. Listen to Viveca."

Viveca approached Chief Moonshadow. "Is there a safe place for my friend and my son to stay?"

"Come with me, child," Chief Moonshadow beckoned, and she and Dr. Winterhawk led Viveca to small room just to the right of where they stood. When she opened the door, Chief Moonshadow stood aside and allowed Dr. Winterhawk to lead her inside.

"This is a mystic chamber, a place of magic and power. No one uninvited may enter. They will be safe here."

"Thank you." Viveca returned to Richard's side and took Liam from his arms. She hugged him closely and kissed his head repeatedly. "I love you so much, Liam. Remember that. Always." She forced a smile and then handed him back to Richard.

Richard hugged his son. "I love you, Liam," Richard said, kissed his son, and handed Liam to Frank. "Please take care of him, Frank."

"I would die for him, Richard. I won't let anything happen to him."

Viveca walked to Frank and placed an arm around him in a hug. She brought her lips close to his ear. "Remember your promise, Frank."

"It won't come to that, Viv."

Viveca leaned up and kissed Liam again. "You take care of your Uncle Frank. Mommy and Daddy love you so much."

Liam reached out and touched her face. "Love Mommy and Daddy." Viveca smiled and led Frank to the mystic chamber.

"Don't step a foot outside this door for any reason. Not until someone comes to get you." Viveca hugged Frank again. "Thank you, Frank."

Frank placed a hand on the side of her face. "Viv, you and Richard take care. I'll see you both soon."

CHAPTER 2

December 21, 2019, New Orleans, Louisiana, 5:17 a.m.

They had parked their vehicles on the other side of a vast stretch of abandoned farmland. Viveca led the way across with Richard at her side as the visionaries fanned out. Most of them carried bows and swords. Their warrior attire was not lost on her. Brilliant colors splashed in embroidered beads across the soft fabric. The beads, she had come to understand, had been woven with spells of protection.

Cavender House loomed like a dark dragon in the distance. High on the western horizon, the setting moon cast its light down upon the land and crept toward the great house like curious wisps of ghostly fingers which seemed to feel their way across its timeworn stone. Upon its immense veranda, a large ghoulish figure stood. Viveca had seen this ghoul before. Menacing. Without remorse or pity. Gannon Bain.

"Dream walker!" Bain's booming voice sounded around them. They marched forward. Ahead of them a hissing rose in the tall grass.

"Be careful," Viveca whispered. The tigress formed around her and surged through her. The dream walker warrior stepped forward.

"I will," Richard said and called the phoenix. Fiery tendrils formed around him, and the head of the great bird glowed around his head like a fiery helmet. The rings formed on his palms. He joined his wife. Around them, the visionaries drew their weapons. Maxine Ryan pulled a vial from her pocket and proceeded to coat each weapon with her synthesized chemical. If there was to be a field test, it was now or never.

From the sward ahead of them, reptilian ghouls emerged and hissed. Their muscular bodies formed a line of defense between them and Cavender House. A coldblooded screech from the center of their small legion propelled them forward. The visionaries crisscrossed the line, drew their weapons, and fired their bows, then doubled back and drew their swords to slice into the reptilian skin. Where arrows had pierced the ghouls' hearts, the scaly creatures had been thrown to the ground. The visionaries looped around to regroup. If the chemical was working, it was working too slowly to be wielded in battle. Even now, the reptilian ghouls were trying to pull arrows from their wounds to regenerate.

Richard and Viveca stepped forward. Using the tigress and the phoenix, they took advantage of the wounds the visionaries had inflicted. The tigress attacked the first ghoul in front of her, slicing through its abdomen before driving its claws through the ghoul's upper chest and ripping away its heart. Behind her, Richard threw rebirth fire forward, catching the ghouls off guard. Using his strength, he drove his hand into the upper chest of the next ghoul and ripped its heart free.

The visionaries repeated their efforts, creating gaping wounds, trying to aim for the ghouls' hearts. Stephanie swung her sword, and it struck home. She pulled the sword from the ghoul's heart and turned, too late, to take the next one down. The ghoul's clawed hand caught her in the side and ripped her open. She fell to the earth and closed her eyes. Viveca projected the tigress forward, taking the ghoul from the back, and thrusting its claw upward to remove its heart from behind.

The reptilian ghouls were falling, and behind them to the east, the sun began to rise. Light painted the early morning sky in glints of yellow, purple, and red. On the vast veranda, more ghouls joined Bain.

The reptilian ghouls had been defeated to two, and when the sun peeked over the horizon, the ghouls standing on the veranda with Bain made their way to the lawn. Bain stood front center and gave the order to attack. In the ever-diminishing distance, ghouls charged from Cavender House to attack.

The visionaries drew the two remaining reptilian ghouls away and destroyed them, then rejoined Viveca and Richard. "Stay behind us," Richard shouted and stepped forward.

Viveca followed his lead, bringing forth the full embodiment of the warrior. The ghouls closed in. They couldn't defeat them all. Outnumbered, their only hope was to defeat as many as possible and pray the visionaries could defeat the rest. She took a step forward and then felt Richard's hand on her pushing her back behind him.

"What are you doing?" She asked.

When she was effectively behind him, Richard seemed to pull energy into himself, then projected it out again. The flames around him rose. He slammed his hands together, turned his palms and drew his hands apart. Between the rings, a ball of fire formed. He held it out before him and launched it into the approaching ghouls. Turning and slamming his hands together again, he launched fire again. He threw himself into the air, carried by the phoenix, and continued to launch fire at the approaching ghouls, taking them from all angles.

The ghouls attempted to evade the rebirth fire, but each launch caused a backdraft that sucked energy in then blew it out again to destroy everything within a radius of several feet. Each time they changed direction, so did Richard.

The ghouls making it through the line were held back by the tigress and the visionaries who still stood in battle. Gannon Bain turned to retreat, and Richard propelled himself between Bain and Cavender House. Richard held his hands at his sides, the rebirth fire grew around him and Bain stood motionless. Behind Bain, the tigress and the dream walker warrior closed in.

"You may destroy me, but you'll never destroy the master."

"*You!*" The dream walker warrior drew Bain's attention. "You killed Papa and Nana. *You* killed Rainier."

A satisfied smile grew sickly across the ghoul's face.

The tigress suddenly slashed at the large ghoul, opening its chest cavity. Richard drew a small fireball between his palms and shoved it under the ghoul's beating heart. The ball erupted, the ghoul's heart flying into pieces and rebirth fire flowing like lava within its already dying body. When the ghoul fell to the ground, its parts broke away like cigarette ash.

Richard allowed the rebirth fire to subside, and he collapsed to the ground. "Richard!" Viveca was at his side in seconds. "Are you okay?"

"Yeah. Just tired."

Behind them, the visionaries approached them. Kent Battiste knelt beside Richard. "That was something, my friend. Now, you need to rest."

In the distance, the visionaries retrieved the bodies of Stephanie Vaughn and Chief Moonshadow. Tears touched Viveca's eyes. She'd always recognized the bravery in these incredible people. In them, she'd learned so much about herself and about her parents and grandparents. Everything they'd done had kept her and the world safe from evil. She looked back to her husband. She reached out and grasped his hand. "We made it," she said. "We need to get you someplace to rest."

"Malcolm," Richard said.

"It's daylight out. I'll deal with him soon. Right now, you're my priority."

CHAPTER 3

December 21, 2019, New Orleans, Louisiana, 11:17 a.m.

Viveca had left her husband with their son to recover his energy. Even now, she was amazed at how powerful Richard had become. Viveca had only begun to know the phoenix's potential, and in Richard, the rising had brought forth its power to a degree she had yet to accomplish. In Richard's heart, she knew the phoenix had found a home within a good and honorable man. It would reside in him as healer and protector for as long as he lived. She reined in her thoughts as she pulled in front of the massive old mansion.

When Viveca entered Cavender House, the sun was high in the sky. She knew Malcolm would be sleeping. Was she a coward to face him when he was defenseless? *Van Helsing staked vampires in their coffins at high noon, and he was the hero of many a vampire movie,* she mused. Her visionary spirit guided her down. She located the basement door and found it unlocked. Perhaps the element of surprise was still with her. The door opened to a set of stairs that sank resolutely into darkness.

She called upon the tigress to illuminate her vision, and she began her descent. One landing led to another and then another. Each step took her to impossible depths beneath the house. She'd visited this place in her dream walk long ago, when she'd visited Richard in his vampire sleep. Now, she understood how she'd come to find him. Her visionary guidance had led her there as it was leading her now. She kept her thoughts to Malcolm and followed her instincts into the pit.

∞

The slab where she'd visited Richard was devoid of occupancy. *Where are you?* she wondered. Around her, a hissing rose. In an instant, she became the dream walker warrior, ready for battle. Her vision became even keener, and her senses sharpened. She waited on a razor's edge for an attack.

From her left, a figure darted toward her, a fast-moving shape that tried to slash at her. Viveca evaded the attack and turned to face the direction the figure moved. Her vision pulled the figure into focus. Jazz. But not the Jazz she recognized. The vampire had mutated into a powerful reptilian creature. "I figured the coward would send his crony out to fight his battles for him," Viveca challenged.

"I'm no crony. I am my master's queen. How is it you are here during the day? You are the coward, dream walker."

"I'm not a coward. Only using my common sense. I bring news. Your legion is destroyed."

"I'll make more."

"No. Your time is over."

Jazz said no more, but leapt into action, rushing toward Viveca with tremendous force. Her left hand struck Viveca in the center of her chest and sent her flying back several feet. Viveca landed on her back, the breath knocked out of her. Claws had sketched a series of tears across Viveca's shirt and had drawn red marks across her skin.

Viveca made a move to stand, and Jazz sent her down again. "I can't see what all the fuss is about. You are a tired, weak, pathetic excuse for a warrior." She laughed. "And you came down here by yourself. You're also foolish. Battling the legion has exhausted you. When I get done with you, I'll pay your husband and son a visit."

Jazz reached down to take Viveca in hand. The tigress burst forth and rent Jazz's right hand away. Surprise was followed by anguish, then by rage. Blood painted the floor where she stood. "You bitch!" Jazz flew into action again. The tigress outpaced her and slashed through her abdomen.

"You were saying something about my being weak," Viveca taunted, but didn't wait for a reply. The tigress came back around and sliced through the vampire's throat. In the next instant, it sent its claws through Jazz's upper chest and tore her heart away. The vampire imploded into dust.

Viveca called the tigress back and stood up. From behind her, an arm wrapped around her and a hand pressed around her throat. A voice swept cold and harsh against her ear. "You dare come here, dream walker."

"Malcolm," she said.

"Where's my brother? Your Nana made that deal, dream walker. I gave you three years together, and you break a promise."

"You killed my Nana, Malcolm. You broke your promise first. Together meant all of us."

"Not the deal she made, I'm afraid."

"You're a liar!"

"No. The truth is far more fun. Your Nana traded your husband's life for three years of time. Now, give me my brother!"

"Why do you want to take him from his family? I thought you loved him."

"I do love him, but—"

"There shouldn't be any buts to that statement, Malcolm. Either you love him without exception, or you don't love him."

He could feel energy surging within her. "You release your tigress, dream walker, and I'll snap your neck. I am faster than you, Viveca. I'll take you from him, if I must, and then I'll take his son. Alone, he'll come to me, as I always believed he would. He'll beg me to turn him."

"He won't. You kill me, you kill our son, and he'll never be your brother again."

"We'll see. Now, where is he?"

"He's safe, Malcolm. You can't get to him."

"Oh, I will—"

"Malcolm!"

Viveca looked toward the voice. The tigress was building its energy inside her and her vision pulled Richard into sharp focus. "No," she breathed. Not enough time had passed for him to fully recuperate.

Behind her, she could feel Malcolm smile. In another instant, he flung her aside, and she landed to his left. "I keep my promises, dream walker. That tigress emerges, and I will kill you." He hissed the words, but never took his eyes from Richard. "Brother, you've come to keep that promise."

"I have. Let my wife go, Malcolm, and I will come to you."

"No! Don't do it, Richard! You're not strong enough," Viveca cried.

"Now, now, love, we made a deal, did we not?"

"He killed my Nana, Richard! He broke that promise years ago! Don't go to him, Richard. Please! Think of your son. Think of Liam, Richard!"

Malcolm turned his attention briefly to Viveca. "Go, dream walker, and do not dare drive a wedge between me and my brother again."

"He has a son, Malcolm! Please don't take my son's father away."

"I am, my love," Richard said. "I am thinking of our son. This is the only way Liam can be safe. Please, go outside, go home. Don't come back here."

Viveca sobbed. "No, please don't make me go. I love you."

"I love you too, sweetheart. This is the only way. We've known this for three years. Now, go. Keep Liam safe."

"I can't perform the blazing again, Richard. Please."

"I know, love. It will be all right. I promise."

Sobbing and gasping for breath, Viveca stood and made her way to her husband and wrapped her arms around him. From behind her, Malcolm said, "Dream walker, do as your husband says."

"Shut up, you son of a bitch! I just want to tell him goodbye."

"I well remember what happened the last time you wanted to do that. Now, step away from him and go, or I promise you, I—"

"Go to hell! I'm going," she said, then turned back to Richard. She put one hand behind his neck and drew his lips down to her own. She kissed him with the passion of searing the memory into her heart. As a vampire, she knew he would never try to come to her again. "I love you," she said as tears stained her cheeks, and then she made her way out and ascended the stairs. As she reached the upper landing and exited the basement door, she made her way to the front door. And then she stopped. Liam was sitting on the floor by the front door. She scooped him up in her arms and made her way outside.

"Daddy," Liam said, reaching around her toward Cavender House. "Mommy, where Daddy?"

"Daddy's not coming back, love," she said as calmly as she could.

Liam began to cry and wriggle in her arms. She held fast and cradled his head against her shoulder. "I'm sorry, love," she said, and made her way to her car.

CHAPTER 4

December 21, 2019, New Orleans, Louisiana, 1:24 p.m.

"Why are you doing this, Malcolm? Why do you seek such revenge upon me?"

"You betrayed me, brother. I told you, you would come seek me out. And so you have."

"My son will grow up without his father, Malcolm. Do you remember how our father loved us? Do you remember our parents taking you in and giving you shelter and a life? You had me turned against my will, Malcolm. And you deprived our parents of two sons. And here you are, depriving my son of me."

"You belong here with me, brother."

"I belong with my family. I'm not your brother anymore, Malcolm. And you aren't my brother anymore. Hasn't your life and all the death around taught you anything?"

"It's taught me that what is mine should always be mine."

"But I'm not *yours*, Malcolm. I never was. We were friends, then we were brothers, and I loved you as my friend and my brother. But you ceased to be that with Alyssa's first taste of your blood. You weren't the Malcolm I knew anymore. And if you take my life, I will spend eternity fighting it just as I did before."

"You will give in to it this time. I will see to that."

"You can't make me accept it."

"We'll see," Malcolm said.

"I have done all I can to save you, Malcolm. Do what you must, for I can no longer stop you."

Malcolm smiled, then pulled Richard into his embrace and sunk his vampire canines into Richard's neck. Blood flowed into Malcolm's mouth.

Life, Richard's life, sought out the vampire phagocytes within Malcolm's body. Malcolm broke free of Richard's neck and stood back, watching in wonder as Richard neither crumpled to the floor nor seemed to die his mortal's death. "It cannot be!" Malcolm exclaimed.

"I tried all I could to stop you, but you wouldn't listen. Goodbye, Malcolm," Richard said, and allowed the phoenix to form around him.

Inside Malcolm, Richard's blood was carried by the vampire phagocytes through Malcolm's body, sending a searing through each capillary. Malcolm cried out as the first fiery tendril broke through his skin. "What's happening to me!" he cried out.

"I told you. I am no longer your brother, Malcolm," Richard said and watched as more tendrils burst through Malcolm's skin. In another moment, the vampire was engulfed in flames. It blew apart into ash, and the lower levels of the pit caught fire.

Richard raised his hands and formed a fiery ball between his palms, then began to launch fire within the pit. He began to climb the stairs, at each landing, catching it on fire. He rose out of the basement and into the great house itself, bringing explosive destruction with him.

CHAPTER 5

December 21, 2019, New Orleans, Louisiana, 2:13 p.m.

Viveca held her son and rocked him as she sat in the driver's seat of the car. A sound drew her attention to Cavender House, and she watched in horror as the windows and door exploded outward in a powerful blaze. She sat Liam on the front passenger seat and stood from the car.

"Richard! Oh no! Richard!"

From behind her, Liam began to cry again. She could hear his small voice, "Daddy!"

From the flames, a figure came into view and emerged from the house. Viveca dropped to her knees and watched in wonder as the flames died away around her husband. In an instant, she was off of her knees and racing toward him. "Richard!"

She threw herself into his arms, and they sank to the ground each holding the other. "For once, you did as I said," he chuckled.

"This was your plan?"

"It was the only way to destroy him, love."

From behind Viveca, Liam came running. "Daddy! Daddy!"

Richard scooped him up and held him close. "Liam, you don't know how happy I am to see you."

"I love you," Viveca said. "I love you both so much."

"I love you too," Richard replied. "And what about you, little man? Do you love us?"

"To the moon and back, Daddy!" Liam exclaimed and pointed skyward.

They stood. Viveca looked lovingly up at her husband. "I have something to tell you."

"What is it, love?"

She took his free hand and placed it on her abdomen. Then she smiled brightly. "It's a girl," she said.

Richard's eyes grew wide with surprise then held an expression of unabashed caring. He drew his wife into his arms and kissed her softly. Then he and Viveca turned to watch as Cavender House burned into ash. When the walls folded in on themselves, they turned, and Viveca walked with her husband toward the car, their son in Richard's arms. "I can't tell you how happy I am, love," Richard said as he put Liam in his car seat.

"Me too," Viveca said warmly.

"Malcolm is gone. It's finally over."

"Is it?" she asked.

"Yes, my love, I believe it is."

"Who knows what's in store for our daughter, Richard, and Liam is destined to be a great spiritual leader. There will be those who will endeavor to stop him from reaching his potential."

Richard smiled. "No worries, love. I am the phoenix, you the tigress. We'll protect them until they are ready to protect themselves."

"Liam has so much to learn and so much to teach."

"And so he shall. We will learn and teach together."

"Always?"

Richard nodded. "Always. Now let's go home."

"Home," Viveca agreed. The word never seemed as wonderful to her as it did now.

AUTHOR'S NOTE

The idea for *The Blazing: A Vampire Story* and its sequels came to me through a desire to write a story about vampires that was different from any other story I'd read. I believe I've met that goal, and I hope you will agree with me that my vampires are unique. While I stuck to the everyday folklore regarding blood drinking, fangs, and sunlight, I hope I have also given you something to think about regarding spiritual possession, Native American folklore, DNA mutations, and the science behind the very real phagocytes that exist naturally in human blood. I hope I've woven a tapestry that is rich and unique—one that captured your imagination and inspired you to turn the page. I thank you for taking this journey with me. As for Viveca and Richard, I will miss them dearly, but I know they will be just fine as long as they stick together.

Love,
Buffy

Lightning Source UK Ltd.
Milton Keynes UK
UKHW041836180221
379033UK00008B/515/J

9 781664 154681